THE ANARCHIST DETECTIVE

Brought up in England, Jason Webster has lived for several years in Valencia, where two of his Cámara novels are set. His acclaimed non-fiction books about Spain include *Duende: A Journey in Search of Flamenco* and *Sacred Sierra: A Year on a Spanish Mountain*. His first Cámara crime novel, *Or the Bull Kills You*, was longlisted for the CWA Specsavers Crime Thriller Awards New Blood Dagger and was followed by the equally acclaimed *A Death in Valencia*.

JASON WEBSTER

The Anarchist Detective

VINTAGE BOOKS
London

Published by Vintage 2014

2 4 6 8 10 9 7 5 3 1

First published in Great Britain in 2013 by
Chatto & Windus

Vintage
Random House, 20 Vauxhall Bridge Road,
London SW1V 2SA

www.vintage-books.co.uk

Addresses for companies within The Random House Group
Limited can be found at: www.randomhouse.co.uk/offices.htm

The Random House Group Limited Reg. No. 954009

A CIP catalogue record for this book
is available from the British Library

ISBN 9780099565970

The Random House Group Limited supports the Forest
Stewardship Council® (FSC®), the leading international forest-
certification organisation. Our books carrying the FSC label are
printed on FSC®-certified paper. FSC is the only forest-certification
scheme supported by the leading environmental organisations,
including Greenpeace. Our paper procurement policy can be found
at www.randomhouse.co.uk/environment

Typeset i̶n̶ ... Palimpsest Book Production L̶i̶m̶ited,
Falkirk, Stirlingshire

Printed and bound in Great Britain by
... Ltd., Croydon CR0 4YY

FOR TANYA, WITH LOVE

Any life is made up of a single moment, the moment in which a man finds out, once and for all, who he is.

JORGE LUIS BORGES

NOTE

There are several police forces in Spain. Chief Inspector Max Cámara works for the *Policía Nacional*, which deals with major crimes in the larger towns and cities. The *Guardia Civil* is a rural police force, or gendarmerie, covering the countryside and smaller towns and villages. Both the *Policía Nacional* and *Guardia Civil* report to the Interior Ministry, although the *Guardia Civil* is paramilitary and has links with the Defence Ministry.

In addition to these national forces, towns and cities tend to have a local police force – the *Policía Local*, also known as the *Policía Municipal*. This deals with smaller crimes, official engagements and traffic duties, and is under the control of each respective Town Hall. A member of the *Policía Local* may sometimes be referred to as a '*Municipal*'.

Any member of these respective police forces is said to be belonging to the *Policía Judicial* if they are acting under the orders of an investigating judge.

PROLOGUE

He's seen dead bodies before, plenty of them. But never like this.

Slowly, for fear of breaking them, the bones are uncovered, exposed and finally liberated from the earth.

Over two hours have passed since he arrived, watching every step of the delicate operation. And his eyes have barely wandered as the shape of the corpse has gradually emerged. Excavators and forensic scientists work below in the pit, their movements calm and unhurried: this takes patience, and while it is important to uncover and collect every clue, respect for the dead as much as professionalism creates a hushed, almost church-like atmosphere.

A flash goes off from time to time as the photographer records their progress. From a distance, a handful of visitors to the cemetery tiptoe around the makeshift wire fencing designed to create a sense of privacy for this sacred act. What's happening here is an important story for the city, but many will be content to catch a glimpse of it on the local television news: a cameraman and reporter are setting up now.

A short break. The forensic team are discussing how best to carry on – whether to concentrate on this one body or extend the digging area and perhaps reveal more of the dead gripped by the greedy fingers of the soil.

He lifts his gaze and looks around at the walls of memory surrounding them. Cemetery names etched on metal plates bolted to niche coverings; an occasional black-and-white photo in a rusty iron frame; some dried flowers tied to a railing; others fading in the sunlight, their nylon petals only providing a temporary permanence against the elements.

Until this moment there has been no record, no remembering of this man lying a few feet away in the ground. No plaques, no tearful relatives, no flowers of any kind. No years of honouring his name and life: small yet important steps to ensure that his death did not mean immediate forgetting and silence.

No. This man was extinguished and cast into a nameless pit. His existence blotted out, as though he had never lived, should never have lived. And for years the earth had kept its promise, never speaking a word, never letting on about the secret lives and deaths it held close to its breast.

Except that it never was a true secret. There was always someone who knew, someone whispering, someone who could point to the guilty.

It has taken years, but now, finally, it is time to see, to show and to speak.

The excavators begin again, deciding to continue working on this first body. With brushes and small scrapers, they resume the task of removing the dirt that has compacted around his sullen bones.

A patch of fraying material covering what was once a shoulder begins to push up into the sunlight. The team moves on, along the breastbone towards the deformed sphere of a head. A few stiff hairs begin to show through the mud. One of the team bends down and carefully cuts a few strands and places them with pincers into a transparent plastic bag. She holds them up to the light, then passes them to a man standing at the edge of the pit, who examines them before placing the bag in a metal briefcase.

More minutes pass. There would once have been a face where their tools are picking and smoothing away, he thinks. Now it is a featureless skull: no smile or frown, no worry lines on the brow, no shining eyes. Just holes. And a few teeth.

Activity around the corpse's face intensifies: the team have found something – something that might help identify the person who once lived in these bones. He peers in, but the excavators' bodies block his view.

He looks up at the cold, cloudless November sky. No birds, no wind, not even a plane cutting through the blue. Was he right coming here? Perhaps he should have stayed at the hospital. But he wanted to see for himself. There is no one else to mark this moment. Only him. He is the last of them, the last of the line. Not long, and he might be entirely on his own.

The man with the metal briefcase is talking to the team leader again. He nods as she comments on what they've found near the dead man's face. After a moment, he gets up and walks over.

'What is it?'

'Glasses,' the man says. 'The same model, the same shape as the ones in the photograph.'

'And the hair? That was his hair you were looking at earlier on.'

'Yes.'

Neither of them speaks for a moment. He looks over again at the body.

'You think it's him?'

'A DNA test will tell us for sure. We can take a sample from you now. Then we'll do the procedure, just to be a hundred per cent. But it will take a few weeks.'

The man puts his hands on his hips and looks over at the body.

'But for my money, that's him. That's Maximiliano Cámara.'

ONE

Wednesday 28th October

A door opened.

'Max?'

He turned and saw a small, badger-like woman shuffling along the corridor towards him.

'Hello, Pilar.'

'I saw you coming. The window looks over the entrance.'

'Is he . . . ?'

'He was on the kitchen floor, couldn't move.'

She shook her head.

'And he'd messed himself. I had to clean that up. But they were quick about it. Only five or ten minutes after I called. I didn't like to tell anyone, the neighbours. But what with the sirens, and them banging up and down the stairway, well, of course, people hear noises, and they open their doors to see what's going on. I had to tell them something. Said he'd taken a turn. Didn't know myself for sure till the doctor said. But I did wonder, when I saw him, saw that he couldn't move properly. I thought, this looks like one of those *embolias*.' A stroke.

An orderly was slowly pushing a cleaning trolley down the corridor, preparing for a final sweep and mop before leaving the ward in the hands of the night shift. Cámara glanced up at a clock on the wall: it was gone eleven.

'I came straight from the station,' he said.

'I rang you as soon as I got a chance. Had to get him here and make sure he was all right first. I didn't know . . . well, I didn't know if he was about to head over to the other *barrio*.' To the other side.

She frowned at him.

'It's them funny plants he's got growing on the patio, Max. They're evil. And they make the flat smell appalling. It's just not right. You should know, being a policeman. You should arrest him. I know he's your own grandfather, and he brought you up, but it's the only way. It'll just kill him otherwise.'

That being arrested might change Hilario's views on anything brought a fleeting smile to Cámara's face. But he was anxious to go in and see his grandfather; he was still alive, that much was clear, if little else was.

And Pilar should head back home. Their housekeeper had been with them since the beginning, since Cámara had moved in to live with Hilario as a shocked, angry twelve-year-old, and she was the closest he had to an extended family in Albacete – a bustling, dark-eyed widow, coming and going from the flat at will, cleaning, cooking, tidying, and prodding them along, fulfilling a role she felt she had to perform in the absence of any wife or mother in the house. She had no family, and neither did they, and so the three of them had made a curious trinity.

Cámara looked in the direction of Hilario's room.

'Is anyone in there with him now?'

'No. The doctors came this afternoon. They stabilised him, or something. Gave him pills to clear his blood. Because it's a clot. Gets into the brain. But they say he's all right now. Got him under observation. On his own in there, which is nice. You don't really want to be sharing a room when you're not feeling good.'

'But we can go in and out?'

'Oh, yes, it's fine. They seem to think the company does him good. Familiar people, like me or you. Helps him, they said.'

'You should go. Get some sleep. You'll have been here for hours.'

'He needs someone here, as I said. And you made it as quickly as you could.'

She made to move. They kissed on both cheeks and he stepped to one side to allow her to shuffle down the corridor.

'I know my way out. I'll be back in the morning.'

From behind he heard the wheels of the cleaning trolley squeaking as the orderly started heading towards the exit. The lights in the corridor dimmed as the woman passed through the swing doors and he was left on his own.

He took a step towards Hilario's room, then checked himself. A sound of papers being shuffled had come from further up. Following his ears, he turned and walked towards the ward reception area. A nurse was sitting behind the counter, writing notes on a form.

'Did you want something?'

Cámara leaned in over the counter.

'I've just arrived from Madrid. My grandfather, Hilario Cámara—'

'Room four.'

'I know. I just wanted to talk to someone about him before going in to see him.'

The nurse reached over for a card from a box file at the side of the counter.

'Brought in just after eleven this morning,' he read off the report. 'Mild stroke, blood clot in the left hemisphere of the brain. Partial paralysis of the right side of the body. He's under observation.'

'Prognosis?' Cámara asked.

The nurse looked up.

'I've seen worse cases, but someone his age?'

He glanced back down at the report.

'Does he suffer from MS?'

Cámara shook his head.

'No. Not that I know of. Why?'

'Blood tests show traces of cannabinoids. Some MS sufferers take it. It's illegal, I know, but it's supposed to help relieve the symptoms.'

Cámara sniffed.

'Look, is there anyone else I can talk to?'

'The doctor will be making her round at half-past nine tomorrow morning.'

The nurse put the card back in the box and turned back to his forms.

'You can talk to her then.'

Room four was in partial darkness: an emergency light on the wall gave a dull, yellowy glow. Cámara opened and closed the door as quietly as he could.

'Max!'

The voice was slurred, but loud enough to wake most of the ward.

'Is that you? Turn the fucking lights on. Like the Dark Ages in here.'

Cámara found the switch.

'Took your time. I've been in here for days.'

Cámara moved towards the bed. A drip was feeding into the back of Hilario's hand, while an oxygen mask was hanging loosely below his chin.

'Or at least it feels like it.'

Cámara leaned over his grandfather and put a hand on his arm. Hilario's face had changed: tenser, paler, as though the skin had been stretched in some places yet lay hanging in folds in others.

'You might want to keep your voice down,' Cámara said.

'*El tiempo es oro y la vida un tesoro.*' Time is gold and life is a treasure. 'Besides, what's the good of keeping quiet? Frightened I might wake up the neighbours? They're all brain dead in here. A seventeen-gun salute couldn't wake them. Have you seen them? They're all old and decrepit. Glad they haven't put me in with any of them.'

'I just don't want you to get tired, that's all. And you're slurring your words.'

'Course I'm slurring my words. So would you if a blood clot the size of a tennis ball had got stuck in your brain. What am I supposed to do? Get up and dance a tango?'

'All right. Calm down.'

'I am calm. Just these wires and masks and things they cover you with. Makes me nervous.'

He motioned towards the side of the bed.

'Here, have a seat. It's good to see you. Come from Madrid?'

Cámara reached out for the plastic chair and placed it at Hilario's side.

'Still with Alicia? Is that going well? Give her my love.'

'You haven't met her yet.'

'Doesn't matter. Don't be so rational. Always was your problem. I feel like I've met her. In fact, I reckon I know her better than you. She's good for you, that girl. You should stick around with her.'

'We're doing all right.'

'That will have to do. A good relationship, good sex, these things are important. And I'm not just talking about relieving physical urges. It's more than that. Gives meaning to life. And that's not easy.'

Cámara grinned. Alicia had already left for work at the newspaper by the time he got the call from Pilar, and he was just getting ready to start his shift at the bar. He rang her as soon as he got to Atocha station. He would have to wait for a couple of hours before he could get the first train down to Albacete. She said she would try to make it over before he left, and ran in just as he was making his way to the platform. Enough time to kiss him and hope Hilario would be all right.

'She sends her love,' Cámara said.

'See? And she hasn't met me, either.'

'Perhaps. One day.'

'Get her down here. I'm not going to be here for long.'

Cámara twitched.

'What was that?'

'I mean here in the hospital, idiot. I'm not planning on checking out of anywhere else in the near future.'

'You should take it slowly. I'll talk to the doctors in the morning, but in case you hadn't noticed, half your body's paralysed. You're not going anywhere in a hurry.'

From behind the contorted mask of his face, a hard, unwavering stare settled in Hilario's eyes.

'I'll go where I like, whenever I like.'

Cámara shrugged.

'Anyone would think you're adopted,' Hilario said. 'Can't believe you're flesh and blood sometimes. Didn't you learn anything? It's all that bollocks they've filled your head with in the police. Taking orders. Doctors are just the same. They call me a patient but I'm really an inmate in here.'

Cámara saw the bait clearly, and refused to bite. He'd been on extended sick leave from his job as a homicide detective with the *Policía Nacional* in Valencia for almost four months. He didn't know himself if he was still really police or not, or if he'd ever go back. But the last person he was going to talk to about it was Hilario, with his strong, anti-authoritarian beliefs.

'They're trying to make you better.'

'Funny way of going about it, making me lie down and shoving bits of plastic piping into me. If you make someone act dead for long enough you'll kill them in the end. It's sympathetic magic. They should have me up and about, making my brain work again.'

'I don't think there's much to worry about there,' Cámara mumbled.

'What's that?'

'I think your brain's fine,' he said more loudly.

'I've got to get my brain communicating with my body properly again. Build some new neurological pathways. Because at the moment there's a bunch of grey cells up here that looks like something you might spread on your toast.'

He tried waving a hand in the direction of his head, but it failed to budge. Cámara wasn't sure what was happening at first, until he saw the frustration in Hilario's eyes, the veins bulging in his neck as his hand merely quivered on the bed sheet where it refused to lift up.

'Stop, stop!' he cried.

'*¡Me cago en la hostia!*' Fucking hell!

'Take it easy. You want to give yourself a heart attack as well?'

'It was moving. Did you see it? It was moving. Idiots say I'm paralysed, but it was definitely moving.'

Cámara nodded, pursing his lips.

'You're right, it moved. A little bit. But you need to rest.'

The door opened and the nurse walked in.

'What's going on? He needs to sleep, you know. You can't stay if you're going to excite him.'

'Who are you?' Hilario growled.

'There's a chair here for you to sleep on,' the nurse indicated to Cámara. 'But I need you to be quiet. You're waking up the other patients with all this noise.'

'Piss off.'

'Rest, Señor Cámara. The doctor will be round in the morning.'

The nurse switched off the light and closed the door behind him.

'He's a cheery sort.'

'I'll turn on the light again.'

'Don't bother. There's a lamp here somewhere by the bed.'

Cámara fumbled around until he found a switch, and a pool of harsh, bluish light shone down on them.

'It's these low-wattage bulbs,' Hilario said, squinting.

Cámara stood up and walked to the window. He pushed the blinds back and looked out at an occasional car streaming past, a solitary smoker outside the hospital entrance stubbing out his cigarette before heading back inside to watch over a loved one for the night. An ill wife? A child?

'I can't sleep,' Hilario said. 'Too much going on in this damaged brain of mine. Repairing itself, I shouldn't reckon. Nothing to do with the pills they're giving me. Just let nature take its course.'

'Do you want anything?' Cámara asked, turning back to the room. 'Some water?'

'I'm fine. You can read to me if you like. There's a copy of today's paper around somewhere. I saw Pilar with it earlier.'

The newspaper was resting on a ledge opposite the bed. Cámara picked it up, sat down, and started flicking through the pages.

'A new kindergarten's been opened on Calle Cervantes.'

'Stop showing off. I know you hate newspapers. Doesn't stop you going out with a journalist, though.'

'I don't hate the media. I just don't like the way they manipulate people.'

'A story about a new kindergarten is hardly major propaganda.'

'Albacete FC lost again.'

'That's not news. More like the weather report.'

The pages ruffled as Cámara flicked through. He paused.

'What's that?' Hilario said.

'They're digging up part of the cemetery.'

'Run out of space, have they? Too many dead people round here. Some of them still walking the streets.'

Cámara continued reading.

'Something to do with people executed under Franco, after the war. They reckon many were buried in an unmarked mass grave, right in the middle of the cemetery. It's just a patch of wasteland now. The Town Hall's behind it, putting up the money. Say it's time to heal the wounds from the past.'

'Funny way to heal wounds by opening them up again. These Socialists just want to remind everyone how nasty the right-wingers were. Forget that they were capable of killing a few people themselves in their time. It's just vote grabbing. There'll be elections coming up soon. Otherwise they wouldn't bother.'

Cámara was silent.

'Anything else?'

Cámara folded the paper and let it fall on to the floor below his chair.

'A murder,' he said. 'Fifteen-year-old girl. Found her body near the tip by the industrial estate.'

He closed his eyes.

'She'd been raped.'

TWO

Thursday 29th October

Getting out of the hospital proved difficult. The morning brought a wave of visiting doctors, nurses, more doctors, and people who didn't identify themselves, but walked in, peered and prodded at Hilario in various ways and then left, without a word. Afterwards he had to track some of these creatures down, trying to get them to say something coherent about his grandfather's condition. After several hours' shadowing and buttonholing, it seemed that medical opinion was that the patient was 'stable', 'improving' even, but would need 'continued observation'. The stroke had been mild, thankfully, but he was still at risk.

Pilar turned up after lunch, in time to find a nurse showing Cámara how to put a bedpan in place.

'He hasn't eaten since his last bowel movement. What's he need that for?'

'In case of emergency,' Cámara said. 'During the night, when I'm here. They're putting him on to solids later this afternoon.'

'He'll be constipated after all that's happened. And the drugs they've filled him with won't help. Always bung you up.'

Hilario fell in and out of sleep. Cámara had tried putting the television on during the night to help his grandfather through his insomnia, but you needed a special plastic card-key from reception, and no one could give him one till the morning shift had started. So they'd chatted, and Cámara had read articles in the sports pages building up to the week-end's matches, until he had fallen into uncomfortable, shallow sleep on the black, sweaty chair. Both he and Hilario were woken at dawn by the first morning rounds.

'Idiots. Leave me alone.'

Hilario had waved his hand – his right hand, the one that was supposed to be paralysed. Not very high, and it had quickly flopped back on to the bed. Was he regaining some movement there?

Cámara had managed to get some coffee from the canteen on the ground floor, and then a sandwich and a flavourless chocolate doughnut from a vending machine near the lifts, but by the afternoon he was ready to head over to the flat, have a shower and lie down for an hour or two while Pilar relieved him.

But Pilar wanted to talk; she was nervous about sitting here on her own with Hilario. Life at the flat was different – there she had things to do, and a certain power. Here in the hospital she was jumpy, anxiously looking for little tasks to perform. And in this state she talked at him, as though nailing him to the chair, ignoring Hilario. Not waiting for her to pause, Cámara got up and walked out the door. A few minutes later, with the card-key from reception in its allocated slot, the television was on and Pilar was absorbed in a Venezuelan soap opera.

'Yes, you go. We'll be fine.'

Hilario had fallen asleep again.

'I'll be back in a few hours.'

'Don't you worry. Take your time. There's some meat stew in the fridge, left over from Tuesday. Should still be all right.'

It was getting dark by the time he stepped outside. The first street lamps were flickering and cars were driving with their sidelights on.

He breathed in deeply and leaned against a railing for a second, wondering to himself about suddenly being back here, in Albacete. What would happen to Hilario? He'd been livelier the night before. Today he'd barely spoken, acting out far better the role of ill old person than was expected of him. There would be time for rebuilding connections in his brain later. If he made it.

He pulled himself away from the railings and started to walk. He needed to stretch his legs, get some air back inside him after hours on the train and then in the hospital. Albacete was a small city, and the flat was no more than a fifteen-minute walk from where he was, but he decided to strike out into the streets in another direction first. Exercise, not more sitting and lying down, would set him up better for another night on duty.

It was gone seven and the shops were busy with last-minute buyers before eight-o'clock closing time. Cars were left double-parked with flashing emergency lights on as people dashed in and out of grocers', stationers' and the shops run by Chinese immigrants selling cheap plastic household goods. He was always surprised that there could be so much bustle in this small urban space. Just a few streets away, where the suburbs ended, the flat, featureless light brown fields of the Albacete basin – La Mancha – stretched for long distances. The city felt like an oasis in the desert, or an island many, many miles from any other civilised land mass, and yet you were almost unaware of this as the cars and the people created a bubble of noise and energy. As if to protect themselves, he thought. To protect themselves from remembering that they were afloat, lost, and alone.

It could almost have been a place worth visiting. There were a few interesting little corners, and a large, attractive public garden, known simply by locals as *El Parque*, although it did have some official, more long-winded title. Yet in reality there was nothing to recommend the city – no riverbanks, no museums of note, no great public buildings. If anyone did associate it with anything, it was with knives: Albacete was, for reasons that no one could explain convincingly, a centre of knife manufacture, and knife shops, selling anything from mediaeval-style swords to fat short blades for cutting off a pig's testicles, catered to the odd tourist who happened to have got lost and found himself in this unloved part of the country.

Albacete – caga y vete, went the phrase. Albacete – shit there and get out. It was a motto Cámara himself had tried to live by.

Except that now he was back.

Not for long, he tried telling himself. But the truth was that he couldn't be sure. Much depended on Hilario, and how he recovered. If he remained partially paralysed it would be too much for Pilar to look after him on her own. And there was no way they would ever get him into an old people's home. Not that he really wanted that anyway, but the idea of Hilario sitting quietly in some television lounge surrounded by other OAPs was ludicrous. He'd either be trying to sleep with the nurses or digging a tunnel to get out before the sun had set on the first day.

So what would happen? Would he have to stay here in Albacete indefinitely, acting as a home help? They could move together, go elsewhere. But where? Madrid? Valencia? That would mean taking up his job with the police again.

And Alicia? What happened to her in this scenario? She'd texted him a couple of times during the day to see how things were going, and he thought about giving her a ring now, but he was still working things out. Time to think and digest first.

These had been a good few months with her. If circumstances had been different he would never have moved in like that with any woman. And he told himself that he hadn't – not really. It was just that he didn't have a home at that moment – the last one in Valencia had collapsed into a heap of rubble after work on a nearby metro line had sent cracks running up the walls. So really he'd only bedded down for a while, until he could set himself up again, and decide what he was going to do.

But weeks had passed, and vivified by an erotic energy that had quickly reignited between them – and which had surprised them both by its force – he had ended up staying in Alicia's small attic apartment for the entire summer, enduring the intensity of the Madrid heat, splashing their bodies cool with water in between bouts of lovemaking.

When the heat began to lessen, and Madrileños returned from their beach holidays, he got a job working at a bar in the next street. The late shifts coincided well with Alicia's work at the newspaper, and they usually got part of the morning together before she had to leave again. Then at weekends he tried taking photographs with a new digital camera he'd bought. Shots of the city, of faces in the street, of details that caught his eye – a griffin statue on top of a facade, a broken 'No Entry' sign, anti-capitalist graffiti on the walls. Nothing anyone else would be interested in seeing, perhaps, but he enjoyed watching the city through a lens for a while.

Yet the question remained: would he return to his job in the police? His boss in Valencia, Commissioner Pardo, had placed him on 'indefinite' sick leave at the end of the Sofía Bodí case back in July, but he knew that couldn't last. It was late October already. Some time soon, he could tell, a phone call would come from someone in Personnel making enquiries about his state of health, hinting that his salary – or the 80 per cent of it that he was still getting paid – might not continue beyond the New Year. Money was tight; they were making big cuts. He would have to take a decision. But life with Alicia, enjoying a mini late adolescence, had drawn him in, and he was reluctant for it to end.

Except that now, it seemed, decisions were being made for him.

He checked the time: Pilar would be all right for another couple of hours at least.

He'd meandered through the city centre. The flat was close by now, but rather than continue down the avenue that took him almost to his old front door, he turned right and pushed up through streets lined with tightly packed dark-brick blocks of flats. On his left he saw the cemetery, while up ahead, where the street ended, metallic grey warehouses closed off the view, like city walls. Skirting around them, he skipped over some bollards and headed into the industrial area. The streets here were built for lorries and vans; pedestrians weren't catered for, and so he had to walk close to the edge, standing out of the way as articulated trucks came bearing down, their headlamps shining brightly in his eyes, returning to their depots after a day out on the road.

After a few hundred metres he crossed the street and stepped over the kerb to strike out over a patch of wasteland.

It was completely dark by now, and he had to watch his feet to avoid stepping in dog turds, but the street lamps on the far side of the plot dimly showed him where he was heading, while the blackness beyond marked the end of the city and the beginning of the La Mancha emptiness.

Old shoes, broken chairs, crushed empty yoghurt pots and shredded tyres littered the ground. They had never got round to building anything here. Some said there was a legal dispute over who owned it that had never been resolved. Others that no one wanted to buy: it was haunted. The memory of what had happened here over thirty years before had still not faded. Neither for him nor for the rest of the city.

There was the same feeling that he always had whenever he came this way, as though being hit on the head by a slab of ice. He could feel his cheek muscles tensing, the knot somewhere in his gut.

A dark green rubbish container stood on the far side. A curious place to put one, for a plot of land everyone used as a makeshift dump in the first place. But from the police tape that had been stuck around it, he concluded that that was where the girl's body had been left.

Once he was about twenty metres away from it, he slowed his pace, looking closely at the ground, then back up at the container. Edging around it in a circle, gradually getting nearer, he kept glancing between the floor and the bin, checking for anything that might catch his eye. The problem in this littered environment was finding anything, any clue. The wealth of material almost obliterated the evidence. And if something was found that could be linked, there was a high chance of it being contaminated and unusable.

There was simply too much, and it was too dark to make anything out. What was he doing here, anyway?

Stupid question.

He took a couple of steps forward and drew closer to the rubbish container. Blue-and-white tape had been wrapped around it a few times, as though marking territory, and then more had been placed around the top edge, to seal it down. The local *científicos* – the crime scene squad – would already have been round, but they might want to make more inspections in the morning. In the meantime it had to be kept closed. He was surprised they hadn't placed a guard to watch over it for the night.

He leaned in, pulling at the tape to see if it would come off. He just wanted to see. Just needed to catch a glimpse of where the girl had been left. He had already caught the smell of the decomposing corpse that had been pulled out of here . . .

By the time he understood what the noise was, the squad car was drawing up behind him, screeching to a halt as it braked hard.

Cámara sniffed and turned round, but already a policeman was grabbing his shoulders, pulling him down to the ground and jerking his arm behind his back.

'Hold on,' he said. 'Just hold on a minute.'

The other officer had jumped out of the car and was approaching with a pair of handcuffs.

'Keep him down, Fuentes.'

'He's struggling.'

'I am not struggling,' Cámara called up. 'Calm down and let me explain. I'm police. Chief Inspector Cámara.'

There was a blow to the back of his head.

'Disturbing a crime scene and impersonating a police officer. I'd keep quiet if I were you.'

But Cámara had blacked out.

THREE

Friday 30th October

He knew that smell, of stale metallic sweat born of fear and anger. The difference was that in the past he had always been able to walk away from it, to climb back up the steps to the ground floor, with a nod to the poor sods on guard duty, and away into the corridors and offices of his ordinary existence. Police station cells might change superficially from one city to the next, but they were the same in essence: rank, frustrating and filthy, a greying chill like the slime on a rotting fish seeping out of the brickwork and penetrating your skin.

He'd avoided them as best he could, leaving it wherever possible to others, further down the chain of command, to deposit and fetch men from the foetid dungeons. It was the stench more than anything else that seemed to reach into his stomach. Yet this time there was no walking away: he was on the other side of the square, grey iron bars, closing his eyes, his face, as much of himself as he could, against the oppressive weight of the tiny cell he had woken up in.

He heard movement outside, a key slotting into a hole.

Clarity of thought was eluding him that morning, but he felt certain the policeman now looking down at him as he sat on the bed was different from either of those who had brought him in. The lump on the back of his head still throbbed.

'The commissioner wants to see you.'

Despite the fugginess, he noted the surprise, even a begrudging respect, in the officer's voice as they went upstairs and he handed him back his money, keys and mobile phone.

He was taken to another room. Two glasses of coffee were on a tray on the main desk, next to a plate of *madalena* cakes and a couple of croissants. The officer indicated for him to sit down, then left, closing the door behind him. Cámara lifted his arm up and smelt at his clothes: the cell odour had come with him.

The office was well lit, with two large windows: he was in a corner room on what appeared to be the second floor of the Jefatura – the city's main police station – judging by the treetops just visible from a busy street outside. Cupboards trimmed in light oak-effect panels sat beneath the windows, a half-open sliding door giving him a glimpse of the cardboard box files filling the space inside. On top, a couple of plaques for merit and service to the *Policía Nacional* squatted next to a photo of a smiling woman in her forties with dyed blonde hair.

Cámara stretched out in his chair, breathing life into his limbs. He was being made to wait. The officer who had brought him up from the cells had clearly mentioned a 'commissioner'. In a small city like Albacete such high-ranking policemen were a rarity. Whoever was expecting him to share an impromptu breakfast was going to be a big fish.

Meanwhile, the coffee was going cold. Should he wait politely until his host appeared?

Bollocks to that. He was going to drink it while it was still hot.

The door opened as he chewed on his first mouthful of croissant.

'Oh, good. You've already started. My apologies. I got waylaid.'

Cámara lifted a hand to wipe the crumbs from his mouth; there was something familiar about that voice.

He turned to see. A tall, slender man in a grey suit with a white shirt and red tie was walking towards him, both arms outstretched.

'Max, Max, Max.'

They embraced.

'If they'd said the next time I saw you I'd be fishing you out of the cells, you know what? Somehow I would have believed them.'

He patted Cámara on the cheek affectionately.

'Getting into trouble. Always getting into trouble. I think that's why I always wanted to play with you when we were kids. For you it comes naturally – for me it's a lot more hard work.'

Cámara hadn't seen Ernesto Yago for over twenty years. They'd both finished their law degrees at the local university and were going up to the national police academy at Avila. The same glimmer of guarded humour shone in his eyes, yet he seemed wrapped in his position and authority, and the cloth fitted him well, as though he had always known he was destined for high rank.

'*Commissioner* Yago?' Cámara asked with a grin. '*Eres un hijo de puta.*' You son of a bitch. 'I'm not going to ask how many arses you had to lick to get here.'

'Back in my home town too. You could do it as well, Max. Come home to Albacete. I could speak to a few people.'

Cámara laughed. It was just like Yago to hit a grey area between irony and innocent seriousness. And as ever Cámara found himself taking him at his word, yet wondering if he was the butt of the joke. Falling instantly back into patterns between them that he'd forgotten existed.

'Ernesto, I've never stopped running from here. I'm out of it, and doing all right.'

Yago slapped him on the arm and walked round to the other side of the desk, picking up the second glass of coffee and downing it in one.

'You sure?' he said, lowering himself into his chair.

Cámara sat down on a low sofa, lifting his feet and putting them on Yago's desk.

'I heard you had a bit of trouble.'

'Is that why you kept me waiting? On the phone to Valencia?'

Yago shrugged.

'Look, Max, you were arrested tampering with a crime scene.'

'Well, your officers didn't really give me a chance to explain myself.'

'I know why you were there,' Yago said. 'And it's all going to be OK, but of course I've got to make some enquiries. There's got to be some paperwork here, even if it's so I can see my old schoolmate again, give him breakfast, a pat on the back and send him on his way.'

He opened the palms of his hands, as though asking forgiveness.

'You know how this works.'

Cámara finished the croissant and leaned over to grab a *madalena*, dipping it into the dregs of his coffee.

'So how much did they tell you?'

'Indefinite sick leave. The Bodí case. You made Homicide. I'm happy for you.'

Cámara pulled a face.

'All right. "Happy" might not be the right word for it. But your career's looking good. Valencia – that's a big city.'

'I haven't been back for a few months,' Cámara said. 'Been in Madrid.'

'Looking for something else?'

Cámara shook his head.

'I don't know. Looking and not looking. Trying to think about it by not thinking about it, if you see what I mean.'

'Wondering whether to go back at all. Whether it's all worth it. Everyone goes through it at some stage. Like some kind of natural law.'

'I killed someone,' Cámara said. 'Shot him. The murderer.'

'The councillor in the Bodí case. Yeah, it was on the news.'

There was a pause for a moment before Yago spoke again.

'You did the right thing. The man was a monster – he was running away.'

'That's what I tell myself,' Cámara said. 'And it sort of works.'

'Is there anyone?' Yago asked. 'A woman? A wife?'

'In Madrid. Recent thing. We'll see how it goes.'

'Well, some things haven't changed then. But it helps, you know, even if it isn't for ever. You never were a settling sort, but they say it's good for your health. Especially for men. A long-term relationship gives you another two or three years, they say. Patricia and I are still going strong.'

Cámara smiled.

'You're still together?' he said. 'That's wonderful. But then with you I'd say I'm not surprised at all. How long have you been together? Since school, right?'

'I was eighteen, she was seventeen. Twenty-five years.'

'Kids?'

'Nah,' Yago frowned. 'One of those things.'

'And she's followed you around all this time just for love?'

'I was in Seville at first, after Avila.'

'Must have been the last time we saw each other.'

'There for seven or eight years, then I made inspector and moved to Madrid. Which was where I stayed until a couple of years ago. Then this came up and I jumped. Patricia always wanted us to come back one day.'

'So she's happy?'

'I could have stayed,' Yago said. 'Forwarded my career some more.'

'But now you're head of the *Policía Judicial*' – the investigating police – 'for the whole of Albacete,' Cámara said. 'I saw the sign on the door. That's not bad.'

'It's fine,' Yago said. 'I won't be going any further, though. But I did it for Patricia's sake. Like you said, she's been following me around all this time, and I promised we'd come back home as soon as we could.'

'But still, you wonder sometimes about how much higher you could have climbed.'

Yago wrinkled his nose.

'It's history. The point is I'm here now, and in a position to help out my old mate in his hour of need.'

'I didn't know being made a commissioner gave you superpowers.'

Yago wheezed a laugh.

'Shut up, you bastard. You want some more coffee?'

'Yeah,' Cámara drawled. 'Why not?'

The two of them eyed one another conspiratorially as a junior member of staff was called to bring them some more breakfast.

Perks of the job, Yago mouthed silently to Cámara as fresh cups and croissants were brought in.

'You're just trying to convince me that police work is a cushy job,' Cámara said once the door had been closed again. He leaned over and sank his teeth into the pastry. 'And you may be succeeding.'

Yago smiled.

'Aren't you going to have one?' Cámara asked. 'You look a lot slimmer than you used to be. You were always a bit overweight.'

'Between you and me,' Yago said, 'the doctor's put me on some pep-up pills.'

Cámara raised an eyebrow.

'Dip in my energy levels. Fatigue, working too hard. I don't know.'

'Responsibility?'

'Maybe. Or just getting old. But anyway, these pills keep me ticking along better. And one of the side effects is a bit of weight loss.'

'Magic pills? Sounds like a nice doctor.'

'And they make you hornier as well.'

'Sounds like a *really* nice doctor.'

'I'll introduce you to him.'

'So that's why Patricia's happy to be back home.'

Yago put his coffee cup on the desk and stood up, flexing his legs a little.

'So why are you back here anyway?' he asked. 'Albacete can't be that bad if you came all this way from Madrid.'

Cámara told him about Hilario's stroke.

'I'm sorry. I didn't realise.'

He took a deep breath and sighed, reaching into a drawer for a form.

'Makes sense, though, I suppose.'

From the other side of the desk, Cámara remained silent.

'Look, I'm going to have to say something,' Yago said. 'I think it makes sense to spell it out. Just tell them.'

He began writing on the form.

'Chief Inspector Max Cámara, of the Valencia Homicide Group and currently on indefinite leave, was arrested on suspicion of tampering with a crime scene near the industrial quarter on the night of 28th October. He admitted that he had acted in error and was subsequently released without charge.'

Cámara closed his eyes as Yago continued.

'We believe it is pertinent to add that Chief Inspector Cámara's current circumstances mitigate any unintended wrongdoing in this case, owing to a grave and sudden family crisis which has impaired – no – temporarily impaired his judgement.'

Cámara was about to say something, but stopped.

Yago paused to look at him, then started writing again.

'Furthermore, the nature of the crime scene – a murder of a young woman – gives extra weight to excusing the chief inspector, as the location, victim and MO of the murderer are all very similar to a murder that took place in this city over thirty years ago: that of Concha Cámara, Chief Inspector Max Cámara's sister.'

Yago scribbled a signature and glanced up. Cámara had opened his eyes, but was looking away.

'There,' Yago said. 'That should do it.'

FOUR

It was still quite early in the morning, and a dusty breeze was playing with the leaves in the plane trees as he walked away from the Jefatura. The hospital was ten minutes away; he needed to get over, to check on Hilario, and to relieve Pilar. She would be annoyed that he hadn't shown up the night before, but he knew she wouldn't leave the patient on his own. Some sweet words, perhaps a kiss on her cheek, and all would be forgiven.

Yago had wanted Cámara to meet Diego Jiménez, his head of Homicide and the inspector in charge of the murder case. They were working on the assumption that Mirella Faro, the girl whose body had been found in the rubbish container, had been taking drugs: the forensic team had found needle marks on her arms, and the area was known as a spot for dealing.

Inspector Jiménez appeared competent and thorough enough, Cámara thought, the steady sort happiest when dealing with something straightforward and routine. They didn't get many murders in Albacete, thank God, but at least when they came in they were easily categorised into the usual varieties: wife killings, revenge attacks, or, as in this case, drug related. Some kind of *ajuste de cuentas*, Yago and Jiménez both agreed – a settling of scores. The poor girl was probably just some unlucky pawn in a bigger struggle. Jiménez was already liaising with his colleagues in Narcotics, and they had some leads.

We've got some leads. It was the kind of line Cámara himself had been forced to use on occasion. Usually when he didn't have a fucking clue where to start.

Medium height, balding, his remaining hair turning grey, a moustache, bit of a paunch developing. Mid-fifties perhaps. Jiménez was a middling sort of middle-grade police officer. Let's just hope his case turns out to be of the middling sort as well, Cámara thought.

A magpie was cackling somewhere in the branches overhead, and for a moment his attention was diverted as it dived down in front of him and swooped over the road before finding a perch on the rooftop of a yellow-brick block of flats opposite, sending a small group of sparrows flying off in a flurry.

Of course he himself had his doubts: there was too much oddness about the case. Why strip the girl and leave her in the rubbish? That wasn't just murder; that was a statement. And perhaps a settling of scores could explain that in some way. Or was it a serial killer? Too much time had passed, but the similarities with the murder of his sister Concha, over thirty years before, were obvious.

Or at least for him. But attacking, raping, strangling, stripping and finally dumping an adolescent girl in the rubbish was perhaps an MO that wasn't so rare or extra-ordinary: there was a basic structure there, one that could arise spontaneously at almost any time and in any place.

Except that this wasn't any place: Mirella Faro had been

found in almost the same spot where he himself had found Concha back then. Just an eleven-year-old kid trying to help out as search parties made up of neighbours, friends, policemen and even their off-duty colleagues scoured the city looking for the girl who'd gone missing three days before. A fifteen-year-old just didn't do that in 1977. Not in Albacete. Something must have gone badly wrong. They hoped that they could find her in time, but already fear was growing stronger in them. Cámara remembered his mother's face, pale and tight like a screwed-up fist. Perhaps she already knew by then that Concha was dead.

And so attention had started moving out to the wasteland areas around the city centre. Only a handful of the new apartment blocks had been built by that stage, yet areas of land had been divided up for more to come, some already with streets, pavements and street lighting, waiting for the builders to move in and start laying their concrete. In the meantime boys kicked balls around, weeds grew, and people dumped their rubbish on corners. When they turned to look for Concha there, the fear was already turning to anger.

A friend had tagged along, one of the other kids from Cámara's street. Ernesto Yago was one of those boys who wanted to break the rules like the others, but never quite had the courage to pick up a stone and throw it at a window. But Concha's disappearance had disturbed him, and he'd been at the flat for much of the time, staying with Cámara, not saying a lot, playing cards with him on his bedroom floor, watching television.

The two of them broke away a little from the main group when they reached the outskirts of the city. Yago wanted to show Cámara an ants' nest he'd seen there a few days before. They grabbed a couple of sticks and started poking at it, watching the black creatures wriggle up towards their hands before shaking the sticks clean. A few yards away the searchers were using sticks to beat away the weeds, looking for clues, anything. Concha had been wearing a blue denim dress the last time anyone had seen her. Even just finding that, or a scrap of it, could prove useful.

Cámara got up from the ants and started swishing away himself at the long grass, his eyes focused down on the ground, but his thoughts were elsewhere: the mournful, fearful sadness rose and fell in him at will, it seemed. And he hated the moodiness that now gripped at his feelings, his behaviour.

Yago fell in at his side, and they flicked a path through the wasteland, moving this way and that as the inclination took them. The other seekers were further away now, while in front of them was a fly tip. Broken tiles lay scattered around their feet, crowned with rusting, dirty household goods – a fridge with no door, metal railing shelves bent; an armchair with faded geometrical patterns and loose stuffing. It lay on its back. Yago climbed the pile of rubbish and kicked at it, watching it roll down on to the unused pavement at the side. It landed on its feet and he went to sit on it, grinning as though assuming a throne.

'You'll get flea-bitten, idiot,' Cámara said, kicking away at the other detritus at his feet.

And it was then that he saw her hair, dusty and stiff-looking as it lay mingling with the broken pots and empty cans of tuna. Nothing moved, and he tried to speak, but couldn't. Yago had understood at once, and came bounding over from the chair.

'Where?' he said.

Cámara pointed down with his foot; it was the best he could do.

Yago had started at once, reaching down and pulling away the loose cardboard, rubble and shredded plastic bags that covered her face. Her eyes were closed, her features discoloured and misshapen, but there was no doubt who it was.

'Step away,' Yago said. 'We shouldn't touch it.'

He waved to the other searchers silently.

'This is a crime scene.'

Years later, at one of the last times they were together before leaving the Avila academy, they admitted to each other that it had been the moment they both had become policemen.

Arriving at the hospital, he took the lift up to Hilario's floor. There was a different person at reception, glasses perched on her nose as she dialled a phone number. Cámara walked past and down the corridor to Hilario's room. The door was closed; he opened it and walked in.

The first thing he saw was a pair of female buttocks poking through the back opening of a regulation hospital gown.

'Oh. I'm sorry,' Cámara said, looking away. The other bed in the room must finally have been taken, he thought. But as he glanced over he saw that in the bed where Hilario was supposed to be, another woman was lying down, peering up at him from over her oxygen mask.

He looked back at the door: he was in the right room, unless . . .

'Who are you?' a male voice asked. A man had stood up, perhaps the husband of the young woman whose backside he'd just inadvertently seen. The woman herself was now climbing back into bed, looking over at him suspiciously.

'I . . . er, was looking for someone,' Cámara said. 'Hilario, an elderly man. He was here . . .'

'We just got here this morning,' the man said. 'And she was already here,' he said, pointing over to the old woman, who was lifting her mask from her face.

'Been here since earlier,' the old woman in the other bed gasped.

'There was a man,' she added. 'Bit grumpy. He left as they were bringing me in. Is he a relative of yours? It's nice to have visitors.'

Cámara made his excuses as quickly as he could and headed out the door.

'Hilario Cámara,' he said to the nurse at reception. 'My grandfather. He was here last night.'

'And he discharged himself about two hours ago,' the nurse said, taking her reading glasses away from her nose.

'What?' Cámara spluttered. 'You can't . . . he can't . . . What about Pilar? Wasn't there a woman with him? Short, middle-aged. Didn't she stop him?'

The nurse shook her head.

'There was no one,' she said. 'He was on his own last night. We tried to call, but there was no reply.'

'I was tied up,' Cámara said.

'Disgrace if you ask me,' the nurse said. 'Leaving the elderly alone like that. Anything could have happened.'

'Look . . .' Cámara hesitated. 'Yes, you're right. It was my fault. So please, let me get this straight. There was no one with him last night, and then this morning, what? He just got up out of bed and walked off?'

'Yes. That's about it. Of course we tried to stop him, but there wasn't much we could do.'

She gave him a tired stare.

'He was on his own. If you had been here we might—'

'And he could walk?'

'He didn't roll away in a wheelchair.'

'He'd just had a stroke.'

'I know. He should still be here. He needs medical attention.

But he got some movement back in the affected side of his body – only partial, mind you – and declared that the doctors were a group of amateurs who didn't have a clue what they were doing and that he was going to cure himself. I know he's a relative of yours, but he's a liability, mentally unstable. You might want to think about having him declared unfit to look after himself, then we could treat him properly, stop him from wandering off. There's only so much we can do.'

'OK,' Cámara said, trying to take it in. 'Did he at least say where he was going?'

'Well, I'm assuming he went home. But no, he didn't leave a forwarding address, if that's what you mean.'

Back outside he called Pilar's mobile.

'Yes?' came the cold reply. He'd known her since he was twelve, and the tone was unmistakeable: he'd been naughty.

'Pilar, it's me?'

'Who?'

'Look, I'm sorry about last night. I got . . . caught up. Police work.'

'Oh, it's you.'

'I'm really sorry. I just couldn't get away.'

'I see.'

'But listen, what happened? I'm at the hospital.'

'Well, I appreciate you've got more important things to do. But I thought you were on leave. Or has that finished now? But I wasn't going to wait for you all night, was I? I mean, a promise is a promise. Or at least it still is for some of us.'

'Pilar, he's not here.'

'So after a while I thought, well, I'm off. I'm not going to wait up all night.'

'Pilar, please. You're not listening.'

'What's that?

'Hilario. Where's Hilario?'

'He's at the hospital.'

'No, he's not. I'm trying to tell you.'

'Oh.'

There was a silence at the other end.

'He discharged himself. This morning. Where are you now? Are you at the flat?'

'No,' she said. 'I came back home. I'm out shopping now, I'm in the supermarket. I can, oh, I . . . *Jolines*!' Oh, blast!

'Forget it. Don't worry. Just carry on. I'll head home straight away. I'm sure he'll be there.'

'Oh, I hope so. I hope so. I should never have left him. I'm so sorry.'

A couple of taxis were at the rank by the hospital entrance, the drivers smoking and chatting. Cámara signalled to one and jumped in. Less than five minutes later they'd crossed the city centre and arrived outside Hilario's flat.

Cámara pushed the key into the lock and sprinted up the stairs.

Opening the door he was hit by a smell he hadn't come across for many years – the scent of saffron, mixing with fish heads, onion, garlic and a healthy slug of white wine. It was the way Hilario always made his fish stock.

The door clicked behind him and he walked down the dark corridor to the kitchen.

Hilario was standing with his back to him, an apron tied roughly around his waist, stirring with a wooden spoon as the blue gas flame burnt underneath.

'You've made it at last,' he said, turning around. 'I was beginning to get worried.'

FIVE

'What are you doing here? You're supposed to be in hospital.'

'So you're a doctor now, as well as a policeman.'

Hilario turned his back on him, giving the fish stock another stir and then taking his apron off. He was humming a tune merrily.

'You do remember you had a stroke, right?' Cámara asked.

Hilario picked up a knife from the counter, spun on his heel and waved the blade in his grandson's face.

'I haven't got bloody Alzheimer's, you know. Here I am, back home, getting better by the minute, and you're trying to tell me there's something wrong with me.'

'You were in hospital,' Cámara countered. 'You had a bloody stroke.'

'And now I feel fine.'

Still holding the knife, Hilario brushed past. Cámara followed him to the patio — a triangular patch of terrace where their apartment block butted against another. The bathroom windows of half a dozen neighbours looked out on to the same area from higher up, but years before Hilario had built a little gazebo with a translucent corrugated roof, allowing the light to get through while preventing prying eyes from seeing the less-than-entirely-legal crop he cultivated in a range of large terracotta pots. There were no marihuana plants now, though. This year's harvest would already have been collected and would be drying in the spare room.

'Didn't get round to pulling the roots out,' Hilario said. 'Been meaning to do it.' And he started hacking at the soil in the pots with the knife, cutting at the tendrils in order to loosen the root balls from the earth.

'Bring me a rubbish bag, will you?'

Cámara sniffed, then headed back inside.

'They're in the kitchen, in the second drawer,' Hilario called.

He'd ceased to be amazed years before by the strength of Hilario's willpower. So dismissing illness and simply getting out of bed was, if extraordinary by anyone else's standards, relatively routine with him. There was a story that, as a boy, he'd come down with pneumonia – a life-threatening illness then – and been effectively written off by the doctor. The young Hilario's response had been to get out of bed and do twenty press-ups, to everyone's surprise except his own. And the next day he'd woken up at the regular time and gone to school as if nothing had happened.

Nonetheless, as he started rummaging in the drawer, Cámara couldn't help being worried; his grandfather should still be in that hospital bed. It would be impossible to get him back there, though: a stubborn refusal to give in to any weakness made certain of that. And so here he was, at home, as though nothing had happened. Perhaps Cámara should call a doctor. But springing a medical man on Hilario like that might make him worse. At the very least it would enrage him, and Cámara's instinct told him that emotional stability as much as anything else would be important if they were going to get him through this.

Besides, you didn't tell a man like Hilario what to do. You allowed him to get on with things his way, and if possible tried to persuade him to take this course or that. Although now that he thought about it, he couldn't say if he'd ever managed to change his mind on anything. It had always been Hilario influencing him, never the other way around.

The rubbish bags weren't in the second drawer, or even the third. He opened the cupboard to check the shelves, eventually spotting a roll of black plastic on the upper shelf.

'So what happened to you last night?' Hilario called from the patio. 'Had a bit of an adventure, did you?'

Cámara headed back outside, rubbish bag in hand.

'Something like that.'

'Being coy, are you? That's good.'

He cut away a little more with the knife, before reaching over and taking the bag, stuffing it with the marihuana-plant roots.

'The thing is, I know exactly where you went.'

He shook the soil off his hands, wiping the knife clean on his trousers.

'I was there myself this morning. Passed by before coming back home.'

'It's almost exactly the same place,' Cámara said.

'I know. Which is why I know where you went.'

'And the same MO.'

'Don't use that silly police talk with me.'

'So why were you there?'

41

'Same reason as you. You deal with these things, you manage them. But that doesn't mean they go away. You can't buy peace of mind. Not with money or by solving all the crimes and murders you run around investigating. It's what I've been trying to tell you for years, if you've been listening. So yes, I was there as well at first light.'

He took a deep breath.

'It's amazing what you find on rubbish tips these days.'

'Were there any police there?'

'Of course there were police there. Came just after I arrived.'

'And they didn't bother you?'

'Who's going to bother an old man like me? Anyway,' he carried on. 'I wasn't going to stick around for long once they got there. You know how I am around policemen.'

He looked at Cámara, as though scrutinising him, a question in his eyes.

'Is that what happened to you, then?' he said. 'Had a bit of a brush-up with the local law enforcers? Didn't like you sniffing around their murder scene? You've been fighting, I can tell. You always get that stupid look on your face afterwards.'

Cámara held his hands up in submission: he was guilty as charged.

Hilario chuckled, proud to have proved to himself, once again, that his grandson held no secrets for him.

'I saw Yago,' Cámara said.

Hilario gave a grunt of only partial interest.

'He's back in Albacete. Head of the Judicial Police now.'

'Still not grown up, then.'

'Maybe not. Perhaps none of us are.'

'Speak for yourself.'

Cámara sighed.

'Of course. How could I forget.'

'So Yago's spent his life kissing police arse around the country so he could come back home one day and be leader of the gang. Do you want me to be pleased with him? Are you pleased with him? Is that what you want for yourself?'

'Said he was in Seville for a bit. Madrid . . .'

'Ah, Madrid. So that's it. You're thinking about her, about Alicia.'

'Maybe.'

Hilario crouched down.

'Those doctors don't have a clue,' he said, casting a glance at his plant pots. '*Donde entra el sol, no entra el médico.*' Where the sun shines the doctor never enters.

He stood up and held the knife out in front of him, his eyes fixed ahead.

'Look,' he said. 'Steady as a—'

The knife fell out of his hand, clattering on the ground by his feet. Cámara laughed; it was typical of his grandfather to play around like that.

Until he saw the expression in his eyes, and sensed the sudden lack of strength in him. He stepped forwards, just in time to catch Hilario's arm as he tottered over.

Hilario felt behind him for the edge of a plant pot, and sat down on it, shaking Cámara's hand off his arm, breathing heavily through his mouth.

'I'll be all right,' he said. 'I'm all right.'

We need to call someone, a doctor, Cámara thought. But Hilario was a step ahead.

'Don't you start,' he said. 'There'll be no doctors in this house. Just get me some of those pills they gave me. They thin the blood.'

In the end the fatigue was too much. Cámara helped him inside and he went to lie down on the sofa.

'Bloody springs,' he said as his head flopped down on to the cushion. 'Remind me to take a look at it later.'

And he fell into an instant doze.

The local health centre was three streets away. He could call and try to get someone to come round . . .

The doorbell rang as he was looking for the phone number. Hilario didn't stir, so he walked the length of the corridor to the front door.

'It's Eduardo García,' said a voice on the intercom. 'I've come about our meeting.'

Cámara buzzed the main door open, then stepped out into the stairwell to look over the bannister. A small, dark-haired man wearing jeans and a thin leather jacket was coming up the stairs, carrying a folder.

'Señor Cámara?' he said, looking up. 'Oh!'

'Are you looking for Hilario?' Cámara asked.

The visitor came up the last few steps to the landing.

'Yes. My name's Eduardo García, from the Historical Memory Association. We arranged to meet.'

'I'm Max,' Cámara said. 'Hilario's grandson. I'm afraid this isn't a very good time.'

He held out a hand and they shook. García was about the same age as Cámara, hair beginning to thin, with fine features and sideburns that stretched down the length of his cheeks. His hands looked pale and somehow unused.

'I see,' he said. 'I can come back another time.'

'What's this about?' Cámara asked. 'Historical memory?'

'Your grandfather hasn't mentioned anything?'

Cámara shook his head.

'Between you and me, he's not very well right now,' he

said in a low voice. 'I've just come down from Madrid. Got in yesterday.'

'Well, as you're family I think you have a right to know as well,' García said.

'A right to know?'

García looked around, as though checking for anyone overhearing.

'I would ask you in, but . . .' Cámara said. 'Perhaps you could tell me what this is about.'

García opened his folder and pulled out a couple of sheets of paper.

'Have you heard about a mass grave that's being opened up at the cemetery?' he said.

Cámara took the papers, glancing at the title – something about the Civil War and people buried in unmarked pits.

'I saw something in the newspaper. Yesterday or the day before, I think.'

'The Town Hall has finally decided to go ahead and open it up. We've been pressing them to do so for several years now.'

The grave, he said, occupied an area near the centre of the cemetery, what was now a weed-filled patch of land that no one had taken care of for decades. This, according to their research, was where people executed by the Franco regime had been buried during the reprisals following the end of the Civil War, in 1939. It was thought that as many as fifty or sixty men and women were there, their graves unmarked, their bodies thrown in a pit. It was only now, after a new law had been passed, that some of the graves could be opened and the dead finally given proper burial.

'Most of the shootings came in the immediate aftermath of the city being taken over by Franco,' García said. 'But the executions continued well into the 1940s.'

Cámara was silent as he listened, glancing down at the papers with their black-and-white photos of the supposed grave site.

'This is interesting, fascinating, really,' he said. He wanted to get back to Hilario inside the flat, and for some reason he couldn't quite explain he was feeling uncomfortable. He'd heard others talking about this; it had been on the news a couple of times, and he'd caught the tail end of a television documentary about it a while ago. Back in Valencia he remembered a few colleagues making comments about it, about how it was better to leave all this Civil War stuff undisturbed. Let people mourn their dead, yes, no one was against that. But was the country really ready to rake over all that Franco business? Better to get on with things, otherwise the old enmities could resurface.

'So Hilario said he was interested in this?' Cámara asked. What was it? Another political act, another way to hit out at the establishment? Except that Hilario's anarchism had been less political over the past years, and more ontological, more about fighting the tyrannies within than without, he felt. So why get involved in this of a sudden?

'He hasn't told you anything, then?' García said.

'No.'

'Well . . .' He paused. 'We have very strong reason,' he said, 'to think that Hilario's father, Maximiliano Cámara, is buried in that grave. He was an activist in the Civil War in the anarchist CNT trade union.'

Cámara felt a coldness rushing through him.

'He was executed in 1943,' García continued. 'Hilario got in touch with us last week when he heard about the dig. Said he wanted to help, give us a description of his father, perhaps some photos, even a DNA sample. Then if we find him we can properly identify him, and he can finally have a decent burial.'

'My great-grandfather,' Cámara said. 'You're talking about my great-grandfather.'

'You didn't know,' García said.

Cámara shook his head.

'I'm sorry to be the one to tell you.'

Cámara glanced back over his shoulder; he felt certain that Hilario was still asleep, but he wanted to go and check.

'Look,' he said. 'I'd better go. But I'd like to talk to you more about this. Yes, you can count on my support as well. Whatever you need. It's just . . .'

García pulled out a card.

'Call me whenever you want.'

Cámara gave him his number as well and they promised to be in touch.

'Keep those papers,' García said, heading back down the stairs. 'Perhaps you could show them to your grandfather when he's feeling better. They might help him remember a few things. We can't let these things slip away with time. Horrendous crimes were committed here and hushed up by the government. We owe it to the victims to tell people what really happened.'

SIX

Saturday 31st October

'He needs to see the doctor.'

'Call him, then.'

Pilar was feeling guilty for having left Hilario alone at the hospital – doubtless her priest would be told of it when next she went to confession – and now she was moving nervously around the house, cleaning, cooking and watching over Hilario, as though to make amends by doubling her efforts on household chores.

Cámara was still concerned about his grandfather, but becoming less so: Hilario had slept well, and looked more relaxed than he'd seen him for some time. If anything it was Pilar's anxiety that was causing him more alarm as she scuttled about, chatting incessantly with her nonsensical, operatic delivery.

'We need more cloths for the kitchen, they get ever so

dirty you know, the grime in this place, I don't know how you mess the place up, oops the coffee's burning, forgot to switch the gas off, then I'll do the bathroom, he's looking paler don't you think?'

Hilario had blocked her presence out, like a horse with blinkers, and stared at the screen of his computer in concentration.

'Everyone should be made to do these brain-training exercises,' he said in a momentary lapse while Pilar vacuumed at the other end of the corridor.

'You can actually feel the neurones being forced to work, like muscles. This is what I need. Not a bunch of pills. This, and some sunshine. If they just made everyone do this for half an hour a day from the age of forty – no, make that thirty – they'd cut the health bill in this country by half.'

The apparent contradiction of a sworn libertarian imagining a scenario where others were 'forced' to do something wasn't lost on Cámara, but it wasn't the right moment to pick his grandfather up on the inconsistencies in his thinking. Besides, it often seemed to him that for Hilario 'anarchy' could mean whatever he wanted it to at any given moment. Which was anarchistic, in its own way.

'It's all about neuroplasticity – I read it in a book. Your brain can adapt and change for ever. The only reason people get ill is because they stop using it; they get old, they atrophy. That's the problem. New challenges, new brain exercises, that's what people need. *Para aprender, nunca es tarde.*' It's never too late to learn.

'I'm going out,' Cámara said.

But Hilario wasn't listening, too focused on testing his reactions by moving and clicking the mouse.

It was a Saturday morning and the street was busy with

49

shoppers buying food for the weekend: short, middle-aged couples with brightly coloured trolleys filled with tomatoes and chicken breasts; mothers with children skipping around their feet as they tried to squeeze into the huddle at a butcher's counter.

He'd pick up a few bits and pieces later. For now he needed to walk, to get out of the flat and wander.

The same graceless streets as ever. Developers in the sixties and seventies had ensured that any charm that had remained to Albacete had been all but annihilated. A large square that had once been a focal point now resembled a run-down yard in some characterless suburb. The city felt as though it had been gutted by some loveless god, reducing it to a dried-up husk, its nutrients, its breath, all gone.

He should leave, get back to Madrid. Yet there was more than just Hilario's illness keeping him here. Unexpectedly he was being confronted by stains and dirt from the past, rising like scum into his life. He almost felt like a character in a gangster film, returning to his home town to collect some debts, or avenge an earlier loss.

He'd been getting on with life; he'd never chosen this. Yet Albacete, the place he'd always run from, was pulling him back into its hard, blackened bosom.

And what was he meant to do? Avenge which loss? His sister? That was over thirty years ago. Even if they'd never found her killer, the chances were the man, or men, who'd done it were already dead. Or almost dead.

His parents? They'd killed themselves. How do you avenge that?

And now his great-grandfather . . .

Maximiliano Cámara – they shared the same name. A family name. It was a link, of sorts. And it was strange how

50

he did feel something. Yet three generations separated them. They'd never met. He was Hilario's father. That was link enough. Hilario was more of a father to him than anyone else in his life. So who had *his* father been? What kind of a man was Maximiliano? Another anarchist bore? They'd shot him for that.

He'd never known. Like in so many families across the country, the events of the Civil War and how it had affected them were a murky, unwanted, half-buried memory. Nobody talked about it, nobody had ever said anything more than that Maximiliano had disappeared when Franco's troops had marched triumphantly into the city in April 1939. After three years of war the Republic had simply given up by then, the fight kicked out of it, and Albacete – the former headquarters of the International Brigades – was absorbed into Franco's Spain.

That was when Maximiliano had vanished, they said. What happened? They didn't know. Perhaps he'd managed to escape. No one could say. And no more questions.

Of course, for decades that attitude was necessary to survive. Cámara and his generation had never been taught any of this at school – it was all too fresh in the seventies and eighties, and even though Franco himself had died when Cámara was nine years old, the textbooks at school didn't change for a long time after that. If any mention had been made of the Civil War, it was still couched in Francoist terminology where the Generalísimo had waged a 'Crusade' against the 'Reds'.

Enough information about what had actually happened was now making its way into popular consciousness, thanks to a plethora of books and a number of television documentaries. Organisations like the one Eduardo García belonged to, trying to preserve the 'historical memory' of the events of the period, had been established all over the country.

Much of this Cámara now knew without exactly knowing how: he'd never read anything on the war, but somehow it had filtered in. Enough for his policeman's brain immediately to realise there was a discrepancy there: the war had ended in 1939, which was when the family had said Maximiliano had gone missing. Yet García had said he'd been executed in 1943, presumably here in Albacete, as he was supposedly buried in the mass pit they were now digging up. So what had happened in those four 'missing' years? Where had Maximiliano been? Why hadn't he been executed as soon as Franco's troops arrived? Why the wait?

He gave an involuntary shrug as he realised he was now mulling over three deaths, three killings: that of Maximiliano, Concha, and the girl who'd been found in the same spot as his sister just a few days before, Mirella Faro. If Albacete was reaching out to pull him in, so the policeman within him was coughing and hacking itself back into wakefulness.

A life outside the *Policía Nacional*? What the hell had he been thinking?

It was coming up for twelve o'clock and an urge, like a twitch, was beginning to kick in. Turning a corner he spotted a sign for Mahou beer on a wall above a neighbourhood bar that looked just dirty enough to be the kind of place that didn't overprice you for a *caña*.

He stepped in and found a stool at one end of the bar where a couple of the day's newspapers were neatly folded next to the trays of roasted peanuts and anchovies in vinegar. The television in the corner was switched off – a rarity – while an old woman was sitting in the corner, defiantly smoking as she drank a glass of vermouth. In another couple of months the ban on cigarettes in bars would be complete; in the meantime clients were savouring these last precious moments when they could enjoy a drink and a smoke at the same time without having to crowd the pavement outside.

Out of solidarity as much as anything else, Cámara reached into his own pocket and pulled out his Ducados, surprised at himself that it had taken so long to have the first of the day; back in Valencia he'd have got through half a packet by now. That was another strange side effect of not working: he was smoking far less.

He drew the nicotine deep into his lungs as the barwoman eventually spotted him and ambled over.

He nodded at the beer tap.

'Max?'

For a moment his attention was distracted from thoughts of cool lager, and he looked the woman in the face.

A smile broke out as her name flooded into his memory.

'Estrella.'

They both laughed.

'Dear, dear Estrella.'

She was older – so much older, but there was no mistaking her: a small pouting mouth with full lips, shoulder-length black curly hair, and fake eyelashes so long they curled and almost touched her eyebrows.

'I don't believe it. You look . . .'

'I know,' Cámara said. 'We both do.'

'But still the same.'

She beamed.

'Oh, I'm not going to let you out of here in a hurry. Not after so many years.'

She came around the bar and embraced him tightly, and his arms wrapped themselves around her waist.

For over a minute they held each other like this, eyes closed, breathing in each other's presence. He felt the dampness where her face rested in the crook of his neck, tears streaming into his shirt.

'It's all right,' he whispered. 'I know, I know.'

She pulled on him harder still.

'You need to be careful,' he tried to joke. 'You'll loosen those eyelashes of yours.'

'Oh, you!'

She drew herself away, slapping him on the chest, a watery smile on her face.

'I just . . . You caught me by surprise. I never expected to see you again.'

'And neither did I, Estrella. I had no idea you had this place.'

'Well, of course you didn't. I could be running a bar on the moon for all you know.'

'Don't hold it against me.'

'I know why. Everyone knows why.'

She pulled his hands tighter around her waist.

'I've missed you, Max. I miss . . . everything. Still. Even now, after all these years. I've never got over it. There. I've said it. But it's true. How can I? How can anyone get over something like that? I don't think the city was ever the same, you know? Something changed back then.'

Cámara shrugged.

'Oh, Max. It's so wonderful to see you again.'

'And it's good to see you.'

She leaned in, patting him on the cheek with one hand, kissing him on the other.

'This makes me feel very old, you know, seeing you like this. I'm not the same girl I was.'

She placed her hands on her breasts.

'I've got these to remind me of that every morning. Heading closer and closer to the equator.'

She giggled.

'Not quite as firm as when you had your hands on them.'

'May I remind you,' Cámara said, 'that while not a small number of my friends had that pleasure, I never did.'

Estrella leaned away, grasping his hands.

'I can't believe it,' she said. 'Still, you are younger than me. And I suppose it was out of respect for Concha – I didn't want to be responsible for leading her younger brother astray. That must have been it.'

'You needn't have worried. Your very presence, with those tight jumpers of yours, was enough. In my mind, at least.'

'Good,' she said. 'I'm glad I had some influence on you.'

She pulled up a stool and sat down, her knees pressing against the side of his leg, one hand on his arm.

'I've been thinking a lot about her,' Max said. 'Coming back, just walking around the city again.'

He told her about Hilario, and how he had rushed down from Madrid. His police work, and his extended leave period, he left out; there was only so much he could reveal of himself. Although the closeness they had shared as adolescents had been rekindled in a heartbeat, and while both were acutely aware of the distance in years and experiences that separated them, they sat close to each other, enjoying a warming, joyful reconnection.

The opportunity had always been there, but they had never kissed or petted. Yet now Cámara knew that they could quite easily sleep together that night. Not that he would, and nor would it be anything truly passionate or meaningful. But as they sat at the bar, touching each other's hands and faces as though each trying to confirm the presence of the other, he could see a door or a window opening, an immediate future where the two of them lay side by side, comforted, and perhaps a little troubled, by a sexual encounter that they had somehow fallen into. With one part of his mind he watched the scene while he listened intently to her talking, her comments about her life, the bar, a man who had left her a while back, but only after taking most of the money from her bank account to pay for his cocaine addiction. And though temptation was there, a possibility to conquer where his adolescent fantasies had always remained a failure, he chose not to pass through, to remain where he was. Despite what was happening, the unexpected re-engagement of his policing self, he was happy with Alicia; he didn't desire anything else, another woman. He had what he needed. And yes, he thought, he needed what he had.

Estrella had opened a bottle of cava, and they toasted their re-encounter. Customers came and went from the bar, and occasionally she got up to serve them, but mostly her attention was on Cámara.

She spoke about Concha, about her memories of her, how they had played together at school, then become interested more in other things, skipping lessons so they could go and catch a glimpse of a couple of boys in another part of the city. The two of them had meant to go out together the night Concha disappeared. The fair was on, and they'd arranged to meet at one of the stalls. Concha walked alone from her flat – it was only a few blocks away, and it was barely dark. But she never made it. Estrella had been the first one to raise the alarm. Concha had never let her down like that; it just wasn't like her.

'Of course I've wondered over the years if those boys, the

ones we'd been chasing, could have had something to do with it. But you think anything in the end, when there are no answers. They were nice lads anyway, just kids, like us. They couldn't have done anything like that. Wouldn't have been capable. They're both married now. One has a couple of grown-up daughters. The other never had children. I see them around from time to time. It's a small place. You can't hide in a city like Albacete for very long.'

She drank some more cava, her eyes moistening again. Cámara started wondering if he should go; he needed this as well, somehow, bringing up old memories he'd shelved somewhere, but he was concerned that the evening could become maudlin if they continued too long.

'There was a man arrested at one point, wasn't there?' Estrella asked. 'I seem to remember something.'

'Juan Manuel Heredia,' Cámara said. Had that name ever been properly tucked away? It had shot out of his mouth like a bolt.

'What happened?'

'They let him go,' Cámara said. 'He had an alibi – he was somewhere else at the time.'

SEVEN

In the end he was drawn away by a phone call.

'Are you free? Can you come and meet me? Now?'

Cámara pulled himself away as delicately as he could from Estrella. She seemed to understand. But they embraced tightly once more, and she kissed him softly on the mouth – a kiss of goodbye, of departure, less of passion or promise.

And he wiped the mistiness from his eyes as he walked away, breathing deeply and steadily, pacing the few blocks down towards the park.

Yago was already there, standing in the shadows of the trees overhanging the outside railings.

'I need a walk,' he said. 'And what I'm about to tell you can't be said inside the Jefatura.'

They set off along the pavement that circled the park, past the old police headquarters and a handful of the few buildings of note. There was the usual growing hubbub as Albaceteños started heading out for the night's entertainments, but no one noticed the two men in their forties strolling together as the car headlights streamed past them.

Yago loosened his tie. Cámara pulled out his packet of Ducados and offered him one. Yago didn't smoke, never had. But he took one and they smoked in silence for a few minutes.

'It's about this murder,' Yago said at last. 'Mirella Faro, the young girl.'

'What about it?'

Yago put his hands behind his back, pushing his head forwards a little, his eyes focused on the paving stones ahead of them.

'We're beginning to wonder if it really is drug related.'

'You said something about needle marks on her arms.'

'Yes, she was a taker. It showed up in the autopsy, and her family have confirmed that she had a problem. She may even have gone in for some opportunistic prostitution to help pay for the habit – traces of semen from at least two different men have been found on her body.'

'Boyfriends? Clients? Suspects?'

'Yes, that's the point. Any or all of the above. The problem is, it's proving difficult finding anyone here who knew her.'

'Here?'

'In Albacete. She was from Madrid, although she has family living in a town not far away.'

They stopped to allow a couple of women in tight Saturday-night skirts to get past them, then fell into step with each other as they continued.

'Mirella lived with her mother,' Yago said. 'Olga Faro. Single parent. The father left and moved to Venezuela before Mirella was born. We're checking, but it looks as though he's still there. There's been no contact between Olga and the father since they separated. Not even now that Mirella's dead.'

From what Yago was saying, the police's first theory still appeared to fit. A broken home, drug addiction, possible prostitution. Cámara was trying to work out what Yago's doubts were – and why they needed to be expressed out here.

'You think there's a sexual motive? Some kind of sex killer?'

'We've thought about that,' Yago said. 'She's found naked, the semen, light traces of bleeding around the vagina . . . it's a possibility. But apart from the marks around her neck from the strangulation, there was little sign of a struggle, no bruising on her thighs or groin, for example.'

'And the prostitution theory. Are you sure about that?'

'No, personally I'm not. Jiménez suggested it. But the semen could just be the result of some adolescent fumblings. Even the bleeding. It wasn't that heavy. She was fifteen, for heaven's sake. She was probably having her first sexual encounters. So there's semen from more than one boy . . .'

He shrugged.

They fell silent, both policemen aware that they had fallen into the trap of speculating too much with too little information. It was one of the things they had taught them not to do at Avila, but every now and again it happened. Especially in cases such as this one, when something about the murder victim brought on an inevitable desire to wrap it up quickly, to catch the perpetrator and throw him into the darkest cell.

A neighbourhood bar on the other side of the road was in the process of closing up: they didn't look after Saturday-night crowds. With a nod Yago suggested they go over and catch a last drink before the shutters came down.

'There's no one there,' Yago said. 'We can talk without being overheard. By policemen at least.'

The barman looked at them with a sneer as they walked in: it had been a long day and he wanted to go home.

'We won't be long.'

Cámara ordered a brandy; Yago a bottle of alcohol-free beer.

'You said no one here knew her,' Cámara repeated once they'd sat down.

'This is the story as far as we know at the moment.' Yago crossed his arms in front of him on the table.

'Mirella had a drug problem. She also had problems at home – didn't always get on well with her mother. So sometimes she used to come down here from Madrid to stay with this family of hers nearby.'

'Where are they?'

'In a place called Pozoblanco, about five kilometres north. Small village.'

'But she used to come into the city.'

'That's right. The idea was that when things were bad at home she could come here and clean up, get a bit of space from Mum, before making her way back. Obviously it disrupted her schooling, but everyone seems to have thought it was worth it.'

'How often had this happened, then? How many times had she come here like this?'

'Three or four times.'

'And she always made trips to the city when she was down here?'

'That's it.'

Yago took a swig of his beer.

'I knew I did right calling you. Jiménez is good, but . . . You saw what sort he is.'

Cámara shrugged. He knew exactly what Yago meant.

'So Mirella came here every time she stayed in Pozoblanco,' Yago repeated.

'On her own?'

'Yes.'

'What did she tell her family? I'm assuming they're – what? Aunts? Uncles?'

'Grandparents. She always told them she had some Madrid friends in the city and that she was going to see them. Used a moped to get in and out.'

'Has it been found?'

'No. There's been a search, but so far no trace.'

'And these Madrid friends?'

'No one has any idea. She never mentioned any names, just used to tell them she was off and that was it.'

'And they were supposed to be helping this girl with her drug problem?'

Yago let out a sigh.

'So the idea is she's meant to be cleaning herself up, but meanwhile she's riding into town every few days to get another hit.'

'That's about it.'

Cámara frowned.

'The theory about it being drug related still looks plausible,' he said.

The barman had turned off the lights in the kitchen and now came around the bar to start stacking chairs.

'There's something else,' Yago said.

Cámara pulled out his cigarettes again, but Yago refused another one.

'It's to do with this branch of Mirella's family in Pozoblanco. The grandfather is a man called Francisco Faro Oscuro. He's the mayor of the place. There are only a couple of hundred inhabitants, but he's been in power for years, and runs the place like a Maoist collective.'

Cámara spluttered into his brandy.

'What?'

'You heard me right,' Yago said, raising his eyebrows. 'He's hard left. Father was a communist – and mayor as well, in his time. And now Paco runs the show. That's what everyone calls Faro Oscuro in the village, by the way. None of your fancy titles. Just Paco.'

'Now you mention it, I'm beginning to wonder if I've seen something about this on television.'

'You may have done. The guy's a maverick, has his own party after he split from the United Left – set up the Workers' Agrarian Freedom Party. He's been on TV a couple of times. I think there was even some documentary made about him. Anyway, for all his talk of collective power, he rules Pozoblanco like his own fiefdom. Of course he makes sure he gives enough away so that everyone keeps voting for him. Rents are really cheap, for example. Fifteen euros a month. But all property belongs to the village. Which in effect means it belongs to him.'

'And this is Mirella's grandfather.'

'That's right.'

'What does the village live off? That's saffron-growing land, I assume.'

'Exactly. And that's what I need to talk to you about.'

Yago turned and glanced round at the barman, who had gone back behind the bar and was folding up a pile of cloths.

'That's why we had to come out here,' he continued. 'Look, there's a scam going on. It may actually be very big, perhaps even international.'

'With the saffron?'

'You know it can sell for anything up to three thousand euros a kilo, right?'

'I knew it was expensive. But that's as much as some drugs. High-grade Moroccan *kif,* for example.'

'Saffron is highly valued and the freight costs are minimal.'

'And it's legal.'

'Right, well, there's a question. There have been suspicions of something odd going on for a while. The amount of La Mancha saffron actually grown and the amount sold on the international markets don't tally. This kind of thing is happening all the time – the majority of Italian olive oil actually comes from Jaén, just down the road. They ship it off and it gets relabelled, and that's it.'

'And something similar's happening here with the saffron.'

Yago nodded.

'The saffron season's starting now. But you just go out there and try and find some. Yes, there are some fields here and about, but not enough to grow all the stuff that gets sold around the world as Spanish saffron. All the unemployment, people leaving the countryside and coming into the city, or leaving for good, looking for work.'

He gave Cámara a look.

'So what's going on?' Cámara asked.

'I think there's a mafia element. We spoke to Faro Oscuro – Paco – about it a few months ago. Interviewed him myself. He's a tough old thing, wasn't having any of it. Just kept going on about collective farming and the benefit to the community and the environment.'

'And you think there's a connection with Mirella's murder.'

Yago pursed his lips.

'I think it's a line we need to explore. The problem is there's an institutional reluctance to look into the saffron scam. Relabelling foreign imports as La Mancha saffron isn't illegal. But vast amounts of money are being made from it.

And just as with drugs, people get greedy. I reckon customs people are in on it. And I'm certain a number of officers at the Jefatura as well, helping to cover things up, taking kickbacks. Even running the whole thing. That's why we couldn't talk there. Understand?'

Cámara nodded. He was also beginning to understand something else. This wasn't just a chance for his old mate to pick his brains, or bounce some ideas off him. Yago wanted more.

'I don't know who I can trust, honestly,' Yago said. 'It's a sad state of affairs for a head of the *Policía Judicial* to be in, but there you are. But I think we need to look into this. Mirella's death may be a settling of scores, as we said.'

'But not necessarily one to do with the drug world,' Cámara butted in.

'Exactly. Is there an angle here to do with Pozoblanco, and a saffron mafia there?'

'I get it,' Cámara said. He looked Yago in the eye.

'Tell me what you want me to do.'

Yago let out a deep breath.

'Good for you, Max. I knew I could count on you. Look, I know you're on leave, and all that. But really, you could do me a favour here. And it would be good to have some support from someone of your calibre, if you get me.'

'You want me to sniff around? Take a look at Pozoblanco?'

'Yeah,' Yago said. 'That's exactly what I want. If we go in now, officially, everyone's just going to clam up. Especially if they've got people inside the Jefatura as well.'

'I take it someone went up there after Mirella was found.'

'That was just routine. Got a couple of statements – one from the grandmother, another from the mother, who's come down from Madrid – and that was it. No problems. No, what I want you to do is find out anything you can about the saffron business. You could – I don't know – pose as a journalist, or something. I can get you an accreditation if you like.'

'Don't worry about it.'

'Just go in, check it out. It's the harvest period, as I said, so you've got a good excuse. I need a pair of eyes there, Max. Someone I can trust. Find out what you can and then come back to me. Something's happening up there. I just don't know what it is.'

They finished their drinks and headed towards the door.

'But whatever it is, we need to find out how it ties in with Mirella's murder.'

EIGHT

The computer was still switched on, but Hilario was asleep, slumped in an armchair by the window which looked out on to the street. Normally he would have woken at the sound of his grandson walking through the door, but he was in a deep slumber, his breathing slow and heavy.

Cámara lifted his head carefully and placed a cushion between his cheek and the chair, wiping away a dribble of foamy saliva that had fallen from his mouth. Moving the mouse to turn off the screen saver, he looked at what Hilario had been doing on the computer before he'd nodded off. A medical website gave details of the recovery processes after a stroke. Hilario had scrolled down until it reached a paragraph talking about the need for sleep in such circumstances, giving the brain time to heal itself after suffering the damage caused by the blood clot . . .

He could tell from the smell in the flat what Pilar had prepared to eat: chicken with a thick, garlicky sauce with rosemary and white wine. It was a difficult dish to do badly, and even Pilar's version of it was edible, although she did manage to stuff it with small, chipped pieces of chicken bone which you spent most of the meal prising away from your gums.

As he put it on the hob to heat up, Cámara opened the fridge and pulled out a bottle of beer, pouring himself a large glass. Finishing it in one, he opened another before taking out a knife and fork from the drawer and drawing up a stool at the little kitchen table.

He smoked a cigarette as the chicken began to sizzle, watching the smoke lacing itself into messy, unfinished designs above his head. Always the desire to find patterns there, he thought, to give shape, when all there was was smoke, doing what it did, moving according to its own whims, not ours.

He wondered whether he was perhaps one of the last people who would be allowed to smoke, cook and eat in the same space. One day even this, in his own home, would probably come to an end – another prohibition, another law. Time to enjoy the old freedoms while they were still around.

Hilario walked in as he started eating.

'I didn't want to wake you.'

'Well, you did.'

'How are you?'

'You know I hate that question.'

'And I try to remember not to ask you. But you don't have strokes every day, thank God. Saw you've been looking stuff up on the Internet.'

'Snooping around like a policeman, eh? I should have guessed.'

'So sleep is good for you, is it?'

'Sleep is good,' Hilario echoed flatly. 'Makes sense. You

become a child again, it says. Or at least in some ways. Your brain is having to make new connections, like you do when you're young. I think that's why children sleep more – it's part of the process.'

'You were lucky it wasn't more serious. I mean, with you it's just a physical thing, right? A partial loss of coordination on the right side. You're not . . . ?'

'I'm not a vegetable, no. I would have thought that was pretty obvious. Even to a policeman.'

'But there's nothing else,' Cámara said. 'No memory loss or anything.'

'Franco's still dead, isn't he?'

'Er, yes, of course. He died almost forty years ago.'

'Good. Well, I'm fine, then. Wouldn't want to wake up from a stroke and discover it had all been a dream, and that he was still in power. Now that would be a nightmare. Probably give myself a stroke again just to get away from it all.'

'A self-induced stroke,' Cámara said. 'I wonder if that's possible?'

'Well, in my case all I need to do is stop taking the pills. Those blood-thinning ones. Probably be gone in a couple of days' time. What, you thinking about new ways to kill people?'

Cámara curled up his nose as he chewed on the chicken.

'Oh, yes, I forgot. It's your job to catch the killers.'

Hilario sat down heavily in the chair opposite.

'Still, it might make for a nice little mystery,' he said. 'A doctor who can induce a stroke in people so no one ever knows it's him killing them. You should write a book. No, screw that, *I* should write a book. You just fill me in on the police details and all that nonsense. I'll mention you in the acknowledgements.'

'You never told me your father was executed.'

Cámara put his fork down and drained the last of his beer, watching Hilario's reaction from the corner of his eye.

For a moment his grandfather barely reacted at all. His expression hardened a little, as though his eyes had turned to stone. Cámara had seen that in him only two, perhaps three, times before. The last time when he told him he was joining the police.

When finally he moved, Hilario's reaction was to glance quickly at the calendar on the wall, before resting his eyes on Cámara.

'Eduardo García been here, has he?' he said.

Cámara nodded.

They looked at each other for a moment in a curious engagement, threatening and affectionate.

'You didn't need to know,' Hilario said.

'What?'

'That's why I didn't tell you. Because it wasn't important for you to know. Perhaps it is now, perhaps that's why you've already heard something about it. This might be it . . .' His voice began to tail away.

'I suppose I always thought there would be a time when we'd talk about this. It was never something I could just start on my own, though. As though I needed a sign . . .'

'He's buried in the cemetery,' Cámara said. 'Maximiliano, my great-grandfather.'

'Yes, he was your great-grandfather. And a true anarchist. He helped many people, saved many lives . . .'

Cámara held his hand out in time to stop Hilario from falling forwards on to the table. His eyes were heavy and half-closing.

'I'm not feeling . . .'

'It's all right.'

Cámara helped him across the corridor and into the bedroom. Hilario lay down on the bed and immediately turned on to his side, curling up into a foetal position, already asleep again.

Cámara cleared up in the kitchen, then went into the living room. One lamp in the corner was switched on, casting a dark yellowish glow. He went to the windows, opened them, and stepped out on to the balcony. It was cold by now, the night air cooling rapidly as they moved towards winter, but he felt a need to breathe different air, something from outside the flat.

The lights in the street were on, and apart from the parked cars below, it was empty. From behind curtains and blinds he caught the blue flicker of television screens, the clatter of dishes being washed, the sound of a teenage girl complaining to her parents. A couple of doors away a cat was chewing a piece of dirt-smeared bone that had fallen from the rubbish.

Even here, in a city as small as Albacete, a background hum told you that life of a sort was carrying on, despite the wasteland all around. He felt a pang of desire to be somewhere else. Where? Anywhere but here.

His phone rang and he slid it open.

'I was thinking of you,' she said.

'Same here. I was just about to call.'

'How is he?'

'He's here at home.'

He hadn't spoken to Alicia since he'd arrived, and now, hearing her voice, he felt something settling in him. He told her about Hilario, about how he'd found him, and his grandfather's escape from hospital.

'From what you've told me about him it doesn't sound too surprising, somehow.'

'It's the kind of thing I'd expect him to do. Still, I'm not sure if it's right, whether he should be back in hospital. You'd think they'd be wanting to do checks.'

'Get someone to go round.'

'I will. But I have to do it carefully, get the right person. If some interfering doctor or nurse comes in here ordering him about it might set him off again.'

He stepped back into the living room and closed the windows behind him.

'How are things there?' he asked.

'I'm missing you,' she said. 'I'm probably not supposed to say that, but it's true.'

'And I'm missing you. But I meant at work, at the paper.'

'Oh, sorry. It's fine. A bit quiet, strangely.'

'I think I might have a story for you here,' he said.

'You're joking.'

'No, seriously.'

'You're just trying to be nice, to show how much you want me, get me down to Albacete, have a tumble . . .'

'No, wait, really.'

'What?'

'I need your help. I need you.'

He told her about Pozoblanco, and Yago's suspicions about the local saffron trade, and how they might be related to the murder of the young girl Mirella in the city a few days before. Alicia listened silently.

'Yes,' she said at last. 'It's interesting. I'm interested. Let me talk to the boss, but I'm sure there won't be a problem. I can make it down on the train tomorrow, all being well.'

'Let me know what time you're arriving. I'll pick you up.'

'OK.'

This was new, he thought as they said their goodbyes. From lovers they had become like business partners in an instant: he the policeman; she the journalist. And the conversation had become drier, less affectionate.

No matter. It would be good to see her again. It was true – he had been missing her. Being back in Albacete had somehow smothered that in him. Or drowned it out in so much other noise – noise blaring from several directions at once.

Hilario had always kept it in neat little transparent plastic bags for Cámara to take back with him to Valencia. Now that he hadn't been smoking for a while, and with the new crop in, the supply of home-grown would have been enough to at least raise an eyebrow in the local narcotics squad, if not actually get them reaching for their handcuffs.

Cámara plucked one of the bags down from the top shelf in the small room that gave off the living room, and settled down on the sofa, avoiding as best he could the loose spring in the middle. Hilario always kept a packet or two of blond tobacco handy for rolling with: black tobacco Ducados were too strong for making a decent joint.

Cámara went through the motions like an old professional, licking the length of the cigarette to help pull off the paper, rubbing the tobacco in the palm of his hand as he mixed in the marihuana, squeezing the mixture into a sausage shape and then slapping a roll-up paper on top with the palm of his other hand before flipping both hands over while clasped together so that the mix now lay on top of the paper. Then he rolled it, glued it, stuck it in his mouth, lit it, and inhaled.

Smoke poured down his nostrils as he let it out of his

lungs, enjoying the cool rush beginning to work its way into the blood of his brain.

Four months. There had been times when he'd wondered if he'd ever smoke again. Madrid felt different, his life there was different. He could even perceive a different way ahead.

And now he was here, where he had begun, smoking more of his grandfather's home-grown dope.

It felt good. It felt very, very good.

NINE

Sunday 1st November

Hilario slept for most of the morning. At midday, with Pilar's insistent voice ringing in his ears, Cámara called the local doctor's surgery.

After a couple of hours' wait, an ill-tempered middle-aged man rang the doorbell.

Without a word, the doctor sat down on the bed to measure the unconscious Hilario's blood pressure and pulse, checked the pills scattered over the bedside cabinet, then stood up and scowled.

'This man should be in hospital.'

They were wasting his time.

Cámara explained that Hilario had already been in hospital and had discharged himself, but the doctor wasn't listening.

'He should be in hospital. There's nothing to be done here.

He needs constant medical attention. Otherwise he could die at any moment.'

He clicked his fingers as though conjuring the spectre of an instant demise.

It was pointless saying any more. Besides, he gave the impression that he was in a great hurry to get somewhere else.

'The pills?' Cámara said as he showed him to the door.

'He must keep taking them. They're very important.'

He stepped out and wheezed down the stairs.

'But he needs a hospital!'

Pilar worked silently in the kitchen. She didn't need to speak. Cámara knew what she was thinking: the doctor was right – they should call an ambulance and get Hilario transferred back to the hospital immediately. It might mean more vigils for her, more sitting by the bedside, but it was what was expected, what any ordinary person would do.

Cámara resisted the unspoken pressure. If Hilario woke up to find himself back in the hospital he would never forgive him. And besides, he wasn't convinced it was the best place for him. *Mala hierba nunca muere*, he thought. The bad grass – the weeds – never die. There was still too much fiery spark in the old man to think that he was truly close to dying.

So he left Hilario where he was, ignoring Pilar, and sat at the computer to do some research on the Internet. He wished his old police colleague in Valencia, Inspector Torres, was around – he was always better with these things.

Still, if he was going to start playing at freelance detective he would have to start doing this for himself.

The wasteland where Mirella Faro's body had been found was a short detour on his walk to the station to pick up

Alicia. The whole empty block now had police tape around it, tied to street lamps and cordoning off an area of about fifty square metres. A bit excessive, he thought. Would never happen in Valencia.

A solitary man was walking a little dog further along, using the creature's frequent stops to piss along the way as an excuse to peer out at the murder scene, an unsmiling exhilaration in his eyes as he came as close as the law allowed him to this place of violent, sexual death.

Cámara paced slowly, waiting for the man to move on. There were no policemen around now, but a patrol car would probably be swinging around at irregular intervals, and he wanted to be alone here for just a moment, to see it in daylight.

The man with the dog turned and caught sight of Cámara watching him. He twitched on the lead, and pulled the dog along. He'd been seen: a secret guilt urged him to put on an air of respectful disdain.

A low stretch of crumbling breeze-block wall ran along one side of the wasteland. Standing on it Cámara would be pressing against the police tape, but not actually crossing it: a detail that a passing policeman might not care about, but he didn't want a repeat of the other night. Besides, he was working on this crime himself – albeit in an unofficial capacity – and he needed to keep himself removed from the actual police investigation.

Standing a foot or so above the ground he was able to gaze over the whole area – if not quite a bird's-eye perspective, then one as good as he could get for the time being. Any plant life there had turned yellow and brown months before in the summer heat. The rest of it was a scattered mess of household rubbish, rock and scorched patches where people had lit fires – kids playing with matches, mostly, he thought. A centre of attraction while they drank cheap supermarket booze.

The site where Mirella's body had been found lay ten metres away to his right. The rubbish container itself had been taken away now – for forensic examination, he assumed, although he was surprised it had taken them so long. In its place the police tape had been doubled since his last visit, creating a separate cordon inside the larger cordon of the crime scene. There was no point trying to get in there again. Besides, he had come here to see other things.

The wasteland had streets on all four sides – an empty gap in a grid network of city expansion. Behind him and to the left stood the warehouses of the industrial quarter. In front, on the other side of the empty waste area, stood an orange-brick apartment block from the 1980s, six storeys high. The rubbish container might be used by some of the inhabitants, he thought, although he noticed another group of containers closer to the building which was almost certainly their usual place for dumping. No, this rubbish bin, Mirella's, had stood on its own, with no obvious users apart from people driving by: an attempt by the town authorities to prevent the entire area from becoming a tip.

It hadn't worked.

He wondered if Inspector Jiménez had interviewed people in the apartment block. It was the obvious thing to do, but already he could sense an investigation going astray. A murder like this wasn't common in Albacete; he'd have thought more would have been done to prioritise resources to it. Yago could sort that out. But if he was caught in a political struggle inside the Jefatura he'd have his work cut out for him. Nothing could look worse than a cocked-up high-profile murder case.

Cámara had been there himself in the past: the panting sound of colleagues and enemies within the force scrabbling for position and power as they pulled down on any advance in the investigation.

Yago might have landed himself a senior job in his home town, yet the bullshit was the same as anywhere. Better, Cámara thought, to be a policeman in a bigger city, a bigger mess – it gave you more gaps, more holes, to slip through. If you played it right.

He shook himself. It was as if the decision had already been taken. But no, he wasn't back in. Not yet. This was a sideline, helping out an old friend. Nothing more. At least not for now.

So was Mirella killed here? He'd have to see the forensic report, or get to hear about it. But his instinct said not. It was too open, too visible, to assault and strangle her, then strip her and dump her. The murder had happened elsewhere, he felt certain. The killer could easily have brought her body here in a car. A strong man wouldn't have much difficulty lifting a slim fifteen-year-old girl up and throwing her in without attracting too much attention. At night, perhaps. Mid-week, when no one was around.

He wasn't one to pay much attention to police psychologist theories, but it didn't require a great deal of thought to see why she had been brought here: naked and tossed away like that, she had become just another piece of rubbish, more debris, more unwanted waste, like the broken chairs, bottles and grubby milk cartons that lay at his feet. She was nothing, as though the murderer had fed on her in some way, taken all that she was – her life, her spirit, her content – and then cast the container away. He had consumed her, like fast food, and then disposed of the wrapping.

79

Why here, though?

He stepped down off the wall. Somewhere nearby? Had the actual murder taken place near here? Whether she'd been carried or driven in a car, it made sense. Why cross town with a dead body on you? If the idea was to leave her in a rubbish container, finding one close at hand was the most obvious thing to do.

Unless there was something significant about here, about this container . . .

He turned and crossed the road behind him, stepping over a traffic island covered in gravel and dying weeds, and walked into the streets of the industrial area.

It was deserted on this Sunday lunchtime. Grey, dirt-coloured warehouses lined wide avenues designed for lorries to heave in and out with goods. A plumbing supplier had decorated its building facade with replicas of its wares, so that a vertical bathroom complete with washbasin and bidet defied gravity above the main doorway. Elsewhere, pieces of scrap metal and blown tyres lay scattered over the ground, clogging forecourts where businesses had proved to be less recession proof and the doors had closed for good.

Cámara walked slowly through the silent, oppressive shadows, glancing here and there: a padlock over a gateway; broken windows, too high to climb in or out of, with no sign of a ladder or way up; heavy steel shutters barring the entry into almost all the warehouses; a bar – closed now – offering cheap working-men's lunches to the haulage drivers, packers and managers who peopled the place during the week.

Reaching a crossroads he looked both ways and saw more of the same: row after row of warehouses, some in use, the rest abandoned. But in all cases securely locked up. He peered more closely at the sides of the buildings: some, although not all, of these places had closed-circuit TV cameras installed.

The way to his right led back towards the city. Ahead, the avenue continued for a hundred metres before reaching a cul-de-sac. To the left the industrial area carried on for two more blocks before the road swept past what looked like a former petrol station and out into more dusty wastelands beyond the city limits.

I'm a killer, he thought. And I'm looking for a place to kill. Danger to the right – too many people. Danger ahead – only one way out. To the left it has to be.

A flash of red paint at head height on a brick wall some fifty metres away seemed to confirm his decision. It was the first graffiti he'd seen here – even the abandoned warehouses were paint free. But not down here, not on this final stretch.

Only one of the buildings appeared to be still in use – a chemical distributor, by the looks of the name. The rest had been locked up and abandoned. Cámara consciously opened up his senses as he paced along the street, keeping off the pavement and staying close to the middle of the empty road as his eyes moved from side to side and up and down. Anything, any incongruity, might tell him something.

The graffiti was illegible and lazy, but the smell of piss alerted him to a change in his surroundings as he reached the final warehouse. The gate had rusted so much it had been forced open with little effort. Here the graffiti stopped – or perhaps had started.

Turning side on to squeeze through the gap in the gateway, Cámara crossed into the forecourt. A couple of wine bottles stood to one side, half full. Bending down he discovered the source of the smell – someone had used them to relieve themselves. It seemed odd – why not piss against the wall like everyone else?

The metal door into the warehouse was closed, but when he pushed at it with his elbow it opened without resistance. Inside it was dark, with only a small amount of light pouring in from windows high up to alleviate the gloom. He waited for his eyes to adjust, closing them as he allowed his ears, his nose, his skin, his other senses a chance to take the place in before the dominance of sight could overrule them.

It felt cool, and dry. No smell of piss in here. But there was something else – a human presence, the smell of bodies, of sweat. Sex? Perhaps. A place people came to fuck.

And get stoned. A sharp, drowsy smell hung in the air, although it wasn't recent – he knew from the silence that he was alone. A crack den?

He took a step and felt something underfoot. Only then did he open his eyes. It was a used syringe, grubby and cracked from being trodden on before.

He could see more clearly now: the warehouse was virtually empty except for a foam mattress that had been pushed against one corner. There was a loneliness about this place. It wasn't somewhere to score, or to come to find other takers. It was rarely used – it would have been dirtier, more filled with debris had it been a regular drug haunt.

No. This was somewhere you came to be alone. Perhaps with a friend, nothing more. To hang out, get fucked, and move on. A place where you were fairly certain that you wouldn't be disturbed.

Cámara scratched his feet along the cement floor, breathing the place in. Some instinct in him already knew.

He moved along one side wall, eyes cast down towards his feet. Then he reached the end and turned ninety degrees to follow the back wall. Four or five more needles; an empty cigarette packet; wrappings for sweets; a light blue sock; a crushed beer can; torn sheets from a gossip magazine; a black bra; half a loaf of hard, stale bread; a pair of stone-washed jeans with a broken zip; a denim jacket; a pink-and-yellow stripy T-shirt; a crushed cigarette lighter; a knife; a pair of white knickers, crumpled and dirty.

Cámara knelt down and, taking out a pen from his jacket pocket, fished the knickers up to see more clearly. It had darkened now, but the slight bloodstain around the groin area was still visible.

Back outside he texted Yago. A message that he'd found a possible scene for Mirella's murder, and its location, would be enough. Let the official police investigation take its course. No one needed to know where the information had originated.

Besides, he had somewhere to go.

He walked back the way he'd come, heading out of the industrial area towards the wasteland again. The phone buzzed. It was Yago: message received. Was he all right?

He slid the phone shut and put it back into his pocket.

Coming out on to the wasteland, he paused before taking the street heading back towards the city centre. Five metres away, to his right, lay the patch of ground where he'd found Concha over thirty years before.

He remembered how the curtain had flapped at his bedroom window that morning, before the search party had assembled, slapping the side of the wall in an incoherent, staccato fashion, as though trying to warn him that something was about to happen.

TEN

'Have you been crying?'

He'd kissed her hard and long at the station, but now, as they rode the short distance in the taxi, he merely held her hand as he stared out the window.

'Thanks for coming,' he said. 'I'm glad you're here.'

Pilar had left, but Hilario was out on the balcony when they got to the flat, stuffing his bed sheets into the washing machine. Cámara sniffed the air.

'He's wet himself,' he said in a low whisper.

Alicia raised an eyebrow.

'A visitor!' Hilario cried when he saw them. 'He doesn't talk about you much, but I can tell he's very much in love. It's very nice to meet you at last, Alicia.'

He leaned towards her and kissed her on the cheeks.

'You must forgive me,' he said. 'I've just pissed myself in bed and I need to get this washed right away. It's this stroke, you see. Does funny things to you. But it won't last long. I'll be back to normal by tomorrow, I reckon.'

Alicia bent down and started helping him load the machine.

'It's all right, my dear. I can manage. Although I appreciate it. You don't really want to be touching this. Not very pleasant.'

Alicia carried on regardless.

'Ho, ho, yes. I can see why you're so good for him. He needs someone who can't be pushed around.'

Alicia giggled.

'And a sense of humour, too. You're pretty, you're smart. My only question is why you've ended up with him.'

Cámara rolled his eyes.

'He's got hidden depths,' Alicia said as she stood up. 'As you know.'

'Keeps them very hidden, though. Frightened of them. Still, you've seen it. That's good. Might get him loosened up a bit. If he only realised who he really is.'

'Drink?' Cámara said.

'There's a bottle of cava in the freezer,' Hilario said. 'Put it in about twenty minutes ago. Should be cool enough now.'

Cámara cooked fish for dinner – fillets of John Dory sautéed with olive oil and a squeeze of lemon juice. He sat in amused silence for most of the meal as Alicia and his grandfather chatted like old friends. Hilario rolled out much-used tales from the past, about how he'd survived the harsh post-Civil War years by working three jobs simultaneously – cleaning a school in the morning, helping out at a mechanic's during the day and then searching for sellable scrap at night – as he and his mother struggled to survive under Franco.

'It's about keeping going,' he said. 'That's it. Whatever happens. That's the only secret.'

Cámara was surprised, though, that Hilario didn't pour himself a glass when the brandy bottle came out at the end of the meal.

'Not for now. Not tonight.'

He got up from the table. Cámara stood up, making to help him.

'I'm fine,' Hilario waved him away.

He turned at the door.

'It's been wonderful meeting you. I'll be off to bed, my dear,' he said. 'It's all right, the new sheets are already there.'

He nodded in Cámara's direction, without looking at him.

'There's some *maría* up on the shelf. Max knows where it is. You two will be wanting to have sex. I don't recommend the sofa, though. It's got a loose spring, needs fixing.'

The door closed and they were left alone.

Cámara pulled out a cigarette and offered one to Alicia, then wordlessly he opened the balcony door and signalled her to follow him.

'Not allowed to smoke inside the house?' Alicia asked.

'It's not that. It's a bit more private here. At least until he falls asleep.'

A couple were walking along the street below, the woman wrapping both hands around her husband's arm.

'Is he a light sleeper?' Alicia said. 'Will I have to keep my voice down?'

'You can scream as much as you like,' Cámara said. 'He's sleeping more than ever at the moment. Something to do with the recovery after a stroke. Give him another five minutes and he'll be out.'

She rested her head on his shoulder and he leaned down to kiss her hair. The smoke from their cigarettes turned into a haze against the orange glow of the street lamps.

'Something's going on,' she said. 'I suppose you'll tell me eventually. Although I might have to prise it out of you, as always.'

'It's about Concha,' he said.

She lifted her head up and looked him in the eye. She was the only woman he'd ever told.

'The young girl's body – Mirella – was found in almost exactly the same spot.'

They finished their cigarettes, extinguishing them on the balcony railing, before carrying the stubs back inside. Cámara carried them down to the kitchen to throw them in the bin, then came back with a couple of shot glasses. Opening a cabinet he took out a bottle of *orujo* and poured.

He handed her the glass and paused.

'Oh, I forgot,' he said. 'You don't really like . . .'

'Here. Give it to me,' she said. And she drank it in one.

'Give me another one.'

'I've got some other stuff. Whisky, vodka . . .'

'It's fine.'

He poured, and sat down next to her on the sofa.

'Do you think . . . ?' she started.

'It was over thirty years ago,' he said.

The liquid in his glass was rippling from the tremble in his hand, and he raised it to his lips, dissimulating.

'So it's just a coincidence.'

He didn't reply.

Alicia took another drink and got up from the sofa. Her black canvas briefcase was sitting on one of the chairs.

'The arrangements for tomorrow,' she said, pulling out some papers.

Despite it being a weekend, she'd managed to get a lot organised. Cámara was impressed. They were to go to Pozoblanco in the morning; she'd set up an interview with Paco Faro Oscuro, the mayor, and they were to be shown around as part of her research for an article on the saffron business.

'It's harvest season, so it makes sense. The official I spoke to was more than happy for us to come along.'

'Was Mirella mentioned at all?' Cámara asked. 'Did you, or they, bring it up?'

'No. I thought they might give it as a reason for not going ahead with the interview. But no, they didn't say anything.'

Not wanting to stay on the sofa, yet unable to reignite the intimacy of a few moments before, he got up and stared out the window for a moment, then reached again for his packet of Ducados.

'I've started looking into this saffron mafia thing,' Alicia said.

Cámara drew on his cigarette, and coughed.

'I know a man who deals in it, based in Madrid,' she went on. 'He was fine at first, talking about the quality of La Mancha saffron, best in the world, that kind of thing. He does pretty well out of it – wholesales it to China and Australia. And he's well connected – I'm not sure if he's an actual member of the ruling party, but he's friendly enough with them. The kind of face you see at official events, VIP balconies for fiestas, that kind of thing.'

'So what did he say?'

'Well, nothing, really. That's the point. I'd done some research before I spoke to him. The problem is that according to the Ministry of Industry, each year Spain produces about fifteen hundred kilos of saffron.'

'So?'

'But then we export a hundred and ninety thousand kilos of it, worth almost fifty million euros.'

'Big difference.'

'It seems much of the shortfall is shipped in from abroad.

88

But when I brought this discrepancy up with my contact – the difference between actual production of saffron and how much of it is sold each year as "Spanish" – he clammed up on me.'

'What, he refused to say anything?'

'He changed the subject. Wasn't interested.'

'Giving imported saffron a Spanish label isn't illegal in itself.'

'So why not give me a comment, even off the record?'

'We haven't got very far, then.'

'The gap, the discrepancy, is there. I checked. I'm amazed no one's noticed it before. And it seems people in the trade are reluctant to talk about it. There's something else, though. What are they hiding?'

She reached into her briefcase and pulled out a camera.

'I brought this as well,' she said. 'It helps play the part.'

'So I'm your *cámara*?' Your photographer.

'Yes,' she said decisively. 'Yes, you are.'

'I can practise some of the techniques I've been picking up recently.'

She smiled.

'Strange,' he said. 'It's only been a few days, but already it feels like a long time since I was in Madrid.'

'Nothing's changed,' she said. 'Your things are still where you left them.'

His 'things' were just a few clothes, a dozen books, the camera and a handful of personal effects. Almost all his possessions had been lost when his block of flats in Valencia had collapsed earlier in the year. Since then he'd held back from buying any more than the purely necessary. He might be on paid leave from the police, but things were uncertain: he'd thought he might need the little money he had to help make a change, move into a new life. Although what that might be had never crystallised in any way.

In fact the months had passed quickly since he'd left Valencia and gone to Madrid. Days spent in Alicia's flat, cooking, talking, reading, having sex. Living at a slower pace, different from the one that was demanded of him as a policeman. And he'd thought that that in itself could bring about change in him, that simply by trying a different way of being, savouring daily pleasures, a shower of sensual impacts – that this would show him a way forward, that something would emerge which he could grab on to.

Yet the questions had remained – whether to return to the police or not. Whether to stay in Madrid. To stay in Alicia's flat . . .

It worked between them: the powerful sexual attraction tended to make up for any tensions that living together had brought. Yet each was aware that their situation had come about through external factors, not because they had really chosen it themselves. Cámara had been homeless and – temporarily, at least – without a job. Alicia had opened the door to him – a chance to start again what had begun almost two years previously as an aborted, abortive, relationship. And so he'd jumped – left Valencia, the ruins of his flat and career, behind, and caught the train to Madrid.

And days and weeks had become months.

No hay mal que por bien no venga, he'd say. Every cloud had its silver lining – and the good that had come out of the broken chaos of his life had been reconnecting with her, physically, emotionally and mentally. Her month of annual leave had come in August, and unlike the rest of Madrid, they stayed in the city, sleeping during the day, sweating through the night.

It wasn't enough, though, and neither could it last for ever. They both knew that. But the question of what was to happen to *them* had seemed to be wrapped up in the question of what he did next, what decisions he made about his life. In the erotic fog it had been easy to forget that, but he knew it annoyed her. She wasn't in control – but neither was he.

The point was, though, that very little appeared to have changed during his 'interlude'. At least on some more profound level inside him. His life, much of who he considered himself to be, had crumbled around his feet back in Valencia. Yet a love affair, passionate and fulfilling though it was, was not the jewel waiting to be found in the rubble. Yes, it was life. Yes, it was something he hadn't experienced before – not to the same degree, not with the same intensity.

Was he in love? Yes. Absolutely.

Would it last?

That depended on many things. Or did it? Perhaps it only depended on this one thing – on where he decided to go, what he decided to do. He felt as sure as anyone ever can be that his feelings for her were reciprocated. But she was strong-willed, independent. As things stood he sometimes felt as though he were feeding off her. And he hated himself for it.

It couldn't last.

Now he was back in Albacete and life had become denser, thicker. The months in Madrid had flown by; these past few days had moved powerfully, like a surging tide.

He walked over to the shelf, reached up and pulled down the tin of home-grown, unleashing a sweet smell into the room as he opened it up.

'Do you want some?'

She stepped across, put her arms around his neck, and kissed him hard.

'Not right now.'

ELEVEN

Monday 2nd November

They left early. Cámara took Alicia to a bar across the street where they drank *café con leche*. She had a croissant; he ate toast with olive oil and salt, watching as she flicked through a copy of the local newspaper.

'It's like a drug for you. The news,' he said.

'I consume it,' she said without looking up. 'As you consume crime.'

Both had woken up feeling heavy and drowsy. Eschewing the sofa on Hilario's advice, they'd moved to the bedroom, where sex had barred the door to sleep for much of the night.

'I need another coffee, a strong one.'

'Me too.'

After a few more minutes with the paper, she looked up.

'I like your grandfather.'

'He likes you.'

'If he weren't so old . . .'

'Oh, come on.'

'I'm serious. He's got something. A spark, an energy.'

'You want me to be jealous of Hilario?'

'You've got it as well. A bit of it. Not always, though. It's as if you're frightened of it.'

'You're beginning to sound like him.'

'He says that as well, does he?'

Cámara sipped his coffee wordlessly.

Afterwards they walked three blocks south to a mechanic's garage.

'Gerardo is an old school friend,' Cámara said as they stepped inside.

'I didn't realise you had any.'

The mechanic was a small, compact man with light blue eyes and a heavy black beard.

'You son of a bitch. I don't hear from you for twenty years and then you call up asking me to give you a car.'

The two men punched each other affectionately on the shoulder, then embraced.

'This is payback for all the times I helped you cheat through school,' Cámara said. 'Think of it as a debt repaid.'

'You with him?' Gerardo asked Alicia with a grin. 'You've got to watch this one. Never forgets.'

Alicia gave him a knowing smile.

'So what have you got us?' Cámara asked. 'Something that's not going to break down on us, I hope.'

'Don't you worry,' Gerardo said, leading them outside on to the street. 'It's a little black BMW.'

'You're joking.'

'No, I'm serious. Look, it's over there.'

Cámara saw a shiny two-door sports car on the other side of the street.

'You *are* joking.'

Gerardo threw him the keys.

'I just bought it off a guy,' he said. 'Lost his job, needed the money. So I've fixed it up a bit. But I can sell it on, make a bit of extra cash.'

Cámara opened the door to a scent of leather seats.

'It's done over a hundred thousand – it's hardly brand new or anything. But I can get five or six grand for it.'

Alicia had walked round to the other side and was climbing in.

'Help clear some of my own debts. Know what I mean?'

Cámara's phone rang; he reached into his pocket.

'All right,' Gerardo said, heading back inside.

'I'll bring it back later on this evening,' Cámara said.

The phone clicked as he brought it to his ear.

'Hello?'

He sat down in the driver's seat. Next to him Alicia was going through her notes.

'Yes,' he said as the voice on the other end began to speak.

'I see . . . I understand.'

Alicia looked over at him, detecting the change in his tone.

'Fine,' he said into the mouthpiece. 'I'll be in touch.'

He put the phone back in his pocket, then slotted the key into the ignition and started the engine.

'It was the Jefatura in Valencia,' he said, putting the car into gear.

'They've given me until next Monday to make a decision. Either go back, or leave the police for good.'

* * *

Soon they were leaving the confines of the town and heading out into the countryside. The flat 'basin', after which the Moors had given the city its name, spread itself out with barely an undulation in all directions, a vast blanket, its colour blanched by the sun.

They headed north, neither of them speaking. Cámara had seen it often enough, a landscape that had felt at times to be an extension of himself, as it was of everyone from Albacete. And which you fled from, and always took with you.

Pozoblanco was a fifteen-minute drive away. As they were arriving, saffron fields with short green plants in rows, but no flowers visible, appeared. A tree-lined avenue off the main road led them towards a cluster of low, mostly white houses, a stone church bell tower stretching high above the other buildings. A sign where the village officially began welcomed them to '*the collectivist utopia of Pozoblanco, a founding member of the Republican Towns Network*'.

'I'm not sure if a BMW is the right kind of car for a place like this,' Cámara said as they left the tarmac and started bobbing up and down cobbled streets.

The plan was to head straight to the town hall, where Alicia had arranged to meet the mayor, Francisco Faro Oscuro. A Republican red-yellow-and-purple tricolour flag hanging from the walls of an official-looking building seemed the likeliest place, and they pulled in opposite, slotting the car into a space between two others.

'We could ask if this is it,' Cámara said, 'but I can't see anyone around.'

The streets were deserted, and the shops closed. But there were no metal security shutters over the doors and windows, as there were in most towns, Cámara noticed.

They got out of the car and climbed a few steps. Alicia

nodded at some modest lettering on a side wall: 'Town Hall'.

They stepped inside to an entrance hall with a pale marble floor. A staircase led up to the storey above. No one was at the reception desk. Alicia stopped and stood expectantly, waiting for someone to appear, while Cámara snooped around.

'There must be a bell, or something.'

He glanced at the papers strewn on the reception desk – official forms, pamphlets relating to water rights, and a map of the town, which he quickly glanced at, then folded and placed in his pocket. A little black metal box with a key was unlocked. He opened it and found a colourful array of papers inside, including bright green 100-euro and yellow 200-euro notes. About 3,000-euros in total, he quickly calculated.

'Anything interesting?' Alicia asked.

'What time did you say we'd be here?'

'We're on time.'

She pulled her phone out.

'I'll give them a call.'

They heard footsteps coming from above, scuffing the floor as they moved towards the top of the staircase. Alicia took a step forwards. Cámara closed the metal cash box and stayed where he was. Then remembering he was meant to be a photographer, not a policeman, he stepped away from behind the desk and came out into the centre of the hall.

A tall, slim man with black hair appeared on the staircase, pausing as he caught sight of them before continuing downwards. Reaching the hall, he started to cross towards the main doors leading out into the square, not glancing at the two strangers.

'Excuse me,' Alicia called out as the man reached the door. He hesitated, then half-turned to her.

'I'm looking for the mayor,' she said. 'I was supposed to meet him here now. Do you know where he is?'

The man already had his hand on the door handle.

'The mayor?' he repeated. Both Cámara and Alicia noted the accent. Middle Eastern, perhaps, given his appearance.

'Francisco Faro Oscuro,' Alicia said.

The man looked puzzled.

'Ah, Paco,' he said eventually.

'Do you know where he is?' Alicia asked again.

'No,' the man said. And he turned to leave.

'Do you know where we might find him?' Alicia butted in before he could get out the door.

The man shrugged.

'Somewhere in the village,' he said. 'He walks around. You'll find him. It's not big.'

And he shuffled outside and disappeared.

Alicia and Cámara gave each other a look.

'I don't think there's anyone else here,' Cámara said.

'Well, it looks like the mayor certainly isn't,' Alicia answered. 'Fancy a stroll?'

Stepping out into bright November sunshine, Cámara reached for the map.

'I can work out where we are,' he said with a frown. 'I just don't know where we're going.'

'Down here,' Alicia said, pulling on his arm.

They walked down what appeared to be the high street. Again, no one was around.

'Perhaps everyone's out working on the saffron harvest,' Alicia said.

'Or the place has been hit overnight by the plague,' Cámara murmured.

He glanced up at a sign on a nearby house.

'We're on Calle Che Guevara,' he said, 'which leads on to Avenida Salvador Allende,' he looked at his map. 'And you'll be happy to hear we're just a stone's throw from the Karl Marx Civic Centre. Perhaps they've all gone there for a collective read of *Das Kapital*.'

Alicia ignored him and carried on walking.

'Are you taking photos?' she called back.

Cámara shrugged, then reached for the camera slung around his neck, pulled off the lens cap, and started taking snaps. Peering through the viewfinder, he circled around, pausing, clicking, moving, pausing and clicking again, trying to capture a 360-degree view from where he was standing. A wooden door with black iron studs; an agricultural supplies shopfront; a dusty tall window with old, thin glass; a view back down the street to the town hall square.

He stopped, and quickly darted the camera back up to the window. He'd seen something there, a movement, a person. Through the viewfinder he saw only rain-streaked glass and a dirt-white curtain: no one was there. Pulling the camera away from his eye he looked up. No: nothing.

He was about to start scrolling through the photos he'd taken, to see if he'd caught anything with his shot, when Alicia beckoned him over.

'Come on. Over here.'

Turning a corner, he saw her standing in front of what looked a bit like a police car. It was light blue and white, and had the town emblem stamped on the door, but the only word written on it was that for '*Town Hall*'; nothing to indicate *police*.

'What do you reckon?' she said.

Cámara shrugged.

'Not like any *Municipales* car I've ever seen,' he said.

'That's because it's not really a police car,' a voice said behind him.

Cámara turned to find a man in uniform approaching them from the other side of the street. He was bareheaded – no cap – and the black belt above his hips lacked a gun of any kind.

'We don't have any police in Pozoblanco,' the man said. He was in his mid-thirties, with three days of stubble covering his chin.

'You don't need them in a utopia.'

'You work for the Town Hall?' Alicia asked.

The man nodded.

Alicia explained who she was, how she'd arranged to meet Paco, the mayor, to do a report for a major national newspaper.

'We were told to walk around,' Cámara said, 'and see if we could find him. Some guy at the town hall. Tall, foreign.'

'That'll be Ahmed,' the non-policeman said. 'Yeah, but if you want Paco you're better off going to the Peace Co-op. It's harvest time, so everyone's up there.'

Cámara checked the map.

'That's in Federico García Lorca Square?'

'That's right. Keep going straight, then swing round to the left.'

He turned to go.

'Just one thing,' Cámara said. 'If you're not the municipal policeman, what do you do?'

'Deliver the mail,' the man said. 'That and a few other odd jobs around the place.'

'Give out parking tickets?'

'Nah! Nothing like that.'

He grinned.

'We don't need any police. It's very peaceful here. People just get on with their lives.'

99

TWELVE

It was obvious which one of them was Paco. The town might have been a collective utopia with no police force, but Mayor Faro Oscuro's body language spoke of authority and of himself being in charge.

He wasn't tall, but then neither were the dozens of other people milling about inside the Peace Co-op. He was physically strong, however, and the thick, forked greying beard jutting from his jaw gave him presence.

When he turned and caught sight of them, Cámara immediately registered two things: an animal liveliness in his eyes that seemed incongruous with one who had recently lost a granddaughter; and a white T-shirt pulled over the man's black top showing a picture of Franco's face with a red line drawn over it. He would have to get Hilario one of those.

Finishing his conversation with a middle-aged woman, Faro Oscuro walked over to them, shaking hands first with Alicia and then with Cámara.

'It's harvest time, the most important moment of the year for us. We have to pick the flowers early the very morning they bloom, otherwise the stigmas dry out and become worthless.'

He swept a hand out, indicating the bustling activity around them.

The Peace Co-op was a simple barn-like structure made from breeze block and brick, with a corrugated roof. Around them were a dozen tables, each with four or five women and children sitting in front of piles of violet saffron flowers. With quick, deft movements, they were plucking at the red stigmas inside each flower, dropping them into baskets, and then tossing the remains of the flower on to the floor, chatting and joking as they worked.

'We started yesterday. It's hard work, but it has to be done. Can't be kept waiting. It's what keeps this town alive.'

Cámara detected an impediment in Faro Oscuro's voice, an inability to roll his 'r's properly. At their feet lay a thick, undulating carpet of flowers, while the air was rich with an intense, sharp, hay-like saffron aroma. It made him think of paella, of Valencia, of his old police colleague Inspector Torres. They'd had more than a few paellas together, nipping out at lunchtime for an hour or two. It was usually when they came up with breakthroughs in a case. Or at least that's what they told themselves.

Torres. He wondered how he was doing. They hadn't spoken for months. Perhaps he should give him a call.

A man with a greasy wrinkled neck was backing in towards him as he swept up. Cámara stepped out of the way to let him pass. The man looked up as he pushed a great swathe of petals with his broom, and smiled; two front teeth missing, but Cámara saw a sparkle in one of the remaining incisors:

a diamond stud, clean and shiny in an otherwise rotting mouth.

'This is very impressive,' Alicia was saying to Faro Oscuro. 'Can we take some shots in here?'

It was his cue: Cámara reached for his camera again.

'We tried looking for you at the town hall,' Alicia said.

'I left Ahmed in charge.'

'Yes, we spoke to him.'

Snap went the camera.

'Moroccan. Landed up here one day needing a job, so we took him in. Helps around the place – harvests, security, whatever's going.'

'That seems to be how things work here.'

Snap, snap.

'Yes, we do things a bit differently.'

Faro Oscuro smiled.

'Here, come and have a look around. You can come as well,' he called over to Cámara.

They walked around the tables. Some of the women looked up in greeting, others kept their eyes on the flowers in their hands, not breaking their concentration or the chatter.

'It's communal – we try to rotate work duties,' Faro Oscuro explained. 'But you have to recognise that certain people are better at some things than others.'

He leaned down, picked up a saffron flower, and showed it to them.

'We only want these red strands, the stigmas. The rest of the flower, the stamens, the petals, everything, gets thrown away. That's what ends up on the floor. Although we use it to mix with fertiliser. No waste. You have to give back to nature what you take from her.'

With thick forefinger and thumb, he pulled at the stigmas,

ripping them from the flower, and then tossed them into a nearby basket.

'It's delicate work, and you need small, delicate hands for it. Which is why we mostly have the women and children doing this part. It's not sexist, it's just how things work better. I could do it, the other men could do it, but we'd take longer. Haven't got the right touch.'

'I wouldn't say that, Paco,' one of the women at the table grinned up at him. 'You've got the touch, all right.'

And the rest of the table laughed and giggled.

Faro Oscuro pulled affectionately at the woman's ear.

'I love them all,' he said to Alicia. 'And they certainly know how to keep me in my place.'

They moved around the tables, other women calling up to Faro Oscuro, joking with him as they passed around the barn.

'You see, we're happy here. Elsewhere in the country people are getting laid off, not finding jobs. But you give people work – work they can believe in, that's part of the community, that they feel involved with – and they're happy. That's how we do things here, that's the philosophy. It's been going for over twenty years, and it just gets better. I'm more of a believer now than I was when we started.'

'So how does this operate?' Alicia was jotting down notes. 'You must have something of a production line.'

'We try to avoid using phrases like that – makes it sound like exploitation. But there is a system, voted on by everyone taking part.'

At one side of the barn, open doors looked out over a yard with a cement floor and the fields beyond.

'The saffron gets brought in through here. We're out before dawn picking the stuff. They'll be bringing in the last of it now. You tend to stop picking around ten o'clock – have to get it early in the day.'

He pointed at the tables.

'The flowers get distributed here, where the stigmas get plucked out, as you can see. Then as the baskets of stigmas get filled up, we store them in that container standing against the back wall.'

Snap.

The container appeared to be an aluminium box, perhaps two metres by one metre, and a metre high. Already it was close to being full.

'That looks like a very large amount.'

'We'll get almost three hundred kilos by the time we've finished.'

Alicia paused.

'That's about a million euros' worth.'

'It's what we live on, as I said. And why the whole town chips in for the harvest. It belongs to everyone.'

He clapped his hands, and after a while the chattering hubbub inside the barn faded into near silence.

'Now as you all know,' Faro Oscuro called out to the women, 'we have visitors today from Madrid, doing a report on us for a national newspaper.'

Calls of 'Ooh, aren't we grand.'

Faro Oscuro held his hands out for silence.

'They're very impressed by what we're doing, and I want to make sure you all smile for the camera. In a few days' time you're all going to be famous!'

The women laughed; some of the children cheered.

'But seriously, I was thinking we might offer our guests a sample of our important work here. So I propose a vote to decide if we should give them a present of some of our famous – soon to be even more famous – Pozoblanco saffron.'

The chatter rose in volume as the women took the idea on board.

'We'll have a show of hands. All those in favour?'

All the women, it seemed, raised an arm, along with Faro Oscuro himself.

'All those against?'

No arm was raised.

'Abstentions?'

A couple of arms went up at the back of the barn.

'Right. Thank you for your cooperation.'

Faro Oscuro stuck a hand into his trouser pocket and fished out a small plastic box with a pinch of saffron stigmas inside. On the label it said, in English, '*Spanish saffron, La Mancha*'.

He handed it to Alicia and started clapping, along with the rest of the people inside the barn.

Alicia nodded her thanks.

'Democracy in action?'

'It's how we like to do things around here.'

Cámara stepped up to have a look at the box in Alicia's hand.

'Where's the packaging done?' he asked.

Faro Oscuro indicated a door at the back of the barn, near the saffron container.

'There's another team in there. They'll be starting this afternoon.'

He led them through the open barn doors and out into the yard.

'These are the fields where we pick the flowers. La Mancha saffron is the best in the world; that's why it commands such a high price. It's like gold.'

Cámara looked out on to fields of a light, creamy brown. Green shoots running in rows were all that remained of the flowers that had been picked earlier that morning.

'With only three stigmas per plant it's pretty labour intensive, I should imagine,' Alicia said.

'You need two hundred and fifty thousand flowers to produce a kilo of saffron, so yes, it is very definitely labour intensive.'

'And you manage to grow all that here?'

'The town has five hundred hectares, owned collectively. And that's thanks to our struggle over the years. Almost all this land was owned by the Duke of Puertollano thirty years ago – didn't do anything with it, and he refused to let us farm it. So that's when it all started.'

They walked out of the yard, along the edge of one of the fields, before connecting with a street and turning back in towards the town centre.

'It was when my father was mayor,' Faro Oscuro said. 'The whole town went on hunger strike, demanding access to the land. And we staged sit-ins, and occupied some of the fields.'

Cámara had stopped taking photographs by this point, and was lighting a cigarette. He hovered a step or two behind as Alicia prompted Faro Oscuro to tell more.

'What happened?'

'They sent the police in. Some of us got beaten up, sent to jail. It was back in the early eighties. Franco hadn't been dead for long. Things were moving very slowly. People were frightened. But we had no work, nothing, here. So we went on hunger strike. The only thing we could do.'

He stopped to talk to a couple of men who were carrying baskets of saffron flowers. Across the street was a large white lorry with the name of an export company stamped on the side. Cámara stuck the cigarette in his mouth and took another shot.

The conversation finished and the two men headed up the road in the direction of the Peace Co-op.

'That's the last of it today,' Faro Oscuro said. 'We'll pick up again tomorrow at dawn.'

'So the hunger strike?' Alicia said.

'Lasted thirteen days. The regional government had to give in in the end. Well, of course, we were in the right. We were starving here, children, babies, everyone. So they expropriated the land and gave it to the town. And we've been doing nicely ever since.'

'As a collective?'

'As a collective. Everyone takes part, everyone owns everything. Schools, parks, civic centres, houses – we've built them all ourselves. That's why it's so cheap. An ordinary rent in Madrid is – what? Eight hundred, a thousand euros a month?'

Alicia nodded.

'Here we pay fifteen euros. That's it.'

'That's incredible.'

'But true!' Faro Oscuro raised his arms in the air. 'You help to build it, so you get the reward. It's simple.'

They came out into the main square, where the town hall building stood. Some of the shops had opened now, making up for the lost hours of the early morning.

'But the struggle continues?' Alicia asked.

'Yes, it's not always easy,' Faro Oscuro said with a grin. 'But as I said, I'm even more of a believer now than I was at the beginning.'

'But for you, personally, I mean.'

Faro Oscuro looked at her questioningly, his small, intense eyes fixed on her.

'I heard there has been a family tragedy recently,' Alicia said. 'Your granddaughter?'

Faro Oscuro breathed heavily through his nostrils, the hairs in his thick beard vibrating. He looked more solid, harder, of a sudden.

'This way,' he said finally, turning towards one of the houses lining the square.

'Come with me.'

THIRTEEN

A dark passageway led through to a patio where dusty glazed pots were held against the walls in iron brackets – geraniums, mostly devoid of their flowers by now, the leaves looking tired and heavy as though calling out to be pruned before the winter cold. An outdoor stairway led to a second floor, while two rooms opened out to where they stood: one shrouded in heavy curtains; the other, a kitchen, with its glass-pane doors slung back.

Inside, three women sat around a table. Two of them looked to be in their sixties, although one was greyer both of hair and skin than the other. They sat on either side of the table, dipping their hands into a large bowl in the centre to pull out potatoes for peeling.

Between them, at the far end of the table, sat a younger woman with long black hair that fell over her face as she leaned forwards, her back curled as though trying to make herself into a ball. It was difficult to see her features, but a thin mouth was just visible as she drew on a cigarette in short, rapid bursts.

All three of the women were dressed in black. Simple skirts and polyester jumpers for the elder two, trousers and a black leather jacket for the younger woman. They sat in silence, the only sound coming from their hands as they dipped into the bowl and then cut into the potato skin with small knives.

'I know there are exceptions,' Faro Oscuro said, 'which is why I'm showing you this.'

He pointed at the women.

'Newspapers, the TV – they concentrate on the story of a death, of a killing. It's dramatic, it's shocking . . .'

He sighed.

'But this is the reality. This, what's left behind.'

He took a step forwards towards the kitchen.

'But no one wants to know about this.'

Alicia followed after him. Cámara glanced up at the rooms on the floor above: the shutters were all closed. Then he fell in step with the others.

The women barely reacted when they reached the kitchen doorway.

'Maribel, my wife,' Faro Oscuro said, indicating the elder of the two middle-aged women.

'Marta, my sister-in-law, and Olga, my daughter.'

The woman in the leather jacket stubbed her cigarette out on a small tin ashtray, then reached over for her packet to light another one, pulling it out with long, thin, pale fingers.

'Police?'

Marta had raised her head from the potatoes for a moment and directed her question to Alicia.

'I'm a journalist,' Alicia said.

'And him?'

'He's my photographer. From the newspaper.'

Marta nodded and turned her attention back to the potatoes. Maribel and Olga remained silent.

At a signal from Faro Oscuro, Alicia and Cámara turned to walk away.

'I'm very sorry for your loss,' Alicia said.

The knives scraped and cut, the smoke curling above their heads.

'Is that the real reason why you came?' Faro Oscuro said when they got back outside.

'It's not my intention to intrude,' Alicia said. 'You can show us and tell us as much or as little as you want.'

'I want people to see what grief really looks like, what death means. It's not about the crying, the sadness, the destruction of life. It's what you just saw – it's the obligation to survive when all you want to do is die yourself. It's carrying on in an empty world. Thank God I have my work, and my wife and daughter. Otherwise . . .'

His eyes closed for a moment, then sprang open.

'It was probably something to do with drugs. Olga has had her problems in the past. It seems my granddaughter did as well. We knew, of course, but we thought it could be kept under control. Recreational drug taking is what has kept humans sane for thousands of years. Even cavemen were eating hallucinogens in the Stone Age.'

He looked at Cámara.

'But Mirella was all right. Perhaps she took too much, I don't know. But it wasn't the drugs that did it. A person killed her, a man. Not some chemical substance.'

He started crossing the road, heading back towards the town hall.

'She needed some space, some time on her own. It's what

Olga never understood. So we let her go, when she said she wanted to go to the city. She was old enough. It would be good for her. There were problems at home with her mother. It's why she was here in the first place, to get away for a while.'

He paused on the step outside the front door.

'And so we let her go. Now she's never coming back. The worst thing is that no matter how I reason it out to myself, I still feel guilty. Some bastard out there killed her, yet I'm the one to blame.'

Alicia took the keys from Cámara's hand and sat behind the wheel.

'I've never driven a BMW. Let's see what all the fuss is about.'

The car rolled along the cobbled streets until reaching tarmac again on the outskirts of the village, and she pressed down the accelerator. Their heads pushed back against the rests as the engine surged.

'Not bad. Thrilling, actually. Is this something to do with penis envy?'

'If you want mine, it's yours.'

'Oh, I know that.'

She giggled as they passed the last of the trees lining the road out of the village, and broke out into the empty landscape once more.

'I have a theory,' Cámara said as field after field of light brown soil flew past. 'The madness round here actually comes from the land itself, as though it runs through the earth like some invisible current, or underground rivers and streams, and it seeps into you if you stay here too long, soaking into your feet and up your body until it reaches your brain.'

Alicia swerved a little to avoid a lorry driving almost in the middle of the road.

'I mean, Cervantes had to make Don Quixote a madman – or at least he had to make his madman come from La Mancha. Nothing else would make sense. Look around you.'

He waved a hand out of the open window.

'Even the rocks and stones here are insane. Just look at them.'

Alicia gave him a quizzical look.

'And another thing, where are all the saffron fields? There was a lot of saffron in that warehouse, but I don't see much of it being grown around here. Certainly not enough to justify the piles of it we've just—'

CRACK!

For a moment the car sped on, neither of them speaking.

'What . . . ?'

Cámara turned around: the back window had shattered.

'Did we just hit a stone, or something?'

'DRIVE DRIVE DRIVE!' he shouted.

'What?'

'Put your foot down. Now! Drive!'

There was no hesitation. Immediately the car pulled away faster as Alicia accelerated. Cámara looked round at the back window once more: the bullet had left a neat hole on the left side, but the rest of the glass was about to fall in from the impact.

'We're being shot at. Don't stay on a straight line. Swerve the car.'

Unbuckling his seat belt, he climbed on to the back seat and pushed away at the glass, scattering bits of it over the road as they sped along. No one was following them – the lorry had disappeared and there was no other car visible.

Whoever it was was almost certainly shooting from a fixed position.

'This is a long straight road,' Alicia said, her voice steady but nervous.

'Keep going. Don't stop. But move the car around.'

He was thrown to one side as the vehicle pulled to the right and then the left.

'Not too regularly,' he said. 'You have to make yourself a difficult target.'

CRACK!

Another shot. They both felt the impact as the bullet seemed to hit some part of the car.

'Are you all right? Are you all right?' Cámara screamed.

'I'm OK,' Alicia said. Their eyes met in the rear-view mirror for a second.

'Keep going.'

The car swerved again.

'There's a turning ahead.'

'He's shooting from behind us. Go, go, GO!'

He couldn't tell where the bullets were being fired from, but it seemed a reasonable guess. And he had to reassure Alicia somehow, tell her that if they could get to the corner and off the straight they would be all right. But would they?

He looked back through the hole he'd punched in the glass, then ducked his head again. The car bodywork offered little protection, but it was better than nothing. Alicia, however, was exposed. He heaved himself over to her side of the car: if the firing was indeed coming from behind, he might at least offer some protection with his own body.

He glanced quickly ahead: the turning was only metres away.

CRACK!

It felt like a very hard punch in the hip, as though someone had taken a large heavy stick and hit him at the top of the thigh. He let out a low grunt and surged forwards, his hands gripping at the pain.

The car turned the corner, Alicia accelerating harder as they pulled out of it and away down another straight. Shorter this time: in a few seconds they would reach another corner.

'Keep going. Don't slow down.'

He tried to disguise the strain in his voice.

'Max?'

'I'm fine. Keep driving. Don't look back.'

She turned to look down at him curled up in the well of the back seat.

'I'm fine.'

The car sped along. Cámara pulled his hand away from his leg: it was dry.

A minute later they joined the main road and were heading back towards the city.

'Just take us back to the centre,' Cámara said. 'We're safe now. Trust me.'

'Are you all right?'

He undid his zip and pulled his trousers down a fraction: the skin at the side of his upper thigh was red and mottled with burst capillaries, but there was no blood. He heard something fall to the floor. Reaching down with a grunt he lifted up the bullet that had struck him. A hole in the upholstery beside him showed where it had come through the bodywork of the car.

His head fell back against the door and he closed his eyes, cold shock swimming through him with a steady pulse.

While the bullet warmed in the palm of his hand.

FOURTEEN

'We need to get that seen to.'

'I'm all right. Let me . . .'

Alicia had pulled the car to the side of the road on a quiet street. The smashed back window was attracting suspicious looks from passers-by.

Cámara opened the door and hauled himself out. Alicia jumped out from the driver's seat and went to help him.

'I'm OK.'

He took a step forward, grimacing at the pain shooting through his leg and hip as it took the weight.

'It's all right. I'll be fine.'

'Let me see.'

Gently, she pulled his shirt tail up where it was covering his upper leg, letting out an uncontrolled gasp when she saw the swelling skin.

'It's bruised, that's all. It's going to hurt for a bit, but I can take some anti-inflammatories.'

She stood up and kissed him tenderly near the mouth, her eyes tearful.

'Oh, Max.'

He kissed her hair where she rested her head on his shoulder.

A bar stood a couple of doors from where she'd parked. Brushing herself down, she walked in and a couple of minutes later emerged with two plastic cups with large doses of brandy inside.

They drank in silence, both looking at each other, feeling the warmth of the liquor trickle its way down. Bit by bit, they began to breathe more deeply again, drawing cool air into their lungs.

'I need to sit down.'

She led him round to the passenger seat, then sat back down in the driver's seat beside him.

'Someone was shooting at us,' she said.

Cámara nodded.

'Were they trying to kill us?'

'I don't know.'

Had someone been trying to frighten them? Or was it a serious, if failed, attempt on their lives? He couldn't say. Perhaps the bullet, now nestling in his trouser pocket, would give a clue.

'We need to go to the police.'

She turned to him, but he didn't move.

'Shouldn't we?'

After a pause, he shook his head.

'No. At least not now.'

She slumped back into her seat, closing her eyes and sipping on her brandy. Cámara reached into his jacket pocket, lit two cigarettes and then placed one between her lips. She accepted it without looking at him.

'What's going on?' she said at last. 'What haven't you told me?'

A couple of teenage boys were staring in at the back of the car, where odd shards of glass were scattered over the bodywork and inside on the seats.

'Fuck, look at that!'

'Looks like they had a crash or something.'

'What, reversing?'

'Shut it.'

'We'll have to take this back to your friend Gerardo at the garage,' Alicia said. 'Or is that off the cards as well?'

'We're safer here than we would be at the Jefatura,' Cámara said.

Alicia drew on her cigarette, watching the boys as they walked down the street and glanced back at the strangely damaged car.

'It's not clear who can be trusted.'

He finished the brandy; his leg was aching and he longed for a refill.

'What's going on?' Alicia said.

'I don't know. There's at least one corrupt officer, perhaps more. I haven't had the full story myself.'

'We were set up?'

His cigarette was burning close to the skin of his fingers.

'I don't know.'

'You don't know? We've just been shot at. We could have been killed. You could have been killed. And you don't know? Where the hell have we just been? Some scam involving the saffron business, was what you said. I didn't know we were heading into some kind of gang warfare.'

'Neither did I.'

'Didn't you? Didn't you really? You mean you had no suspicions?'

'Look!' He turned to face her. 'The police may be involved in some saffron mafia. That's what I was told. That's what I'm telling you now. If I'd known it was going to be so dangerous I would have taken precautions. I had no idea this was going to happen. No idea.'

She stared out of the window, taking a last drag of the cigarette before throwing it out on to the road.

'God knows I would never have brought you along if I'd known.'

She reached over and took his empty cup. A few minutes later she had returned from the bar with more brandy for both of them.

'They're talking about us in there,' she said.

'We'll have to move.'

'Where are we going?'

'For the moment, it's back to Gerardo's'.

They manoeuvred past scattered spare parts and left the BMW in the centre of the garage, next to the office.

Gerardo grinned when he saw them. Only when he caught the expression in their eyes did he begin to have doubts.

He stood up and walked out into the workshop.

'What happened? No, no, no. Please, tell me it's all right.'

Wordlessly, Cámara walked him around to the back of the car. Gerardo's face dropped when he saw the smashed rear window.

'A stone hit you on the back?' he asked incredulously.

Cámara sighed. With his finger he traced over the

bodywork, searching, then stood up and pointed when he found the hole. Gerardo looked at him, then bent down to have a look.

He stayed there for almost a minute, then very slowly lifted himself up, still gazing down at the curious mark on the metalwork.

'Now you're going to tell me that it isn't what I think it is.'

Cámara lifted his hands up and shrugged.

Gerardo gave him a look of fear and surprise.

'Tell me that sudden limp you've developed isn't anything to do with this, either,' he said.

Cámara said nothing.

Gerardo nodded towards Alicia, who was still sitting behind the wheel.

'Fine,' Cámara said. 'We're both fine.'

Gerardo let out a deep breath.

'Well,' he said, 'that's good news. I don't know what's been going on. And I don't want to know.'

He glanced back down at the hole.

'I never realised I was living in such a dangerous city.'

Cámara patted him on the shoulder.

'Clean it up and you could get an extra grand for it,' he said. 'Goes faster than a bullet.'

He sniffed.

'Well, almost.'

FIFTEEN

'I'll try some of that home-grown now.'

Pilar was leaving when they reached the flat. There was no sign of Hilario.

'He said he was going for a walk. There's some stock on the counter. You can use it to make a consommé.'

The door clicked shut and they were left alone.

'Is she always like that?' Alicia asked.

'It's probably the sight of another woman in the flat. You're an intruder.'

He limped his way to the living room and fell down on to the sofa. Alicia followed after him.

'How are you feeling?'

'I've had worse.'

Earlier that year, at the start of the summer, Alicia had seen for herself the cuts Cámara had received on his hands after warding off a knife attack. She'd helped clean and dress the wounds until they had healed: the scars were still there.

'It's up on the shelf,' Cámara said. 'I'll make you one if you don't mind getting it.'

She reached up and passed him the box. Cámara opened it, pulled out a cigarette paper and a pinch of *maría*, and started preparing the joint. A few moments later he lit it and passed it over to her. Still standing, she took it and paced around the room, inhaling deeply.

'This is a place of secrets,' she said.

Cámara was silent. After a couple more drags, she sat down next to him on the sofa, curling up and resting her head on his chest. Cámara took the joint from her outstretched hand and drew in hard.

'I've never been shot at before,' Alicia said. 'I'm still not sure what I'm supposed to feel. Fear is too simple, it doesn't quite describe it properly.'

'Did you see your life flash before you?'

'I'm serious.'

'So am I.'

She sighed.

'Yes. No. I'm not sure. I felt so many things. I'm still trying to unravel it all.'

She sat up and looked at him.

'Did you?'

Cámara shrugged.

'No, I don't think so. I was too busy trying to work out what to do.'

'Is that what they teach you?' Alicia asked, placing her head back on his chest. 'At police academy? How to dodge bullets if someone shoots at you? All that swerving from side to side you told me about.'

'No,' Cámara said. 'There's nothing as useful as that. I probably got the idea from some TV programme.'

She laughed.

'I don't know,' Cámara said. 'A friend of mine is in the GEO – the special police. He may have mentioned something. Although come to think of it it was something about how little protection a car can give you against a sniper. Bullets go right through the bodywork. Unless it's bulletproof, of course.'

'Which BMWs aren't.'

'Not normally.'

'You'd have thought they might be, what with the way people go on about them.'

Cámara leaned over to hand her the last of the joint.

'How many shots were there?'

'Three, I think. The first one hit the back window, the second impacted in the car somewhere, and the third . . .'

'The third went into your leg. Or nearly.'

She took a final drag and lifted the joint up to offer him, but he shook his head. Pulling the ashtray closer on the little table in front of them, she stubbed the burning end out and watched the trail of dying smoke rise up into the foggy living-room air.

'I have a feeling we've had a lucky escape,' she said.

Cámara said nothing.

'They were trying to kill us, weren't they? I mean, whoever it was shooting at us. That wasn't just a warning. You can warn in other ways. But those bullets came very close. They were shooting to kill.'

'Possibly.'

'So we're still in danger.'

She stood up and turned to look down at him.

'Here we are getting stoned in your grandfather's flat when we should be . . . OK, I know you don't want to go to the police, but come on, Max. We've got to do something. We can't just sit here and wait for them to come knocking on the door to finish the job off.'

He beckoned her to sit down again.

'They're not coming here. No one's coming here. We're fine.'

She remained on her feet, her nervousness kicking against the slowing, dulling effect of the marihuana.

'How can you be so sure?'

'Look, you're being paranoid. Perhaps the joint wasn't such a good idea. This stuff's pretty gentle, though. I just know, all right. I had a sense we were in danger when we were in Pozoblanco, although not quite to what degree. I don't have that now, all right? Trust me on this. It's a kind of sixth sense you develop.'

'I'm supposed to stop fearing for my life because of some gut feeling of yours?'

Cámara shrugged. She sat down on the sofa again and leaned in against him, punching him softly in the ribs.

'Bastard.'

'They may have been trying to kill us,' Cámara said, 'but it wasn't a very sophisticated attempt. So I don't think we're dealing with a professional contract killer. Which means they're not going to be clever enough to track us down here. There was something more than a little bit botched about it, as though it was dreamt up at the last minute. If they'd really wanted to kill us they could have done so. Driving on ahead and then shooting from the front, rather than behind, would have increased their chances by a huge amount. Or a car bomb, or a—'

'OK, I get it.'

Her words were beginning to slur as she moved towards

sleep. Cámara stopped talking, and in a few moments he could hear her breathing slowly and deeply as she reached unconsciousness.

The drug was working on him as well, but rather than making him drowsy, as ever when he found himself in situations such as this, it helped silence some of the screaming, to lower the noise and allow quieter voices to be heard.

And he found his thoughts turning to Hilario. Did he know about Pozoblanco, about this collective farming village just a few miles up the road? He imagined it would be the kind of place he would like, or admire at least. Weren't those anarchist ideas Faro Oscuro was implementing? Anarchist, communist – he had never been entirely certain what the difference was, despite the years of living with Hilario. But his grandfather wasn't a preacher – he had never tried to 'convert' Cámara in any way. If anything he'd simply made him uncomfortable – nothing was stable, nothing was quite what it seemed with him. The moment he thought he'd worked something out, Hilario would come along and change the rules, never allowing stasis to descend on them and their life. Atrophy – that had been a common word used during his adolescence. He didn't hear it in other households, but it was often on Hilario's lips, something to be avoided, to dodge and outwit. Stay still and atrophy would get you, like a disease of the world.

So was that anarchism, Hilario's anarchism? Being mercurial, staying ahead in some inexplicable way, never allowing anyone to pin you down, to nail you?

Sometimes he'd wondered if an anarchist was simply a communist who didn't have any power. Give a man a gun and authority and you'd see the anarchist in him evaporate in an instant, almost like the spirit leaving his body.

He tried to imagine Hilario with a gun. Would he still hold on to his ideas and ideals with his finger wrapped around a trigger? Anyone would succumb, even him.

But then again, what were his ideas exactly? It wasn't the kind of anarchism others might easily recognise – one that involved abolishing private property and collectivising the land. As a Spaniard of his generation, growing up during the tail-end years of the Franco regime in the 1970s and then through the Transition and the first steps into democracy into the '80s, Max had received practically no education about his country's twentieth-century history. But he'd picked up titbits here and there from conversations with people, unstructured chats with Hilario, a chapter or two of one of the new history books while browsing a bookshop. And he was aware of the experiments that had taken place in Spain during the 1930s, during the early months of the Civil War, when anarchists had insisted that revolution in Republican-held territory was more important than fighting Franco at the front. Towns and villages had been taken over and collectivised, money abolished and all signs of social hierarchy done away with. Some of these experiments had been pacific, in others wealthier townspeople had been taken out and shot before the workers' utopia had been established.

Had Maximiliano, his great-grandfather, been involved in any of that? Had he gone around shooting people because they wore suits, or went to church? He tried to look inside himself, as though some memory of the times might have been passed down to him in his blood, or his DNA as people said now. Could he himself have done that? Would he, had he been alive then?

He couldn't see it.

So why didn't Hilario ever mention Pozoblanco? He felt sure there was something there, something he should know.

When he woke, Alicia was already up, sitting at the table opposite him, drinking a glass of milk and eating some chocolate biscuits.

'I found them in the kitchen.'

He lifted himself up from the sofa, shaking his head clear.

'Want some?'

The milk was cold and refreshing, the chocolate mellowing.

'It's raining outside,' she said. 'But still no sign of Hilario. Do you think he's all right?'

'Yeah. I think so.'

'It was only a few days ago, you know.'

'I know him. Besides, if he's ever going to go – I mean, when he finally goes – he'd prefer it this way.'

'What do you mean?'

'Out, on his own, free. The more I try and fuss over him the worse he'd get. It's not him. Better to be alive, or dead. But not dead while still alive.'

'You're quite like him in some ways,' she said. 'Not in everything, but I can see it. Now that I've met him as well, I can see characteristics that come from him.'

Cámara smiled. Not too many, he thought to himself.

'I found these as well,' Alicia said, holding up two small boxes. 'Anti-inflammatory pills, and this soothing cream. They were in the bathroom cabinet.'

Cámara swallowed the pill with the last of the milk. He pulled his trousers down to expose the bruising on his upper thigh and Alicia began to work the cream in.

'Sore?'

'No.' He stifled the urge to wince.

'I saw you,' she said. 'Moving to my side of the car behind me on the back seat.'

Cámara had his eyes closed.

'You were trying to shield me.'

He didn't react. She leaned down and kissed him on the thigh. That bullet could have hit her.

He dozed for a little more as she rubbed the cream in until it had been absorbed. It felt good just to have her hands there, taking away some of the pain and tension.

She pulled his trousers back up.

'We could put some ice on it. Might help.'

'The pills will do the trick.'

She cleared away the glasses of milk and biscuit crumbs, then returned to the living room from the kitchen, opening the door out on to the balcony to let in some fresh air.

Cámara watched her as she moved about the room. She'd lost some weight since moving to Madrid, and her trousers were loose around her hips, held in place around her waist by tightening her belt a notch more. She'd talked about getting some new clothes, a size smaller. But running to and from the newspaper, or simply lounging at home, drenched in her new love, had meant she'd never managed to make it to the shops. And the old clothes stayed. She'd fit back into them soon enough, she joked, once Christmas came along.

Or this – their affair – came to an end.

She was behind him now, glancing at the books on the shelves, rummaging around through boxes and drawers. He'd grown used to it – a journalist's curiosity. He could switch it on in himself when needed. With her, however, it was more of a compulsion, if innocent in nature.

There was a rhythm to her movements, but the rummaging came to a sudden stop. And the silence drew his attention.

'What is it?'

She didn't reply.

He tried to turn, but his body felt heavy on the sofa.

'What have you got?'

She took a step towards him, appearing in the full light shining through the open balcony door. Her hand was outstretched, and in it she held a pistol.

It was pointing at his chest.

SIXTEEN

He jumped in his seat.

'What the hell is that?'

She looked him in the eye.

'You tell me.'

'Let me see that. Where was it?'

'In the drawer.'

She pulled her hand away as he tried to snatch at the gun.

'I've seen one of these before,' she said.

There was a click from the other end of the flat as the front door was opened and closed. Footsteps came down the corridor, slow but steady. Alicia gripped the pistol in her hand.

The living-room door opened and Hilario appeared, rain-water dripping from his overcoat on to the floor.

Alicia held the gun up to his face.

'It's a Luger,' she said. 'The Germans used them in the Second World War.'

Hilario didn't flinch.

'Either you're a collector,' she said. 'Or . . .'

'I was in the Blue Division,' Hilario said.

He lowered his eyes and walked over to the table, taking off his coat and draping it over one of the chairs. There, he paused for a moment, as though thinking about what he was going to say, and then walked over to the balcony door.

'The rain's coming in,' he said, closing it shut.

Alicia and Cámara's eyes didn't leave him, but he refused to look at them. Instead, he walked over to the armchair and sat down. Resting his elbows on the arms, he brought his hands together and tapped his fingertips lightly against one another. After a pause, he felt in his pocket and pulled out a small black leather wallet. From it he plucked out a black-and-white photo which he passed to Cámara.

Cámara looked down at a new and instantly recognisable face. He was heavier set, and his cheekbones were more prominent than either his own or Hilario's, but there was no mistaking that he was of the same family. The strong jaw, fleshy nose and an air of physical strength about him. His eyes, dark and penetrating, were framed by round glasses of the kind worn in the 1930s.

'My father,' Hilario said, 'Maximiliano, your great-grand-father, was betrayed.'

Cámara passed the photo to Alicia, who was still standing near the door. Neither of them spoke.

Hilario's eyes became unfocused and he breathed heavily for a moment. Then he opened his mouth, pausing for a second before beginning his story.

'Albacete was a busy place during the Civil War,' he said. 'It's hard to imagine now, but this was the headquarters for the International Brigades – all those young men coming in from around the world to fight for the Republic.'

He sighed heavily as the memories appeared to flicker before his eyes.

Many people were coming into the city, he said, refugees fleeing areas conquered by Franco's troops, volunteers from abroad, and there had been a lot of organising to do.

'The communists were mostly in charge – the International Brigades were under their control – but my father, Maximiliano, was tolerated. He was an anarchist, a member of the CNT trade union. Anarchists, Republicans, communists, socialists, they were all lumped together in the fight against Franco, but they hated each other really.

'Maximiliano was an idealist, though, an intellectual anarchist, a dreamer. Anarchism meant utopia for him – free people and the best of their characters would naturally come to the fore. He was a vegetarian, and believed in free love, although my mother always said he was the most devoted and faithful of men. I think he agreed with the principle of free love, of men and women having relationships on their own terms, without the interference of Church or State.

'And so when Alfonso XIII fled the country and the Republic finally came in 1931 he was there, as enthusiastic as the rest, filled with hope that real change could finally begin.'

Hilario reminded them of what the country had been like back then. Many areas were almost mediaeval, with feudal landowners and peasants sometimes forced to eat grass to survive. Outside the towns and cities it was hard to find anyone who could read or write. But hopes for the new Republican government turned into frustration as reforms were slow to arrive. Anarchist groups spontaneously collectivised the land in some areas, and the police moved in. There were shoot-outs, many deaths.

Then the Civil War had started in the summer of 1936.

'I remember,' Hilario said. 'I was sitting at home with my mother, and we heard the news coming from a neighbour's window on the radio – the army had risen in Spanish Morocco. I think we all knew it was coming.

'Militias were set up almost straight away – people demanding weapons so they could go and fight the rebels, to defend the Republic. Maximiliano wanted to go too, but he was already old for fighting. Some of his CNT colleagues suggested he stay behind – they knew he was a good organiser. He'd been a committee chairman at the furniture factory where he worked, calling for strikes for better conditions. Some of them had been beaten during the stoppage, Maximiliano included. I remember him coming home one night with bandages around his hands and head – two of his fingers were broken. The police, again. But those men followed him, they believed in him, and they stuck to it. And got what they were asking for in the end.'

By now Alicia had sat down next to Cámara, crossing her legs under her on the sofa. Hilario averted his eyes from them, staring at the wall as he remembered.

'They made mistakes, though, the CNT. When the war began they opened the prisons in many places. All crimes, went the theory, were caused by the greater crime of class struggle and repression. Now that revolution was breaking out in the face of Franco's military uprising, that cause had been removed. So all prisoners should be freed. Besides, the very concept of a prison is anathema to the anarchist ideal.

'But the result was that murderers and thieves were suddenly let loose. And many of them joined the CNT – perhaps out of gratitude to their liberators, or just opportunism. I don't know.

'Those first few months were a bloody time. People were

settling old scores, killings became commonplace. Someone would get hauled up, accused of some crime or other, and then get taken out and shot by the side of the road and left there. Priests, businessmen, known right-wingers.

'It was a bloodbath. The same was happening on the other side, worse, even – Franco's men slaughtering left-wingers wherever they were in control. But it was no excuse.

'Maximiliano was disgusted. He did what he could to stop it, but no one listens when they've got a gun in their hand and you don't. I think he feared for his own life at times.'

Hilario closed his eyes for a moment, his chest heaving as though he were catching his breath, before opening them again to continue.

'Then new battles started breaking out – not just the ones against the fascists, but between the different groups fighting for the Republic. The communists started becoming more important – they had money and support from Stalin. They wanted to take over, and lots of people liked them because they seemed more organised than the rabble that had been in charge at the beginning. No more militias, they said. We need a proper army, like Franco's, if we're going to win this.

'But what was the point of fighting fascism if you were letting a new form of it come in through the back door? Stalin was just as bad – worse, even – than Franco. In the end being set free is the most frightening thing you can do to a person. They almost always bring back whatever it was they've been freed from. Under a different name, of course.

'And what could Maximiliano do? So-called anarchists had let him down by shedding innocent blood, and now a new form of tyranny was being set in place. But he felt the need to serve the Republic, the people around him. The communists were rooting out many anarchists and Trotskyists, and anyone else they didn't like. But they let Maximiliano stay. His reputation as an organiser saved him, I think. Not a quality you tend to associate with anarchists, but there you have it. They tried to get him to join the Communist Party, but he refused. Said he could have gone far. But they didn't understand him, they never could.

'And so he stayed, keeping himself out of the fights between the different factions, wondering if he'd betrayed his ideals, but concentrating on helping the refugees flooding into the city as more and more of the country was taken over. Basques, Asturians, Catalans – they all needed somewhere to sleep, something to eat. Our flat became a kind of holding centre – dozens of people passing through, perhaps staying just one night, lying on a spare patch of floor along with the others, before they could be sorted with somewhere to go. My mother gave them what she could to eat, but food was scarce, and getting more so. She suffered a lot in those times, but she believed in Maximiliano and what he was doing. The refugees needed her.

'I remember once watching her stewing bones she'd got from God knows where. The remains of some old horse, perhaps. A little girl from Oviedo was sitting on the floor near her feet. She'd been evacuated before the city had fallen, shipped off to Cartagena, and then brought here. No one knew where her parents were, or if they'd survived. There was just a tag around her neck, with her name and address, and a pathetic appeal scribbled by someone on the back to please look after her. She must have been five years old or so. I was thirteen. All the toys in the house had gone – we'd given them all away. But from somewhere my mother managed to produce a tiny wooden spinning top. I don't know if it had been lost in the pocket of her apron. And she leaned down and handed it to the little girl, who took it without a word and then began to play with it on the floor, spinning it with one hand and then another, watching as it wobbled and tumbled, but always catching it before it came to a halt.

'"Don't stop," she said to it angrily. "Don't stop!" As though giving it an order. And she'd start spinning it again, but again it would run out of momentum, and she'd have to catch it once more in her hands before it stopped altogether.

'"Don't stop. Don't stop."

'She slept in my bed that night – I found a spot on the floor next to the others. The following morning my father took her with him and we never saw her again. And neither my mother nor I asked what had become of her. We couldn't. You couldn't. There were so many of them, so much to think about. We lived in a kind of saturation.

'The end came quite quickly. It was the spring of 1939. What remained of the Republic collapsed – there were barely any guns left even to shoot with. Our soldiers fled the front lines, and the fascists walked in. Albacete was one of the last places they reached.

'Maximiliano was in danger. But there was really only one choice. Surrendering would mean a swift execution – there was nowhere to run to, stuck here in the centre of the country. So he went into hiding, became a *topo*' – a mole – 'hiding in his own home, out of sight, as though he'd vanished. People were doing it all over the city, all over the country. Some of them lived like that for years, decades even. Maximiliano was forced to spend his days in a cupboard that had been used for keeping spare bed linen, hunched up, in the dark, not making a sound. Even a cough could give him away.

'We had to be so careful. People were keen to get in with the new authorities, to get contacts, or favours from the fascists. And one of the best ways was to feed them "Reds" who had escaped. They wanted to cleanse the country, they said, to eliminate the "anti-Spain". That meant anyone who didn't think like them. Sometimes at night we heard the shooting of the execution squads. They'd won the war, but the killing had to continue.'

Max listened, motionless with concentration on Hilario's story. Beside him, Alicia reached over and held his hand.

'We managed it, though. Maximiliano was very disciplined, sleeping through much of the day in his cell, then coming out at night, late, when we felt it was safe. Then he had to wash and shave and eat in total silence. Conversations were held in a whisper, or even on pieces of paper. If any neighbour had heard anything suspicious, we knew they'd come for him straight away. Searches of people's houses were common. And the cupboard kept him out of sight, but it would take only a minute or two to find him if someone tried.

'We managed it for three years. A new European war had started, Hitler had taken over France. Maximiliano didn't break, although perhaps he should have done. My mother kept him alive – I saw them sobbing silently in the dark together a few times. Even his frustration had to be wordless and mute.

'Three years. And then they came one morning, walked straight to the cupboard and fished him out, like an errant schoolboy.

'No one had heard him – we'd been strict about that.

'Someone had told them. Someone who knew.'

SEVENTEEN

Hilario barely moved as he spoke, his body still, apart from a slight heaving in his chest when he breathed. Cámara was aware of a change in him, however: something was different; he was seeing a side of his grandfather he'd never known. Something in his eyes: there was the same liveliness about them, but the spark appeared to be tempered, or alloyed.

He wondered about asking him to stop. Remembering past pain might not be the best thing for an elderly man recovering from a stroke. But Hilario wasn't a man easily dissuaded from anything. And besides, the story wasn't finished; Cámara wanted to know what had happened. Alicia had handed him back the photo of his great-grandfather, and it rested between his fingers. The irony that Hilario, who always shunned any brooding on the past, insisting always on the need to move forwards, should keep this with him at all times wasn't lost on him.

Alicia sat forwards with her elbows on her knees, her

attention focused entirely on Hilario and his story. The Luger now rested on the low table next to the sofa.

'Maximiliano was interrogated, and beaten,' Hilario went on. 'Immediately after the war many who'd been captured by Franco were simply shot, or done away with in whatever fashion. By this time, however, 1942, there was some semblance of order to the killings, or at least they waited a while before executing them.

'I didn't see him, but my mother went every morning to the prison where they held him, taking whatever she could – food, clothes – to help alleviate his captivity. I don't think any of it reached him, and she probably knew that as well, but it helped – helped her to think she was doing something, and perhaps helped by making the guards who were stealing it all be less violent towards my father.

'But I know – she told me later – that they'd treated him roughly. A beating only – he was saved from the more vicious tortures that had been devised.

'Before they even came for him I had decided what I would do if he were found and arrested. Although communists were seen as the main enemy, they were all – anarchists, Republicans, socialists – lumped together as "Reds". Maximiliano had never fought, there was no "blood crime" on him – that was the kind of language they used. But an organiser, an administrator, educated, a leading member of the CNT, an anarchist – it all added up against him.

'Perhaps if he'd told them things – given them names of others who'd worked with him, told them of their hiding places, just something, things could have gone better for him. But he would never do that. We knew – my mother and I. Back then, in the forties, people who were found, or arrested, weren't often seen again. At best they might get life, and their family not even informed until months later.

'So I knew what I had to do, but, well, I waited a couple of days, and then went ahead.

'It was straightforward – there was a recruiting centre in the city. I was still very young, but I went along, said I wanted to join, and that was it. I think they knew why I was there. There were a few others as well, hoping to help some imprisoned relative by joining up. There was something religious about it – a cleansing of your sins, or the sins of someone you loved. Make this sacrifice and maybe, just maybe, something can be done. Like buying indulgences from a priest for a family member suffering in Purgatory.

'So I became a private in the Blue Division. They put me in the Valencia Regiment, gave me a couple of weeks' training, and then I was sent off to the Eastern Front. Stalingrad was just beginning around that time, but we were all in the north. I arrived in Novgorod just in time for the transfer to Leningrad and the siege.

'The division was Franco's gift to Hitler, a thank-you present for everything Hitler had done for him in the Civil War, sending the Condor Legion, and weapons and planes. Spain couldn't become a full ally in the Second World War, like Italy. There was barely enough to eat back then. The country couldn't have gone straight into another conflict. At least that's what people said. I think it was Franco hedging his bets. So the Blue Division was a compromise – the country remained officially neutral but they let Spanish men who wanted to, fight on Hitler's side – a special infantry force as part of the German army. Only on the Eastern Front, though – at Franco's insistence. But they were surprised how many joined up when they announced it was being set up. It had been going for almost a year by the time I went – part of the reinforcements for the new battles ahead. It wasn't going so well for them by then. Novgorod had been fairly easy. Leningrad was something else. But at least we were up there, not south on the Volga, Stalingrad. It could have been much, much worse.

'It got cold that winter. The Germans thought we wouldn't cope, because we were Spanish, from the south. They didn't know how tough the winters are here. We had cold-weather supplies sent in, but even that wasn't enough when it was minus thirty sometimes. You had to watch for frostbite. It's what took up most of your time, inspecting your toes, your fingers. Thrusting your hands down into your groin for warmth. The officers forbade it at first, but then ended up doing it themselves. Some of the men built *mesa camillas*' – round tables – 'with a brazier underneath. The problem was finding fuel for the fires, though. It's not easy making wood burn when it's frozen solid.

'They taught me how to dig trenches, how to dig field latrines. But again, not always easy when the ground is hard as rock with the cold. Your body does strange things at those temperatures, though. You might not shit for days – every turd is lost heat that you have to recuperate. Then going out for a piss was an experience when it hit the ground solid, freezing as it left your body. Just taking your dick out to do it was frightening enough – no one wanted frostbite there.'

He raised his eyebrows. Alicia forced a quick, humourless smile.

'We heard stories, about how bad it could get, that the temperatures could go even lower. Men being eaten alive by wolves because they were too cold and frozen to frighten them away as the animals started sinking their teeth into their feet and legs. I never saw it myself, but I believed it. Still do. You see enough that fantastical things become possible, then real and finally everyday. And you learn not to be shocked by anything.

'And, yes, they taught me to shoot, to use grenades, and to bayonet someone to death. We were infantrymen. Frontline, the brave idiots who got it first – unless they gave it to the other side. That's the thing about being at the front – you're not trying to kill, you're trying to stay alive. And you do that by killing. But that's not your goal, that's not what you're thinking about. At least I wasn't. But then I wasn't good infantry material, as my commanding officer never tired of telling me. I was given a Mauser rifle and told to get on with it, more or less. I was the son of a Red, like a handful of the others. There seeking redemption, and as such they weren't going to waste too much time on me. The best I could do was either kill a large number of Russians, save some of my comrades in an act of heroism, or get killed – preferably having killed as many of the enemy as possible first. There was no point getting ripped apart by a mortar shell if you hadn't killed at least three or four Russians already. It took a lot of Russian blood, I soon learned, to clean the stain on my family.

'So I got good at surviving – and shooting. Small things save you in conditions like that, not heroism, or bravery, or good organisation or all the things you might expect. A sudden itch in your leg makes you bend down just as a bullet passes through the space where your head had been. A slip, a fall, a pause for a smoke – or not smoking at the right time. Our lives became a litany of tiny life-saving or life-taking details. A man could leave his position on some errand and find it shelled and everyone killed on his return. Or else never return, while his comrades remained unscathed for another few hours, or days.

'This Luger, you see. We weren't issued with these. Only the officers. But I found it during a firefight. The hand to which it had once belonged was still clinging to it, but the body it was attached to had scattered and joined the rest of them. A shell burst. I stopped to pick it up. I thought – I don't know – that I'd hand it in to my lieutenant, or perhaps keep it. But in the moment I paused to bend down two of my companions fell, shot by machine-gun fire. I stayed down, pushing myself as hard as I could into the frozen ground till nightfall, dizzy with the cold, willing the blood to flow to my feet and fingers. And the Luger buried in my tunic. Then, when it was totally dark I moved to head back to our positions. And the Luger stayed with me. I felt it had brought me luck.

'I don't know what it was that saved me – intuition? Fate? Perhaps it was just accident, not design. But no – I don't believe that, not entirely. If there is a design then it is so far beyond our understanding that it appears to be accident, randomness. But just because we can't understand it doesn't mean it can't exist. It simply demonstrates the limits of our understanding. But you can, nonetheless, sense something – something moving it all. And you learn very quickly to accept that at any moment you may cease to exist, in an instant. All the while struggling with every breath, every movement, every thought, to stay alive.'

Alicia lit a cigarette, sharing it with Cámara beside her. Hilario told them about a big battle that had begun shortly after, as the Russians tried to break the siege. The Germans were amazed that they had the strength after hearing stories of cannibalism inside the city. It was a difficult period and Hilario's unit lost a lot of men.

'I thought a wound of some sort might help,' he continued. 'But it was looked down on – they could tell if it had been deliberate. Besides, I was in a minority – most of the men were there because they wanted to be, to kill as many Russians as possible. All that fascist fervour. Reds, communists, Russians – they didn't make much distinction. It was a continuation of the Civil War for many of them. Veterans from the Battle of Teruel used to joke that the Aragon winter of 1938 had been colder than Leningrad. So cowardice, absenteeism, self-inflicted wounds or wounds deliberately got from the enemy were virtually unheard of. Later, when reinforcements started including conscripts rather than just volunteers, you heard of a few cases. But Hitler was very happy with us – said we were one of the best divisions in the Wehrmacht – or at least that's what they told us. There was even a Blue Division medal struck, at Hitler's insistence.

'But things were coming to an end by then. Stalingrad was a big blow. The body language of some of the German officers changed. They weren't used to it – big defeats like that. Our lot weren't so bothered – there had been plenty of reverses during the Civil War, they said. You kept going. Victory was certain. We were fighting the forces of evil. How could it not be?

'Not long after Stalingrad Franco began negotiating our retreat. Of course, I had to be up in arms, like the rest. There was already talk of staying behind. It was a ruse, they said. Typical Franco. Let the world know that he wasn't officially supporting Hitler any more, but keep on fighting all the same. They started making preparations – applications to stay on, to be absorbed into SS divisions.

'A lot of them managed to stay behind, but I got drafted back. I was alive, I'd done my bit. Or so I thought. No medal, no mention in dispatches. But I'd killed. More than my fair share of young men just like myself. Except they were fighting to save their homes, their country. I was a foreigner, fighting someone else's war against a people I had no grudge against, no hate for. Yet I'd survived, and in order to do that, I'd killed.

'I was in Barcelona when I heard that Maximiliano had been executed. It had taken place a week before, as we'd been freighted across lands with swastikas flying from every public building. On Franco's personal insistence he'd been shot, rather than garrotted. I had that to thank him for. All those dead Russian boys had bought for my father a second or two less pain and panic in his dying.

'And back to civilian life, a grieving, widowed mother to look after. More surviving – I'd got good at it in Russia. It didn't feel so different in many ways. We both worked where we could – she ended up cleaning for the wife of the military governor, the man who signed Maximiliano's death warrant. I got a job at a mechanic's – oh, there were dozens of jobs I did back then.

'I handed the Mauser rifle in, when we were demobbed. They asked if I had anything else. I still had the Luger, kept it tucked into the back of my trousers, but said no. I don't think the NCO believed me, but they only searched my bags and didn't find anything, so they let me go.

'And I don't know why. Perhaps I should have got rid of it. I've still got a magazine for it, somewhere.

'But I'd grown fond of it, for some reason.

'They're funny like that, guns.'

EIGHTEEN

Tuesday 3rd November

His leg was sore, but he could walk. After taking some more pills and pacing up and down the corridor half a dozen times he could move almost without a limp.

Hilario was still asleep. Cámara went into his room to check he was all right, nodding to Alicia when he came out.

They had some coffee, then Cámara downloaded the photos he'd taken the day before and put them on a memory stick while Alicia showered and got ready to go.

'I'll walk you there.'

'There's no need.'

'It'll be better. It's just going to get stiff otherwise.'

There was a mist that morning and the streets were pale and milky. After the rush of early workers moving around the city, the roads were now scattered with parents and grandparents taking small children to nurseries and play schools. A mother with a pushchair wriggled past them on the narrow pavement, her little girl, perhaps one year old, staring out ahead as she nestled a doll against her chest.

Alicia's hand squeezed around Cámara's. They didn't talk about that now. It had come up once, a few days after he'd arrived with his suitcase at her Madrid flat early in the summer, but the child of his that she'd aborted at the start of their relationship would have been about the same age. Cámara only glanced down briefly at the little girl. His hand tightened instinctively in response to Alicia's grip, but his mind was taken with other things.

Grief and anger over the abortion had consumed him for too long. He'd left that behind in Valencia. It didn't form a part of him any more.

They had ten minutes at the station before her train arrived.

'Time for another coffee?'

'No, thanks. I'm already wired as it is.'

She leaned up to kiss him.

'Let me know what happens.'

'I will.'

'I'm worried.'

'Don't be.'

'It's easy to say that.'

'It'll be fine.'

'I'll . . . I'll give you a call.'

She kissed him again.

'Sometimes it's as if I can't see into your eyes. They're open, yet they're closed. As though a film covers them, made up of all the terrible things you've seen.'

He handed her her bag and watched as she passed through ticket control, found her carriage, and boarded.

She didn't look back.

Cámara was already out on the street again, his hands thrust deep into his pockets.

Had it been a day like this, cold and misty?

He sniffed. Memories were stirring inside him. Something about Hilario's revelations, saying goodbye to Alicia.

It had had this same feel – that day. Although thinking back it had been late summer when Hilario had come for him. The end of the holidays, a new school year about to begin. He hated that time of year.

It should have been a relief. And in some ways it was. July and most of August had gone and he and his father had barely moved from the flat. A couple of times, at the beginning: doing the shopping together, a walk around the park late one evening, when the sun had almost set and the air was beginning to cool. His father had said something about going to the coast, perhaps. Getting the car and driving away, just the two of them. Perhaps down to Valencia. They could find somewhere cheap, a hostel perhaps. Or even sleep rough – in the car, on the beach. Wherever. That was the great thing about the summer – the elements were kinder, at least at night-time.

He was still only twelve, but Cámara had loved the idea. Later he wondered if that had been an early warning sign, his father already showing the decay, the lack of consideration for his only remaining child. Sleeping rough – it sounded fun, and it could have happened. But it was too late. He just couldn't see it then.

He started heading to the shops more on his own. His father seemed to sleep a lot during the day. It was normal in the summer, when the hours of darkness became a refuge from the sharp-eyed sun. But even the young Cámara knew it was excessive: not for his father's sake, but for his own. Friends were avoiding him; they said he stank. After four days slouching around empty bottles and unwashed dishes, he spent half an hour in the shower trying to scrub off the grime.

More orders came in for drink. From his pocket, his father would pull out crumpled peseta notes and hand them to him, telling him to go to the little neighbourhood super-market that had opened on the next street. Wine and beer at first. And Cámara had joined him, sipping cans in secret, then more openly as his father had encouraged him.

The demands for stronger drink became more frequent. Anis and whisky. Then just whisky – DYC, the cheap brand, from Segovia. Cámara tried it in the kitchen one evening while his father slept on the sofa. An hour later – although it could have been less – he just remembered having enough strength to cough and roll on to his side as the vomit stuck in his throat. Some time afterwards he'd found himself in the bath, still clothed, cold water lapping around his groin. The vomit on the kitchen floor had not been cleared up – that was his job.

One night a woman had shown up. He'd never seen her before, or had any idea who she was. Cámara was sitting at the table in the living room, studying for some retakes he had to do in September when he got back to school. His father answered the door when the bell went, and in came this tall, skinny young woman with short black hair and a small brown leather handbag that flapped over her hips as she walked. What was the point of something so small, he thought. What on earth could you put in there? Besides, he was hungry. A day had passed since they'd last eaten properly and he was hoping his father might fix them something. Was the girl here for dinner?

She gave him an intense, odd look as, wordlessly, she

walked past, following his father down the corridor. The bedroom door opened, they stepped inside, and Cámara was left on his own. He never saw the girl leave.

The following morning his father poured whisky on his cereal: the milk had run out.

It was probably around that time that his father lost his job. He hadn't worked properly since Concha's death. And the men at the printing cooperative were very helpful. The printworks had shut down altogether at first, partly out of respect, and partly because all the members were helping in the search for the missing girl. A week after the funeral they'd started again, but orders started slowing up – people said they didn't want to bother them when they were coping with such a tragedy. The real reason, everyone knew, was because they didn't want to be associated with something so dark and painful, as though an evil stain had attached to them through what had happened, and the family and anyone close to them had to be avoided. Superstitious crap, they'd all denounced it as, but they were worried; things would have to improve if the co-op were to survive.

But Ricardo, Cámara's father, was told to take his time; there was no rush. He had other things to think about – keeping the rest of his family going, and looking after a wife quickly crumbling under the strain.

She hadn't lasted long. Poor old Ana, they'd said. Such hardship for a mother to lose her daughter like that. But few had come to the funeral. The doctors made out that it was an accident, but no one fooled themselves it was anything more than an attempt to save face for the family – and for themselves. It was standard practice to give someone in her condition sleeping pills. No one, it appeared, had stopped to think that she might be a suicide risk. She had another

150

child – the boy, Max – to look after. No mother would abandon her son like that.

But she had.

One morning Cámara had woken to find his mother had simply vanished.

'She left,' someone – a family friend he'd found crying in the kitchen – said. 'Last night. She just went.'

He thought she might have gone to the shops, or gone to see friends, or something. But that she would come back. This was a temporary thing. Strange, yes, and the faces that dared to peer down at him wore curious, indescribable expressions. But it would not last for ever. His mother would return.

Finally, when he realised what had happened – although no one told him straight; he remembered having to piece it together for himself – he went into his room and put his fist through the window.

The bandages were in the bathroom, on top of the mirror cabinet. He found a stool, grabbed the box, and bound the wound himself.

The day of his mother's funeral had certainly been cold; he wore a soft black woollen jumper his grandfather had given him for Christmas just a few weeks before. It was as if he'd known he was going to need it. But they said that about Hilario – that sometimes he seemed to see the future, or behave in a way that suggested he knew things. A *brujo*, someone had called him once. And they'd laughed. He was a bit of a joke – fun, a bit strange, kept his distance from his family; there was some suggestion he'd fallen out with Ricardo, his son, years back. No one would say over what. But a wizard? A man of magic? No. He might be lots of things, but not that. He was just a crazy old anarchist, living in the past, quoting proverbs most of the time.

His memories of that spring after his mother's suicide were

unclear. He'd been at school, his father at home most of the time. Perhaps he'd gone to the co-op as well. He couldn't say. They'd simply carried on. The two of them alone in the flat, with neither Concha nor Ana at home with them now. There had been lots of takeway food, he seemed to remember, and cartons crushed in the corner of the kitchen waiting to be thrown out with the rubbish.

Then the summer came, and the removal of the school day took away the last remaining structure to their lives.

The talk of a holiday, of sleeping rough on the beach, came to nothing.

Meanwhile the flat became less and less inhabitable.

It felt as though his father hadn't exchanged a word with him for weeks, perhaps since the beginning of August. He was continuously drunk, either crashing around the flat in occasional rages, or slumped in front of the TV, his eyes burning into the flashing blue screen. They ate bread, crisps, chocolate, stale breakfast cereals . . . Cámara hadn't shat properly for days.

And then Hilario, his mysterious grandfather, had come. He didn't ring, or knock. He'd got his own key from somewhere. This man he barely knew, with a kind, lived-in face, smiled at Cámara and told him to pack his things.

Cámara could hear him talking to his father in the living room as, confused but secretly relieved, he grabbed bundles of unwashed clothes and stuffed them into plastic bags. A couple of books as well – one on Greek myths that he'd read and reread since his mother had given it to him on his seventh birthday; another, a history of El Cid. Somehow he knew he might not be coming back for some time.

Down in the living room Hilario was still talking, but Ricardo remained silent. After a pause, footsteps approached his bedroom door and Hilario's face appeared once more.

'Time to go.'

And so began something new – a life with Hilario, in his flat on the other side of the city. And Pilar, his housekeeper, moving silently around them, like a shadow. He'd hated it at first: his so-called anarchist grandfather had been strict with him, enforcing mealtimes, bedtimes, study times. Later he understood how much he needed it; he'd become almost feral, eating and sleeping whenever the urge took him. A return to a disciplined life proved painful, and he raged against it, while longing for it at the same time.

'You have to learn to control yourself, otherwise your instincts and desires will control you,' Hilario told him. It was nonsense. So much for freedom and anarchy. But his grandfather didn't see it that way.

Then somehow – and no one had been more surprised than him – he passed his retakes at the beginning of the new term. No need to redo the entire school year. It felt good, a relief, and while his moods moved violently in many directions, he knew Hilario was the one to thank. He hated him, but he needed him. He had to stay.

His father lasted three more months. Shortly before Christmas he was found by a neighbour in the same living-room chair, the television still on.

His heart had stopped beating.

He'd told Alicia some of this – the outline – when he'd arrived on her doorstep towards the beginning of the summer. But not all. The details weren't always clear. But they were coming more into focus now, driving a wedge, taking him further away, further into himself.

NINETEEN

The cemetery was divided into several sections, almost like neighbourhoods, with a central 'square', each one surrounded by high walls where coffins were placed in niches before being closed over with a metal plaque with a name and occasionally a small photograph, now curled and blanched in the light.

Cámara walked in, expecting to be the first visitor of the day, but already an elderly woman wearing a black skirt, black stockings and shoes, black woollen jacket pulled over her black blouse and a black scarf wrapped around the back of her short grey hair, was shuffling past the cypress trees. She had a yellow plastic shopping bag in one hand and a bunch of white flowers in the other.

He checked the time on his phone: he had a few minutes.

The path took him down the central avenue before narrowing and veering to the left. It was breezy, and he pulled his coat around him more tightly, hunching his shoulders against the cold of autumn.

Two, perhaps three years had passed since he'd last been here. Hilario had never been one for encouraging regular visits, but he wasn't going to ban them either. Not that banning was something he did, but he'd made it clear that self-pity or wallowing in negative emotion of any kind was looked down on.

Remember, yes. But allow space for forgetting as well.

And so for a few years he'd come on All Saints Day, joining the thousands of other mourners placing flowers in the small metal vases in the niches. Hilario had joined him the first few times, silently to begin with, but then vocalising his criticism more until one year he refused to go. Enough time had passed, he said. The dead were gone, and lived with him every day. He didn't need to make an annual show of caring. Besides, he found the commercialisation of dying, the florists and the expensive undertakers' fees, obscene.

Cámara had gone on his own anyway, cursing, not caring, alone. He was about to turn eighteen; he didn't need his grandfather with him in the first place.

And it was easy to forget, then, that Hilario himself grieved. They were members of his family, too.

Concepción Cámara Reyes.

Concha's niche was low down, on the first row, near the end of the red-brick wall. He'd brought flowers the last time he'd come, he felt sure, but they would have rotted long since. Perhaps someone had removed the dead stems from the vase for him. He'd seen that on occasion – a woman, usually, helping to maintain a niche that had nothing to do with her or her family, but out of a sense of respect, stepping in where others should be doing their duty. And perhaps with a view to keeping the niches around her own loved one's tidy and clean.

Some bypassed the problem by placing plastic flowers in

the vase instead. He could see why they did it, but even plastic flowers weathered badly, gathering dust and looking as old and unloved as the wilting petals of their less ersatz companions. So what could you do? Nothing, just leave the niche bare and unadorned? Or come more regularly and leave fresh blooms by a polished plaque, every week like the black-clad widows who regularly inhabited the place, living more with the dead than the living.

Hilario was right, perhaps. Only those left behind needed cemeteries. But you could choose how to grieve – or not.

He traced his fingers over her name, feeling the tiny ridges of the brass under his fingertips. Only his mother had called her Concepción; he, his father, everyone else, had used the shortened form. Sometimes he'd thought about changing the plaque: it would be more fitting to have 'Concha' written there. It had been one of the ideas that had come to him in late adolescence, part of his attempted move into adulthood when, comparing himself to his school friends, he realised that, parentless, he had a freedom to make decisions, an autonomy, that they couldn't enjoy. Hilario wasn't a parent – at most he was a guardian. Someone he could throw off and disregard with ease. Aged eighteen, nineteen, Cámara could do whatever he wanted, go anywhere.

But the plaque had stayed the same. In fact much had, despite what he told himself. Pinpointing what he didn't like, what needed to go, was one thing; becoming and replacing were something else. Things only changed once he joined the police.

For a moment he wondered if he would ever come here again; there was a sense of terminality about it. And he thought about kissing the plaque. Farewell, you piece of metal covering a hole where something – barely anything – remains of the body my sister once lived in.

No matter – this truth, that truth: at that instant an emotional self needed to make contact, to kiss Concha goodbye.

He got back on to his feet. And thought of Alicia. She would be almost halfway to Madrid by now. He felt a strong urge to hold her, press her tight to him, to kiss her powerfully, completely. He'd been cold with her that morning. She was leaving, going back to Madrid, her home. She'd been here, seen him, a greater part of him – his world, his life, his Albacete. A place which, no matter how hard he tried, he never quite managed to leave.

Was he ashamed? The metropolitan journalist coming to terms with her lover's provincial background? No, it wasn't that. There was as much of that in her as there was in him. Valencia, her home town, could be as provincial as anywhere else in the country.

No, it was something else. They'd shared an intense experience – driving away from Pozoblanco, getting shot at – almost getting killed. There was no need to get overly dramatic – they'd both survived: you either died or you didn't. But she'd seen that side of his existence – the violent side, the danger. The police side of him. And it was something he'd felt close to walking away from. Yet here it was, claiming him once again, like a tide pulling down on a drowning man. She'd seen it, lived through it with him for a brief moment, and then gone.

Could she still love him now?

He tried to look beyond the confusion kicked up inside him like dust, and see more clearly the link between them. She was there, with him, inside him, but would she stay? Would he himself end up pushing her away?

The truth was that he'd never had a relationship like this before. Already in his mid-forties and it was strange to think that – you were expected to have had a wealth of experiences by that age, to be settling down, or coasting along. Yet his past was populated by women who had only ever seemed to penetrate his thoughts and emotions at the time, but who then had slipped away with greater ease than he had imagined. With one, perhaps two, he had even convinced himself that he had been in love. Yet once the relationships ended the pain of separation was no more than transitory, a process of – relatively swift – adaptation.

None of them had sunk into him like Alicia had.

Which, if he admitted it to himself, made him almost afraid.

He wasn't certain which disturbed him most, however: the events at Pozoblanco, or Hilario's story of the night before.

It had felt like a revelation; it was a revelation. His grandfather, the person he loved most in the world, had fought and killed for Hitler. The irony of it was almost absurd, were it not that he had done it trying to save his own father – and failing.

No self-pity – it had been the one message Hilario had managed to get through to him during those first years after he had moved in with him. And Cámara had kicked against it: he'd lost his sister, his mother and his father in less than a couple of years. He had a right to feel self-pity. Yet for all that time he never stopped to think that Hilario had lost a son, a granddaughter and a daughter-in-law. There was no space in Cámara's own grief to allow for someone else's. Besides, Hilario didn't grieve – or didn't show it. So it was easier to get angry with him.

Cámara had never known, however, that it wasn't the first time his grandfather had lost close family members. Anyone looking at his life – father executed, granddaughter murdered, son dead from drink, daughter-in-law a suicide, wife dead from liver cancer – would think he had a curse on him.

Yet . . . he was Hilario. And now, not only was he a priapic marihuana-growing anarchist OAP, but gun-toting Blue Division infantryman and Siege of Leningrad veteran had to be added to complete the picture.

Was there any more?

The surprising thing was that none of this had changed Cámara's opinion of him, or rather, he didn't think any less of him. He'd been surprised, shocked by the story. But he himself had shot and killed another man, at the end of his last case, in Valencia. Not in anger, but to survive, and hoping to save others.

And he understood how much more Hilario understood him than he'd ever realised.

Even his being a policeman, a detective. There was a parallel there, of sorts, with Hilario joining the Blue Division. If you saw it from an anarchist perspective.

Was that why it had disturbed his grandfather so much, when he'd joined? Not for purely ideological reasons to do with tyranny and power, but because Hilario had seen something of himself in him?

Hilario had joined the Blue Division to save his father, and failed.

Cámara had joined the police to solve his sister's murder, as though that might in some way bring her back from the dead.

Both in organisations of violence and authority trying to undo what will be done, or already has been done.

Both struggling against events, against a world that twists and kicks and bites with scarcely a warning.

Hilario's solution was to choose to be the person he wanted to be, in the face of what life threw at him. He couldn't control the world, the events that struck him, but there was one thing he could take decisions on – himself. He could be Hilario, and nothing could change that.

Cámara's solution?

He had no idea. He'd only just identified the problem.

Two other niches demanded attention before he left. Ricardo Cámara Gutiérrez and Ana Reyes Albayzín lay side by side next to their daughter. It was a municipally controlled cemetery – suicides were allowed, although there had been grumblings at the time. Had his mother taken her life a few years earlier, before Franco had finally died, things would have been more complicated. There were no flowers for her or her husband, however. Cámara had placed some once, when he finally decided not to be angry with her any more. Or at least to try. Forgiveness was easy to talk about, even to understand and accept on an intellectual level. The problem was getting that to work its way through all of him, to forgive her with his emotions as well as his mind. He'd felt abandoned by her, that her sadness over Concha had taken precedence over her duty to him as a mother.

But he'd lost as well, like her. Not a grown child like Concha, but the promise of one. And it had struck him harder than he could have imagined at the time.

To forgive you needed to imagine. And imagination fed on experience.

He knelt and touched both the plaques, his father on his right, his mother on his left. This was who he was – a combination of the two, and the actions they had taken, with all the repercussions rippling over the years.

It was time to move on.

He checked his phone again and stood up.

He had to go; Yago would be waiting.

TWENTY

Yago looked even thinner than he had a couple of days before.

'Take any more of those pills and you'll start falling through the cracks in the pavement.'

'Come on, let's walk.'

He looked down at Cámara's leg.

'You got a limp, or something?'

They strolled along the lanes of the dead, birds chirping overhead as they flapped from tree to tree. Yago was wearing a pale-coloured suit that hung loosely from his body, with a strong, spicy smell from his cologne.

A white tent had been erected in one of the squares that made up the cemetery, covering a piece of ground that was normally left barren.

'That's where they're digging up the remains of people shot after the Civil War,' Yago said. 'Perhaps you heard about it.'

Cámara said nothing, but looked over to see if Eduardo

García, the historian, was there. The area was deserted: perhaps they'd gone for coffee.

Was that where Maximiliano lay?

'It's all very well,' Yago said, 'to let people mourn their dead. After all these years, I mean. To be able to do it properly. But are we ready for this? The country? It just throws up old wounds. We got past all that. Now you see these kids wandering around with Republican flags.'

He shook his head.

'We should move on – *pasar página*. With the amount of people there are out of work you'd think there were better things they could do with public money.'

Cámara pulled out his cigarettes, half-heartedly offering one to Yago out of politeness, knowing somehow that this time he'd refuse. Smoke streamed away from him in a quickly vanishing cloud as it got caught up in the wind and blown up and out beyond the cemetery walls.

'Pozoblanco,' Cámara said at last.

'Yes. You went, then?'

'Yeah. I went. Interesting place.'

Yago snorted.

'Say that again. I like the fact that places like that can exist – the anomaly of it all: a little communist enclave in the middle of a capitalist state. I mean, who'd have thought? But I'm not sure I'd want to live there.'

'Faro Oscuro's quite a character.'

'Oh, so you met him, then? Rules the place like it was his own.'

'I got that impression. There's something a bit . . .'

'Sectarian?'

'Yeah, that's it. He's the boss, everyone loves him – or so it seems. And together they've built this amazing utopia.'

162

'No, I don't buy it either. So what did you find?'

'Lots of saffron.'

'It's the season.'

'But not really enough fields to produce the amount we saw being processed.'

'What did he say they have?'

'Five hundred hectares.'

'Doesn't figure.'

'No, not for that quantity. Not even by the figures he gave us.'

'How did he explain it?'

'Said they got saffron from other villages around. Not just Pozoblanco.'

'I can check that. But it sounds like a bluff. Production around here is way down on what it was even ten years ago. People moving to the city. Masses of bulb stocks got sold off. But if the saffron isn't from here, where's it coming from? Or is it really saffron at all? That's the question.'

An elderly man tapping a walking stick on the paving stones passed them as they crossed the main avenue from one half of the cemetery to the other. He nodded to them as they drew close, a melancholy smile on his thin, cracked lips. Cámara nodded in return; Yago kept his eyes looking ahead.

There was a bench a little further on, protected from the wind by a high wall of niches behind. They sat down on it, Yago crossing his legs, Cámara stretching both arms out along the back. He breathed in deeply, then blew the air out, as though expelling some unwanted thought from his body.

'Anything else?' Yago asked.

'There was another man there. Faro Oscuro referred to him as Ahmed the Moroccan.'

'We came across him as well. Our checks threw nothing up, though. It may be a false name.'

'Head of security, Faro Oscuro said.'

'OK.'

'I think he may have tried to kill me.'

Yago turned towards him and looked him hard in the eye.

'You're serious.'

'I'm serious.'

'What happened?'

'Driving away from the village. Bullet smashed the back window. Another went into the bodywork of the car.'

Yago glanced down at Cámara's leg.

'The limp?'

'The last shot was closer than I would have liked.'

'But you got away?'

'I'm here, aren't I?'

Yago stood up, thrusting his hands into his pockets, pacing backwards and forwards in front of the bench.

'All right,' he said. 'I asked too much of you.'

He kicked at a loose piece of paving stone, sending it scuttling into a patch of dead grass.

'*Me cago en la puta!*' For fuck's sake!

'It's all right,' Cámara said, not moving from the bench.

Yago looked down at him, lines of incomprehension on his brow.

'You weren't to know. It's not your fault. The question is why? Why try and kill me? I was there as a journalist, just doing a report. What made them so worried that they thought they had to take me out all of a sudden?'

'Where did it happen?'

'On the road out of Pozoblanco. I said.'

'I can check that.'

'Nothing of this makes sense, though. First of all, why try to kill me? And secondly, why botch it up like that? It was hardly professional. It's as though Ahmed, or whoever it was, was making it up as he went along. There was something almost casual about it.'

'*Me cago en la puta*. Where's the car now?'

'I borrowed it from a friend.'

Cámara put his hands up.

'I've given him enough problems. Don't make him hand it over to your lot.'

'We might need it.'

Cámara sniffed.

'Look, before we do that, we need to check out what's really going on in Pozoblanco. You don't take pot shots at journalists for no reason. Or did they know I'm police? Who else knew I was going?'

'No one. Just me, you idiot. You don't think I was going to tell anyone with the kind of problems I've got at the Jefatura.'

'Jiménez? Did he know you were meeting me the other day?'

'No.'

'Someone might have seen us, and told him.'

Yago stopped pacing.

'Possible. But unlikely. It was dark. Unless . . .'

'What?'

'I don't know. You can get paranoid in situations like this. Not knowing who you can trust. It's why I got you to go in the first place.'

'And I want to go back.'

Yago shook his head.

'Out of the question.'

'I'm not working for you, remember. You asked me a favour.'

'All right. And I'm asking you, as a friend, not to go. You really want to get killed? Give that Ahmed or whatever his name is another shot? I can't do that, Max. I can't let that happen. You're on my watch, however you want to look at it.'

Cámara stroked his chin; he hadn't shaved that morning and nascent stubble dragged against his fingertips.

'You pulled me back in,' he said. 'I was fine, getting along, getting a taste of what it's like outside, not doing this. And then you came and threw me back into it.'

Yago turned on his heel and stared at him.

'It was you, remember. You were the one snooping around a murder scene, getting yourself locked up for the night. Don't give me that.'

Cámara grinned.

'All right. But it was worth a try.'

He got up and punched Yago on the arm.

'Come on. You're taking this too seriously. Stop thinking about it too much. It's driving you mad, I can see. You'll end up getting paranoid, then it'll be me coming round to see you locked up in the loony bin.'

Yago shook him off.

'You're a bastard. You should be dead.'

'Well, I'm not. So get over it.'

They started heading towards the exit, away from the pregnant, stagnant calm of the cemetery and towards the noise and movement of the streets outside.

'I need to think this through.'

'It's what you always did. Not sure if it gets you anywhere, though. You're worried about a leak, about some bent cop on your team? Listen to your guts, your instinct. It might be the last person your thinking would ever consider.'

Yago looked at him and sighed: he was hopeless.

'And please don't go back to Pozoblanco.'

'I want you to do something for me,' Cámara said. 'Something I want to check out.'

'What?'

'That suspect from Concha's case, years back. Juan Manuel Heredia.'

'What about him?'

'Where is he?'

'Torrecica,' Yago said, nodding his head in the direction of the city prison. 'He got done for murder a while back. Some thing between Gypsy families. It caught my eye when I got back here. I've been watching him. You want to go over all that again?'

'Loose ends. I want to go and see him.'

They stepped out into the street. A bus blew its horn loudly at a car blocking the road as it waited for a parking space to become available.

'I can sort that out for you,' Yago said.

They shook hands.

'Be careful, though, Max. Just be careful.'

TWENTY-ONE

Wednesday 4th November

He stepped down on to the platform and joined the stream of passengers making their way towards the exit to the cicada-like accompaniment of a hundred wheeled suitcases being dragged along the ground. Passing under arches decorated with mosaics of orange trees and fertile fields, he stepped out into the square: bullring to his right, Plaza del Ayuntamiento straight ahead.

Valencia, again. Familiar territory.

It was raining and all the taxis were taken, so he ran to the metro station and dived for cover underground. The green line would take him almost all the way to the port, then he could catch a tram for the last section.

Almost four months had passed since he'd last been here. At the time, when he left, he thought he might never return. His former home was a pile of rubble, his career was sinking . . . Valencia already felt like the past by the time he'd boarded the train to Madrid and a new life with Alicia. Yet here he was again.

It was the kind of city which was small enough to make bumping into acquaintances a normal occurrence, and part of his attention was on the lookout for a former colleague or friend to come swimming up, as though from nowhere, asking questions about how he was, what he was doing, what he was going to do.

The first question rarely needed answering with any honesty – thankfully. The second he wasn't prepared to say, and the third – well, that was still undecided.

But the need didn't arise. Surrounded mostly by university students and immigrants, he could let his thoughts drift as they hummed and jolted down the black tunnel of the metro line.

After meeting Yago back in Albacete he'd spent the rest of the day at home with Hilario. His grandfather had got up late, and appeared to be fresher, lighter than he had over the previous few days. Neither had talked much over lunch or clearing up. Hilario's story of the night before, about his experiences in Russia, was there with them, like a third person in the flat, but ignored. Enough had been said. If there was any more to add, then Hilario would do so.

Cámara had questions, but timing, for Hilario, was important: things had to be said, or done, at the right time. And he was usually the arbiter of when that time was. To try to get him to talk about something important outside of that timing was futile: he simply sealed up, not saying anything. Chat was one thing – that could take place at any time and anywhere. Talking – and doing, real action – were different.

So they carried on as normal, two men quietly sharing

this living space as they had done for so many years in the past, slotting back into a rhythm they knew well. Pilar came for a while, but left after an hour. There was nothing that needed doing, she said. The real reason was that she could sense the atmosphere in the flat, one that told her she was on the outside – not exactly unwanted, but temporarily surplus to requirements, as an internal police communiqué would have put it. And so she went.

In the afternoon Cámara made a couple of phone calls, while Hilario lay on the sofa reading Goethe. Then over a quiet dinner of *jamón serrano* with bread, cheese and a salad, Cámara told Hilario he would be going away the next day.

'Back to Valencia,' Hilario said.

Cámara nodded: perhaps Hilario had heard his phone conversations, but more likely he was – as so often – already one step ahead of him.

'Figures.'

'There are some things I want to check out.'

'I suppose you wouldn't be going otherwise.'

'This saffron business.'

And Hilario had munched on his lettuce, not looking up.

The metro reached the terminal and Cámara got out and jumped on to a tram for the final part of the journey.

Something buzzed in his pocket: Alicia had tried to call him while he'd been out of range underground. He stared at her name on the little screen, then put the phone back, burying it under his keys.

The rain had turned into a light drizzle by the time he got to his stop. The port customs office was only a short distance away, and he was able to skip along the pavement without getting too wet.

'Not here. We need to go somewhere else.'

Teniente Antonio Maragall was an old *Guardia Civil* contact from Cámara's days in the drugs squad. While Cámara had moved on to *Homicidios*, Maragall had stayed in the port customs office. There was, he said, more chance of reducing the amount of dope on the streets by stopping it as it came in than by chasing it once it had got out. Cámara had nodded at the time, but it sounded unrealistic to him – another policeman trying to convince himself that his work, his job, really made a difference. There were small victories, even the appearance of sizeable victories at times, but it was a doubt that existed in all their minds – that in the end they were merely managing, never preventing or eradicating, crime. For some it wasn't a problem – the more pragmatic ones, often, the ones who were happy to blur distinctions between police and criminals. There had been plenty of them in the drugs squad – particularly the drugs squad, it seemed. Every few years a colleague or two would get busted for something – either working directly with the narcos, or ignoring certain deals in favour of a cut. There were even police and *Guardias* who started dealing themselves – the stupid ones, the ones you wondered why they had ever become police in the first place. It never took very long to spot them, then weed them out.

Maragall was of the other kind – the ones who saw policing in terms of us and them, of good and bad, who cheered every success, like waving a scarf at a football match, and felt pain and frustration with every reverse. Practical and efficient, nonetheless there was a hero inside him waiting to emerge, a man who could really make a difference, make Valencia – his home city – a better place to live. His friends and neighbours – almost the entire population – were, to him, almost like children, in need of his protection and care.

And it hurt and angered him to see the limits of what he could do.

But something else angered him more, to despair: corrupt police. Not the low-level types – that was almost expected, if not in large numbers. No, what ate away at him was seeing officers like himself, or superiors, on the take. It was a betrayal – to him personally. It was enough, as Cámara had witnessed once years back over a case involving the Colombians, to bring him to tears.

Back out into the drizzle, hopping over puddles as they dived towards a small bar on the other side of the road.

'None of the others come here,' Maragall said, wiping his glasses dry on his jacket as they stepped inside.

'Over there. There's someone I want you to meet.'

In the run-up to the total ban on smoking in bars and restaurants, establishments had been forced to reserve a certain number of tables for non-smokers. And there, in a corner surrounded by unoccupied chairs, sat a man in a dark grey suit with a dentist-white shirt and thin black tie. In his hands he held a tablet computer, its screen reflecting in his eyes.

The man stood up as they approached the table and held a serious hand out to Cámara.

'John Villalobos,' he said before Maragall could introduce them. Cámara could hear his accent. 'FBI.'

His straight black hair and skin tone marked him out as being of Hispanic origin, probably Mexican. On the table in front of him stood a tall glass of water with ice. Cámara immediately felt the urge to pull out his cigarettes, but the no-smoking sign on the table merely underlined what he'd already seen as they'd walked in the door. He'd have to wait.

'Villalobos is a special agent with the FBI,' Maragall added. 'From America.'

They sat down. Cámara noticed that Villalobos didn't bother to greet Maragall.

'The lieutenant here tells me you're looking into the saffron business,' Villalobos said. He had the nasal, sing-song, slightly menacing way of speaking of many Mexicans.

'I told him what you told me,' Maragall said before Cámara could answer. 'Villalobos is head of an international investigation into this. They're trying to pressurise Madrid to start doing something about the scam.'

'How did you two get together?' Cámara asked.

Villalobos smiled briefly before reassuming his studied air of gravitas. Maragall answered for him.

'I heard about the investigation and approached them myself,' he said.

Cámara looked at him. Maragall, so frustrated and angry with his own people that he was prepared to go behind their backs and talk to a foreign police force, one that appeared to be treating their sovereign state like another colony or satellite where they could do as they pleased. Cámara should ask for some bona fides at least, make sure that Villalobos was who he said he was. But there was no surrender in Maragall's countenance, no sense that he had taken this step through defeatism. Desperate, perhaps – some would call it betrayal. But he looked energised, almost; here – at least as far as he believed – there was a chance to actually get something done. For now, Cámara himself would have to ride on his faith in this, in Villalobos. Besides, as a policeman on indefinite leave, he was hardly in any position to question the man himself.

'I understand your concern,' Villalobos said. 'We're all in a situation where it's not clear who can be trusted.'

He lifted a hand and signalled to the barman.

'Now, I don't know about you guys, but I could do with something a little stronger.'

In a moment, two bottles of beer had appeared on the table. Maragall had a coffee.

'I've got to be back in my office soon.'

Villalobos drank his beer straight from the bottle; Cámara poured his into a glass before taking a gulp.

'Let me tell you some of what I know,' Villalobos said.

Cámara sat back in his chair to listen.

'The saffron trade is a big mess,' Villalobos started, mimicking Cámara by sitting back in his chair as well. Cámara was aware of the man's attempt to ingratiate himself with him by changing his style like this – drinking and being more open, copying his body language – but decided to go along with the game.

'There's a lot of money involved – we're talking hundreds of millions of dollars. Saffron is expensive, light, easily shipped and highly sought after. In some cases it's worth more than its weight in gold.

'Now you can imagine that with something like this we're dealing with a situation not at all unlike the drugs trade. And it seems that business practices we tend to associate with narcos are becoming more common with saffron.'

'Wait a minute,' Cámara said. 'Are you saying the narcos are getting in on this?'

'Not exactly. Not yet, at least not in big numbers. But the way things are going it could end up like that. Saffron can sell in the US for up to a hundred and seventy dollars an ounce, which comes out to over seven thousand dollars a kilo. That kind of money for something that's so easy to move around can attract the wrong kind of people. You with me?'

Cámara pretended to take another sip of his beer. Villalobos reached for his bottle.

'Every year around two hundred tons of saffron are produced around the world. One hundred and ninety tons of that is sold as Spanish.'

'So there's almost a monopoly.'

'The only thing is, only one point five tons of saffron are actually produced in Spain each year.'

Cámara put his beer back on the table.

'Where's the rest of it coming from?'

'Various countries,' Villalobos said. 'Greece, Morocco, Kashmir – but from Iran, mostly. The vast majority from Iran.'

He put his bottle of beer on the table next to Cámara's glass.

'Now there's a problem for the Iranians selling their own saffron. They've got bad relations with the international community, first of all. And secondly there's reason to believe there's a risk of radioactivity from their saffron as it's grown near their nuclear reactor plant at Bushehr.'

'We have nuclear reactors here in Spain but no one ever talks of radioactive saffron,' Cámara said.

'The safety levels are nowhere near the same,' Villalobos said with a wave of his hand.

And they were hardly exemplary here, Cámara wanted to say, but Maragall was speaking.

'I've got more than enough evidence that a lot of saffron is being imported and exported out of the port,' he said. 'Large amounts – the numbers tally with what Villalobos is saying. And some of it makes it over to La Mancha, but a lot of it simply goes into warehouses here in Valencia for a while, gets relabelled and sent out again as Spanish. That's just the start of it, though. The saffron's being cut as well, but no one in the top ranks wants to touch this.'

The same old problem, the one that had dogged Maragall his entire career. There was no need to say any more: someone – perhaps several people – in charge was almost certainly on the take. Getting in touch with Villalobos began to make more sense.

Villalobos cleared his throat.

'Now, as the lieutenant outlined,' he said, 'the real problem is not just that Iranian saffron is being shipped here and then repackaged as Spanish to be sold to the US and the rest of the world. That kind of thing is happening all the time. The problem is that, just like heroin or cocaine, the saffron you buy is highly adulterated in order to boost the profit margins. And we're not talking by a small amount. Top-quality saffron you buy in the US regularly comes up in tests as actually only having ten per cent saffron in it, maximum.'

He opened his eyes wide for dramatic effect.

'People are paying a lot of money and getting shit in return.'

TWENTY-TWO

John Villalobos picked up his bottle of beer and drained it in one, placing it back on the table with a loud clunk.

Cámara's fingers had been fiddling inside his pocket for the past few minutes. He decided not to resist any more: he lifted the no-smoking sign off the table and tossed it on to a nearby empty chair. Then taking out his packet of Ducados he picked one out and lit it before offering one to Villalobos. The look of confidence on the American's face showed the first signs of cracking. He glanced down almost longingly at the little sign with its cigarette and a red line running through, then shook his head.

'So how are they bulking it out?' Cámara asked. 'What's in the saffron if it isn't saffron?'

'Other parts of the flower sometimes,' Villalobos said, crossing his hands over his lap. 'Not just the stigmas, I mean, the bits that make saffron. They add colouring to make it look like the real thing – carmoisine, which makes it reddish. Tartazine for the yellow tones.'

'What about the smell?'

'Again, chemicals are being used – derivatives of benzene, mostly. If you don't know the difference you probably wouldn't notice. But the fake stuff smells much more like chemicals. The problem is that it's hard to find anyone who's actually tried or smelt pure saffron in the past fifteen years. Not even what you buy here in Spain. It's almost all fake. Even the expensive stuff.'

Cámara looked in vain for an ashtray, eventually flicking his ash on to the floor. Villalobos turned to the side and executed an exaggerated cough before turning and speaking directly to Cámara.

'Now Lieutenant Maragall here tells me you've recently managed to visit a saffron farm near Albacete.'

'In a place called Pozoblanco,' Cámara said.

Villalobos nodded.

'We know it. Or rather we know of it. It's one of the main production facilities we'd like more information on. Perhaps you could share some of your findings.'

Cámara began to relate his experiences at the commune village, editing the information so as to leave Alicia out. As he spoke, Villalobos picked up his tablet computer and started tapping on it, taking notes. He was particularly interested in what Cámara had to say about what he'd seen inside the barn where the saffron stigmas were being plucked out of the flowers by the villagers. Cámara mentioned the door leading into a section which he hadn't been shown, where he was told the packaging was done. Villalobos looked up at him and then quickly tapped some more.

'And the fields around that you saw didn't look like

they could produce the amount of saffron in the barn?' he asked.

'It seemed that way to me. Much of the land around that area has been abandoned.'

Villalobos stared hard at the screen.

'Satellite-imaging confirms that. But it's always good to have eyes on the ground as well.'

'There was another thing,' Cámara said.

After a pause, Villalobos looked up at him.

'There was a Middle-Eastern man in the village. A Moroccan, they said. Ahmed.'

Villalobos's brow lowered a fraction, his gaze intensifying.

'Did you talk to him?'

'A little. He gave me directions. Why?'

Villalobos lowered his voice.

'This is strictly off the record. I'm not supposed to be telling you this.'

Maragall leaned in, nodding.

'It's a pseudonym,' Villalobos said. 'His name's not Ahmed, it's Reza Amini. And he's not Moroccan, he's Iranian. We've been tracking him for some time. We believe he's a link man between the Iranian and Spanish saffron traders.'

He frowned.

'Former member of the Islamic Revolution militia. And a very dangerous man.'

It was practically hidden under the thick black beard, but a smile, a definite smile, lit up Torres's usually dour expression as he spotted Cámara on the other side of the road. They both crossed and met in the middle, ignoring the cars heading in their direction.

'Hello, chief.'

'Inspector Torres.'

They shook hands formally, then, laughing, opened up into an embrace.

'Good to see you. You're looking very relaxed, I must say. All that time off suits you.'

'Not for much longer,' Cámara said.

Torres frowned.

'I'll tell you about it over lunch.'

A line of six cars was now backed up, unable to get past the two men standing in the middle of the narrow street. A chorus of horns was beginning to blast.

'Eh! Get out of the way!'

'Do you know anywhere around here?' Cámara asked calmly.

'There's a place a couple of blocks away. Someone suggested it – we can try that.'

'All right. Which way?'

'Over here.'

Only when they'd decided in which direction they were going to walk did they step out of the way of the traffic.

'*Gilipollas!*' a driver spat through his open window as he roared past. Pricks! For Torres and Cámara, it was as if the cars weren't there.

They walked in single file down the narrow pavements, Torres leading the way, before heading into a restaurant with frosted glass windows.

'All right, chief?'

'Let's give it a try.'

They sat down at a wooden table covered in a white cloth. Before either of them could say anything a basket of bread, a bottle of house red and some olive oil and vinegar had been placed in front of them.

'I'm wondering,' Cámara said.

'What?'

'You must be the only policeman in the entire force who calls one of his superiors "chief".'

'I only say it to you. And then it's only because I'm such a deeply sarcastic bastard. Chief.'

Cámara sniggered. Torres poured them both some wine.

They were an unlikely couple. Other policemen formed friendships, but this was more an informal partnership where both knew full well that their best policing characteristics were complemented by the other. Torres more thorough, Cámara more instinctive. Each could take on features of the other when they were working together, as though unconsciously performing a balancing act, their moods and personalities almost capable of swapping over according to the needs of a case.

Others in the police were aware of it, which was why they had been allowed to work together for so long before Cámara's period of leave. It was rare, almost unheard of, for an inspector and a chief inspector to team up like this, but it was tolerated: the crimes they'd solved together were ample justification.

Despite Torres's good humour, Cámara could tell that something was bothering him.

'I've been given a deadline,' he said as they both pulled out their cigarettes. When they'd walked in, Cámara had been pleased to see it was one of the places that didn't bother having an area set aside for non-smokers.

'Come back now or leave for good?' Torres said.

'That's it.'

'Well, they weren't going to give you a holiday for the rest of your life. Not now with all the cuts. They're talking about bringing our salaries down again. Ten per cent less. And that's just this year.'

'I thought they loved me so much it might go on for ever and ever.'

'Covering the docking bills for your yacht as well, are they?'

'I reckon it's you. You miss me so much you forced Personnel to call me. They might have forgotten all about me, otherwise. And I could be happily getting on with, er . . .'

'Yeah, right. Not so happily getting on with sweet bugger all. I know you – you'll have been stewing all this time wondering whether to come back or not, trying to convince yourself there's a life for you outside.'

'So you admit it. It was you.'

'If that makes you feel wanted and loved.'

'This is the thanks I get for that medal I recommended you for.'

'I had to show my gratitude somehow.'

They ordered: paella for the first dish, then pork for Torres and anglerfish for Cámara.

'So how is everyone?' Cámara asked.

'Pardo's been moved up,' Torres said. 'Made him head of the whole *Policía Judicial*. Don't see him so much these days.'

As head of *Homicidios*, Pardo had been Cámara's boss. He was foul-mouthed and ambitious, but loyal to his officers if he thought they could bring in results.

'So if Pardo's gone, who's in charge?'

There was only one name on Cámara's mind, the one person in the Valencia Jefatura he couldn't stand the sight of. One man who would have wanted Pardo's job more than anyone else.

He looked at Torres in horror. Torres nodded.

'No, please tell me it's not true.'

'It's all right for you. You're off sailing in the Bahamas. It's me you've got to feel sorry for.'

'I can't believe it.'

'Well, start believing it. He was in there like a shot.'

Calculating and manipulative, Chief Inspector Maldonado had clashed with Cámara on many occasions in the past. Now he would be directly over him if Cámara chose to go back.

'Should make your decision that much easier, I'd say.'

'Here, pass me the wine.'

'I mean, what would police work be if it were all chasing criminals instead of fighting the cunts behind your back?'

'That bad?'

'He's taken my work mobile away from me – it took me three years to get that. He gives me bad progress reports, interferes in everything. You know what he's like. He's pestering us all the time, thinks he has to be there, looking over our shoulders, otherwise we'll start slacking. There's even a suggestion he wants us all to wear uniforms for work. It's ridiculous.'

Torres stubbed out his cigarette and started eating some of the paella that had been placed in front of him.

'No one's happy. I've never known such fucked-up morale. Not anywhere in the police.'

Come back, he was saying. Come back and give us a hand, help us sort him out. If there was anyone who could have taken Pardo's job instead of Maldonado, it was Cámara. And now Cámara was being made to feel some of the blame: he'd abandoned them, gone off on a jolly, leaving them to cope with Maldonado and all his bullshit.

'How long have you got?' Torres asked.

'What?'

'Until you have to tell them what you've decided.'

'Monday.'

'And?'

Cámara ate his yellow paella in silence. Part of him was wondering if there was any saffron in it at all.

'If you don't come back and do your bit I swear I'll come and find you and bite your fucking head off. Don't care where you sail to.'

'Everything all right at home?' Cámara said. 'Wife? Your little boy.'

Torres stopped chewing, sighed, rolled his eyes and put his fork down on his plate. On the face of it, life with his wife and son appeared normal, but Cámara had been vaguely aware that there were tensions from time to time. A few months ago, the last time they were working together, Torres had mumbled something about it. Or at least denied it in such a way as to confirm it.

Torres swallowed, then reached out for the wine and filled both their glasses.

'I'm looking for somewhere else,' he said.

Cámara leaned his elbows on the table and rested his chin on his hands.

'Separation?'

'Separation. Divorce. The whole thing. We're just going through the process.'

'I'm sorry to hear that. How's Iván? How's he taking it?'

'He'll be all right. They're pretty adaptable, kids. I mean, it's tough. And he doesn't really understand what's going on. He's only eight. But, well, we'll have to help him through it, I suppose.'

'Is there someone else?'

Torres started nodding.

'Oh, yes. There's someone else. You know, I used to have my suspicions, sometimes. But I didn't do anything about it. There were times when she was more distant, not really there. Then things changed and she'd be back, you know, more connected. I couldn't say anything because I wasn't around, getting caught up in work and the rest of it. So it didn't bother me. I mean, it bothered me, thinking she might be with someone else, but I didn't have time to let it bother me. Besides, I didn't have any proof.'

He took a long draught of wine.

'But then one day, out of the blue, she hit me with it. I came back, took out a beer from the fridge, sat down, switched the telly on, you know, to relax a bit. And she comes in and starts telling me she wants a divorce, that it's not working. Iván wasn't there – he was at a friend's house, I think. Which is probably why she chose that moment. So we have this long argument, throwing all our shit at each other, years of it. I was amazed – she remembered all kinds of stuff from before we were even married. Like why I hadn't met up with her one evening and went out with some mates instead. I don't know. I can barely remember it myself, but she was there, screaming at me that I never looked after her, or gave her what she needed. And other stuff, all kinds of crap she'd been sitting on for years. And that was it, she couldn't stand it any more; she wanted us to split. And I asked her, I said, is there anyone else? Because, of course, with all this I'm wondering about these doubts I've had in the past, about whether she was sleeping with someone else. And she wouldn't say anything at first, said it was only about us, no one else. But I carried on asking her, wouldn't let it go, until finally she admitted it, she said yes, there was. Another person. And I said, another person? Another man? And that's when it came out. It's not another man. She's with a woman now. She likes women.'

He rubbed his face with his hands and stared out into the distance.

'In your imagination you're always jealous of another man. The scenarios that play out in your head involve other men. It's weird when your wife cheats on you with another woman. You're jealous, but it's not exactly the same. It's almost as if you have to imagine the other woman as a man in order to feel properly jealous, in the way you expect to be.'

The paella remained unfinished when the waiter brought the second course. Torres ignored the pork and lit another cigarette.

'I've got to find somewhere new to live. We're still together for the moment, although I'm on the sofa. It's not easy finding somewhere I can afford, though, especially after the recent pay cut.

'I've got to do it, though. It's my son I have to think about. It's better for him.'

TWENTY-THREE

There was too much of a risk of bumping into Maldonado if they went to the Jefatura, so instead they walked to Zapadores, and the crumbling former military barracks that acted as a secondary police headquarters for the city. With a bit of attention it could have been a grand old place, built in late-nineteenth-century palatial style, but netting had been put up around the upper floor to prevent pieces of masonry falling on people's heads as they walked past, while no one had dared change the flag over the main entrance for years for fear of the balcony collapsing under their weight.

The main square inside the compound – what would have been a parade ground in the past – was now the car pool, filled with weeds and *zeta* squad vehicles, while officers had to park their own cars up round the back, near the foreigners' detention centre, in the ruins of some old outbuildings that had only partially been pulled down.

Cámara and Torres sauntered through, keeping an eye

open for anyone they might know, but the place was relatively quiet during the daytime. At night, when the Jefatura effectively closed down, this became the centre of the police's city operations.

'The *científicos* have got an office round the back. I know the woman who'll be on duty,' Torres said. 'She'll let us use her computer.'

As it turned out, there was no one in the office. They sat down at a terminal and Torres logged on to Webpol, the police intranet, tapping in his ID number and code word before getting on to the main portal.

'I want to check out this man first,' Cámara said, scribbling down a name on a piece of paper and handing it to Torres. 'Iranian.'

There was a section for foreign nationals. Torres clicked on it, then searched under 'Reza Amini' and his country of origin. Within a few seconds his details, including his passport photo, had shown up.

'*Aquí está.*' Here he is.

Cámara looked at the photo. Allowing for the usual distortion that official photos always produced in people, he was certain it was the man he'd seen at Pozoblanco – 'Ahmed the Moroccan'.

'That's the one.'

Torres checked the details on the man's file.

'Entered the country a month ago on a tourist visa.'

'Arriving in time for the harvest?'

'It's his third visit in as many years. Always comes around this time of year. Flies in from Tehran to Madrid.'

'Then makes it down to Albacete on the train.'

'You've come across him, I assume. Well, probably. We could check the railway company records.'

'No need. Criminal record?'

'Nothing here.'

'Anything about a militia?'

Torres scanned the screen.

'Nothing. I can give you the more usual stuff – date of birth, names of parents, where he was born, that kind of thing.'

'How old is he?'

'Well, he's thirty-four going on this.'

'Have we got any idea when he's going back?'

'In previous years he's flown back to Tehran in early November. So assuming he's working on a pattern . . .'

'He could be leaving any day soon.'

Cámara stared into the eyes in the photo.

'If only we could find out a bit more . . . What about the Iranian militia? Can we check on that?'

'I'll see.'

A moment later Torres was reading to him from his screen.

'The Iranian militia, or *Basij*, is a volunteer force set up during the Islamic Revolution in 1979. It is made up mostly of young men, hard-line supporters of the regime. It acts as a moral police force, imposing Islamic behaviour codes, as well as being used as a force for repression against the students' movement and other anti-regime activists. It was a major part of the Iranian war effort in the Iran–Iraq War from 1980 to 1988, when militia members were employed in "human wave" attacks against the enemy.'

'OK, we get it.'

'Sounds like a fun bunch of people. Bet they throw great parties.'

'So they're official, government-linked.'

'Official meat-heads by the sound of it. Violent, repressive.'

'A bit like the *Falange* used to be here under Franco.'

'Yeah, I suppose so.'

'A fanatic.'

'Almost certainly.'

'And he's in Spain for the saffron harvest.'

Cámara stood up and started pacing the room. Torres knew better than to interrupt him when he was in one of his moments.

The door opened and a woman with streaked blonde hair walked in. She gave Cámara a quizzical look, then seeing Torres sitting at her desk smiled broadly.

'Oh, visitors. How nice.'

Torres stood up and kissed her on the cheeks.

'¿*Qué tal?*

She glanced over towards Cámara.

'Chief Inspector Max Cámara,' Torres said. 'This is Teresa Matute, from the *Científica*.'

'Oh,' Teresa said, kissing Cámara as well. 'I've heard about you. Are you back, then?'

Cámara looked away, lost in his thoughts. Torres gave a shrug.

'Well, yes, sure. Anything to help. Can I do anything?'

Cámara turned to her.

'Know anything about ballistics?'

'I used to be in that section,' Teresa said. 'My first job in the police. But I haven't got any of the kit here. It's all at the Jefatura.'

'Could you tell me something about this?'

Cámara fished into his pocket and pulled out the bullet he'd picked up from the inside of the car the day he and Alicia had gone to Pozoblanco.

Teresa took the bullet and glanced up at him slightly nervously, as though it were some kind of test.

'It's, er, a nine-millimetre,' she said, as though everyone would know. 'Almost certainly fired from a semi-automatic.'

'For instance?'

'Well, there are lots of possibilities, but I suppose the most obvious would be an AK-47, because it's such an easy weapon to get hold of.'

'Can you tell me anything else?'

She frowned.

'Not really, not just by looking at it like this. I'd need the equipment.'

'No matter. Listen, tell me, is an AK-47 very accurate?'

'It depends.' Teresa shrugged. 'Over short range it's quite good, if it's set to single shot. It's pretty inaccurate if you're on automatic.'

'Long distance?'

She wrinkled her nose.

'Not really. It's best for close combat.'

'So you wouldn't use it for a sniper weapon.'

'What? An AK-47?'

She laughed. Cámara's expression didn't change.

'Well, no. No, of course not. Not if you actually wanted to hit anything.'

'All right. Thanks.'

'No problem.'

Cámara fell into silence again. Torres had already sat back down at her desk.

'Well, er, I might just go and get some coffee,' Teresa said. 'You want some?'

'Black, please,' Torres said.

Cámara said nothing.

'Same for him.'

The door closed behind her and Cámara went to sit down

next to Torres. He had a glassy, distant look in his eyes, one that Torres was familiar with.

'There's something else I want to look at.'

Torres knew something about the Mirella Faro case in Albacete. Cámara filled him in on the details he had.

'I want to check murders with a similar MO,' he said. 'Can we do that?'

Torres turned to the screen.

'Time frame?'

'How far back can we go?'

'Your sister's murder won't be on there, if that's what you mean.'

'All right, all right. Just see what you can get, will you?'

Torres tapped on the keyboard, trying combinations of search words. A few moments later they were looking at a list of over a dozen killings.

'The victims were all girls between the ages of twelve and sixteen,' Torres said. 'All with some sexual aspect to the attack. I've ruled out ones where the attacker was a member of the family.'

'What about MO? Were they all strangled?'

'No.' Torres looked down the list. 'Two were knifed, one suffocated, and for two others cause of death is unknown.'

'Why?'

'One of them was badly mutilated, the other—'

'That's fine. Can you get rid of those ones. I just want to see the girls who were strangled.'

Torres fiddled with the mouse, then clicked and the screen was refreshed. Cámara pulled out a notebook and pen, ready to jot down some notes.

'Right,' he said. 'Let's start from the first one we've got.'

The door clicked open again and Teresa walked in carrying

three cups of coffee. Cámara and Torres got up to take theirs, thanking her, then all three started blowing and sipping on the hot liquid. Teresa looked a little uncomfortable, not quite sure what to do with these two senior policemen in her office, using her computer in a not-entirely-regulatory fashion.

'Teresa,' Cámara said after a pause. 'I wondered if you could help us.'

He explained briefly about the Mirella Faro case, and what they were doing.

'You're looking for links, patterns. Great. I like that kind of thing.'

Torres looked at her.

'Thanks, Teresa. I suppose I should point out—'

'That neither of you has ever walked into my office, or used my computer. Yeah, I've got it.'

'Thanks.'

'Do you want to use my login, to be safer?'

'No, we're fine.'

There were ten cases left to look at. Torres scrolled down to each one, letting them all read the details over his shoulder and see the photos of the murdered girls. Details included each one's name, date of birth, age when murdered, weight, height, hair and eye colour, what they were wearing – if anything – when found, and what they were last seen wearing when alive. Then there were accounts of how, exactly, they had been sexually assaulted, with a primary murder scene and a secondary in the cases where the body had been moved after death. Except for two, each case had been resolved, with the killer named, a mugshot provided, and information about his sentence and where he was currently being held. No women were involved in the attacks.

The first murder dated back to 1992, in Seville.

'The year of the Expo,' Teresa said.

Julia del Barrio's body had been found near the banks of the Guadalquivir, her dress ripped, although not entirely, from her body. She'd been raped and then strangled with a hemp rope. One of her silver hoop earrings had been torn out in the struggle. The three of them looked at the school photo taken of her a month before she was killed, and then the black-and-white police images taken where they found the body. At the bottom of the file was a picture of a man by the name of Antonio Gabarri. He'd been found guilty of the murder after a shred of the girl's clothing was found in his car, an Opel Astra. Given life, he'd been refused bail for never admitting his guilt. He was still being held in Seville's Number Two Prison, although his term was due to finish in eight months' time.

'Gypsy?' Torres said.

Cámara pursed his lips. It wasn't easy to say.

The next two cases were in Madrid, involving Vanesa Romero Pérez and Rosa Esquivel Fuentes. They had been murdered two months apart in 1998, and at the beginning police had suspected a link, but none had ever been established. The first girl was aged sixteen and had started working as a prostitute only a couple of months before. No one had ever been found guilty of her murder.

The second Madrid victim, Rosa Esquivel, had been found not far from the railway tracks leading out of Atocha station. She'd been assaulted, although not raped, strangled by someone using their hands, and her body stripped and left. No trace of her clothing had ever been found. A young friend of the girl's, with a previous record for drug dealing, was convicted of her murder. He was currently serving at the Valdemoro prison in Madrid.

The following three murders took place from 1999 to 2001, occurring outside the capital. One in Barcelona, another in Badajoz, near the border with Portugal, and the third in Guadalajara, about an hour's drive north-east from Madrid. In each instance the MO was similar or the same – a young adolescent girl assaulted and strangled. No one had been found guilty of the Guadalajara case, while two different men – one an Algerian immigrant, the other another drug dealer – were serving time for the other cases.

The next case had taken place in Albacete seven years previously. Paula Gutiérrez Soria's body had been found in a rubbish container, like Mirella Faro's, although this time it was near the university campus area.

'Not long after they finished building it,' Cámara said.

The name of the murderer was one he had already come across: Juan Manuel Heredia, currently held in Albacete's Torrecica jail. Cámara picked up a pen and paper to jot down a couple of notes before Torres scrolled on.

The last two murders had taken place in Madrid again, one in 2005, the last in 2008. Carmen Montero Ferrero had been fourteen when her killer had attacked her as she left home one Friday night to meet up with friends for a birthday party. Her semi-naked body was found four days later in a tip three kilometres away. A former vagrant she'd been seen with a few times in the run-up to the murder was sentenced to life after it was learned that he'd lost his job as a teacher eight years previously for inappropriate relations with two of his female students. His wife had divorced him and refused to let him see their three children any more, since when he'd lived on the streets.

The last case before Mirella's involved María Teresa Machado Ballesteros, fifteen, a promising basketball player who used to go training on Tuesday and Thursday nights at a sports centre a ten-minute walk from her home in the Leganés district of Madrid. Her trainer's assistant, Raúl Rojas Sánchez, had been found guilty of raping and murdering her after her body was found in pieces inside his freezer.

The final case was that of Mirella Faro in Albacete. A photo of her, taken just a couple of months before, took up a large part of the screen.

'That's it,' Torres said, standing up.

Both he and Cámara reached for their cigarettes.

Teresa coughed.

'Would you mind,' she said, smiling. 'It's just that I have a chest infection that's not going away.

'Oh, yes, of course.'

Torres put his cigarette back in its box; Cámara left his in his mouth, unlit.

'So,' Torres said, 'any thoughts?'

Cámara sniffed.

'The similarities are obvious. It's less obvious similarities I'm wondering about.'

'There's something similar about quite a few of the attackers,' Teresa said.

'You mean they're fringe people,' Torres said.

'Drug dealers, a suspected paedophile, a Gypsy . . .'

'Yes. That's right. Except for the basketball trainer.'

Teresa kept looking at the screen.

'Anything else?' Cámara asked.

'I'm just wondering,' she said. 'Not all of them, but with quite a few of the girls they're of a similar type.'

'What do you mean?'

Cámara looked down at the screen with her as she picked up the mouse and began to scroll over the cases again.

'These ones,' she said, pointing out the Seville murder, the first of the 1998 Madrid cases, the Guadalajara girl, the Albacete girl, the Madrid case from 2005. And then Mirella Faro, the last one they'd looked at.

'There's something quite similar about them,' Teresa said. 'Not so much their colouring – the Guadalajara girl is quite pale and has light brown hair; the others are darker. But there's a look there – they're all quite slim, athletic looking, and there's something strong, almost square about their faces. Perhaps it's their jaws, I'm not sure.'

Torres and Cámara looked at the photos – they had been taken at different times, with different cameras of different quality. But Teresa had seen something they hadn't.

She was right. Something about all of the girls she mentioned was very similar.

'It's almost as if they were related in some way.'

TWENTY-FOUR

Thursday 5th November

Yago had told them to expect him. The guard at the gate checked his name and ID number and then rang through to the administration office. Cámara was made to wait a few minutes; there was nowhere to sit and the guard didn't look like the kind who wanted to make conversation, so he paced around the small room, humming a song by the Flamenco rock band Triana.

'*Abre la Puerta*'. Open the door.

Eventually a second guard appeared to escort him inside the Torrecica prison proper. Cámara followed in silence as they went through a series of entrances and doors that had to be unlocked and locked again each time. Cámara could hear voices as they passed along corridors, groups of men in various rooms hidden behind the brown-painted bars. In fact, the whole place had been decorated – if that was the word – in shades of brown: light, dark, chocolate, coffee, and . . . well. The walls, the doors, the floors, the guards' uniforms – it was all brown. Even the smell, he thought, had a brownness about it.

Another door was opened. The guard stepped through and then stopped, beckoning Cámara wordlessly to follow. Inside, there was a scuffed wooden table at which sat a man in a toffee-coloured shirt, hunched over, his chin resting on his hands.

The guard began to back out.

'I'll call you when I've finished,' Cámara said.

'You've got ten minutes. No more.'

The door slammed behind him, but his face remained at the small window of reinforced glass at the top.

Cámara moved towards the table. The prisoner sat still, looking bored, his eyes unmoving from the wall in front of him. Cámara pulled out a chair and sat down, placing himself in the man's direct line of vision. The eyes rested on him without emotion, and stayed there.

'Do you know who I am?' Cámara asked.

The man didn't move. Cámara had seen photos of Juan Manuel Heredia years before, when he'd been a suspect in Concha's murder. He'd been much younger then – more than thirty years younger – and considerably thinner. But he still wore his hair long, like many Gypsy men, while the walrus moustache he always sported was distinguishable over the thick carpet of black spiky bristles that covered the lower half of his face and neck. There were spots of white there now, as well as in his hair; he was in his mid-fifties, and old age appeared to be making inroads.

'I'm Max Cámara. Does that name mean anything to you?'

Heredia shrugged.

'You must be police,' he said. 'Otherwise they wouldn't let you in. It's not visiting hours.'

'Yes, I'm police.'

Cámara thought for a moment before pulling out his packet of Ducados and lighting a cigarette. People were becoming so tense about smoking, but that also made it useful in certain circumstances. It had worked with the FBI man. Now, for want of a new idea, he would try it again. He took a deep drag before releasing a plume into the air. Seconds later, as though on cue, there was a knocking at the door from behind. Heredia's eyes darted from him to the door and back. The knocking came again, but still Cámara ignored it. Finally the door opened and the guard barked at his back.

'No smoking!'

No reaction. Heredia's eyes were beginning to widen.

'Didn't you hear me?' the guard barked, taking a step forwards. 'This is not a designated smoking area.'

'It is now,' Cámara said. Heredia sniggered.

'If you've got a problem,' Cámara said, 'you'd better go and call your superior officer.'

There was a pause, then eventually the guard backed out, slamming the door behind him and locking it.

'Just you and me,' Cámara said.

'Give me one of those,' Heredia said.

'You still don't know who I am, do you?'

Heredia sighed.

'Look, what do you want? That was good, what you did just now. But you want to play games with me as well?'

'Cámara. Doesn't the name Cámara mean anything to you? Concha Cámara. Think, Heredia, think. Quite some time ago. You were in your twenties then.'

'And you were still wearing nappies. What the fuck!'

'My sister—'

'Yeah, I know what you're talking about. What? You her baby brother? Come to do me in for big sister's murder? Now? Thirty years on? Get the fuck out of here.'

Cámara sat back in his chair. His cigarette packet was on the table in front of him. Heredia leaned forward and grabbed it, taking out half a dozen and shoving them into his shirt pocket.

'They never got me for that. And you know why? Because I never did it. I didn't kill your sister. They never had anything on me, although they tried. They were desperate. No suspects. So they picked up some Gypsy kid and tried to nail it on him. It's what they always do. But they didn't even sit me down in front of the judge. It didn't even get that far. They fucked it up.'

Cámara sucked hard on his cigarette.

'You're in now, though. For murdering and raping a young girl. And her body was found in a rubbish bin. Strange, that. An almost identical murder.'

Heredia began to laugh.

'Yeah, this time I'm inside. God knows, they've been trying to get me in here for years. And they finally managed it. Another Gypsy off the streets.'

'What is it? You just can't keep your hands off young girls? They do it for you?'

There was a loud splitting sound as Heredia smashed both fists down on to the table, cracking the wood.

'I didn't kill any fucking girl, you got it?' he shouted.

'She was from a rival family, a family trying to take over your patch.'

'I've got daughters of my own! You think I could do

something sick to a girl like that, when I've got my own daughters, almost the same age? You stupid fuckers who've never had kids don't get it – all children are your children. You see a kid getting hurt, it could be yours. How the fuck am I going to go round doing sick shit like that? I don't care whose family she's from.'

'The drugs—'

'Yes, I've done drugs. This city was mine. But they never could get me on that. So what do they do? They come up with some crap about murdering this girl.'

'One of your own men had been beaten by them. You had a feud going. You needed to tell them you were in charge.'

Heredia's face hardened.

'I can't believe how fucking stupid you people can be sometimes.'

Cámara took a last drag on his cigarette and let it fall to the floor.

'Tell me.'

Heredia shrugged.

'What's the point.'

'You're innocent. You're here telling me you're innocent.'

Heredia turned his head and spat on the floor, the spit landing with a fizz as it expertly extinguished the burning butt of Cámara's cigarette.

'You didn't kill Concha, and you didn't kill Paula Gutiérrez. You're a wronged man. Perhaps there's something I can do.'

'Fuck you.'

'You see,' Cámara said, 'it seems odd to me that a man like yourself would rape and kill his rival's daughter as part of a feud. So they beat up one of yours? You go back and beat up one of theirs, harder, perhaps even kill him, I don't know. Things can get out of hand.'

Heredia stared at him.

'But to rape and then kill the man's daughter? You see, that doesn't seem to fit for me either. There's an etiquette to these things. I know that. You know it. So what happened?'

The door crashed open behind them.

'Time's up!'

Without looking round, Cámara looked at Heredia quizzically, as if to ask if this time the guard had brought reinforcements. Heredia glanced at the door, then gave an almost invisible nod.

'What happened?' Cámara repeated.

Heredia shuffled in his chair. One of the new guards had entered the room and was coming round to his side of the table to escort him away.

'An *ajuste de cuentas*,' he said. A settling of scores. 'That's all it takes.'

It was getting blustery – strong, cold winds were beginning to blow in from the north.

Estrella's bar was gradually emptying as the last lunchers of the day finished their meals and prepared for the second half of the working day by knocking back strong doses of coffee laced with brandy or whisky.

'*Hola, cariño.*' She greeted him affectionately and nodded him to the same stool at the bar.

'It's your place,' she said. 'Have you eaten? We've got some swordfish fillets left, and pasta, but not much else. It's all gone. I can fix you up a sandwich if you like.'

She poured him a beer and placed it down on the bar in front of him.

'You looked troubled, sweetie. Everything all right?'

He nibbled at the food she offered him. The fish was warm

and seemed to promise a night of poisoned agony, while the pasta was overcooked and going dry. He poured some olive oil over it, to try and make it go down better, but more came out than he'd intended, and the plate swam in golden-green grease.

Half an hour later, when only a couple of customers were left and the girl who helped behind the bar had started cleaning the stove, Estrella came and sat down next to him, an exaggerated frown on her face.

'Tell me all about it.'

She placed a hand on his knee.

Cámara drained the last drop of his beer, trying to encourage the pasta stuck in his gullet to move further down towards his stomach. Smothering a belch with his hand, he looked her in the eye.

'I want to ask you something.'

'Of course. Go ahead, ask anything, my dear.'

Her eyes darted to the side for a second before coming back to his face.

'What kind of thing? You mean police questions?'

Cámara shrugged.

'Oh. Well, if I can help. Is it something to do with Concha?'

'Maybe.'

'OK.'

'This man who left you, your ex . . .'

'Oh, him.'

'He was a dealer, right?'

'Fuck, Max. Did I tell you that?'

'You didn't have to.'

'How did you—? Oh, it doesn't matter. Yes, I'm pretty sure he was. I mean, he is.'

She pulled her hand away from his knee and turned towards the bar, tapping her nails on the metal counter.

'Is that what you wanted to ask me? Are you trying to bust him?'

Cámara didn't say anything. Slowly, she turned back round to face him.

'Or what? You want to bust me? You think I'm dealing as well?'

Cámara held up his hands.

'It's all right, it's all right. Estrella, really, I'm not trying to frighten you. I just need some information. I don't care what you're doing. OK? Trust me. I don't care, and I'm not going to say anything to anyone, all right? I just need to know some things.'

'Christ, Max. If you weren't police I'd fucking throw you out. Fucking cheek.'

She turned back to the bar and rested her head on one hand, looking down at the floor.

'Where do people go these days, to score?'

She shrugged.

'The same old places.'

'And what are they selling these days?'

Estrella gave him a look of disbelief.

'Again, the same old thing.'

'Like what?'

'Like what?'

'Yes.'

'For fuck's sake. Cocaine, hash, amphetamines, crystal . . . same as always. It's a stable market, Max. No one's pushing anything new. Kids are conservative these days. Just want what they've always had. Don't want to experiment any more.'

'What about the gangs? Who's controlling? Who's doing what?'

'The Gypsies,' she said, as though he were stupid. 'Same as ever.'

'No one else? No one new?'

'The Colombians aren't here, if that's what you mean. They're distributing to the Gypsies, probably. I don't know. What are you asking me these things for? Shouldn't you be talking to the narco squad? They'll have all this.'

'That's it? No one else?'

She shrugged.

'I don't know. People talk sometimes about Moroccans coming in. Or some Moroccan guy around. I haven't seen him, so I can't say. Don't know what he's doing here, or what he's selling. It's just been mentioned, that's all.'

'You sure?'

'Yes.'

'Moroccan, you say.'

'Yeah. Some name like Mohammed or Ahmed. But, I mean, they're all called something like that, aren't they?'

TWENTY-FIVE

'Fuck off. I'm not lending *you* another car.'

Gerardo was not pleased to see Cámara's face appearing at his door again. Sitting at his desk, finishing off some paperwork before closing the garage for the evening, he shook his head.

'I can't believe you. Seriously, Max. This is not on.'

Cámara said nothing, leaning against the wall, a cigarette drooping from his lips.

'You're a fucking liability. You lost me a lot of money on that BMW. It was a beautiful car.'

'Still looks pretty good to me.'

Cámara glanced over to the other side of the workshop, where the BMW was parked up against the far corner.

'Look, you don't know anything about cars, right. That's my department. And I'm telling you that at least a couple of grand have been lost thanks to your pissing about with it.'

'If you say so.'

'I *do* say so.'

'I'll make it up to you.'

'How?'

'Are you the only person in the country who doesn't have a favour to ask of a policeman?'

Gerardo looked up from his desk.

'Anything?'

'Anything.'

'No matter how big?'

Cámara shrugged.

'They say you only know your true friends when you show up at their door with a dead body on your hands,' Gerardo said.

'You planning on killing someone?'

'Right now, the only person I'd kill is standing in front of me.'

'Can you lend me a car first? We can sort out the bit about killing me and disposing of the body when I get back.'

'If you get back. Looks like it was a close-run thing the last time.'

'I made it, didn't I?'

'Just make sure this time that when they shoot you, you put yourself between the bullet and the bodywork, all right?'

'So you will, then?'

'What?'

'Lend me a car.'

'No.'

'Come on, Gerardo.'

'I haven't got anything here you could have. I'm not lending you a client's car. Not least because if they're in here it means they're broken. And I'm not lending you my car, for fuck's sake. Not for where you've got in mind. Where are you going, as a matter of interest?'

'I can't tell you.'

'Oh, forget it. If you're going to be like that.'

'Look, it's a place not far away. But it's dangerous.'

'What? In Albacete? You talk as if this was Beirut, or something.'

'Pozoblanco,' Cámara said. 'Heard of it?'

'Pozoblanco? That commie village up the road?'

'That's it.'

'That's where you got shot at?'

Cámara nodded.

'Bloody hell. I had no idea.'

'So can you lend me a car or not? I have to go there tonight.'

'No, I told you. What? Tonight? In the dark, sort of thing? A night raid? You sound like some kind of special forces bloke. Are you blacking up your face as well?'

'I wasn't. But now you mention it . . .'

Gerardo shook his head, laughing.

'That's the thing. I could never tell – none of us could – whether you were joking or being serious.'

'It's too far to walk. I'm not going to catch the bus.'

'Oh, that would be worth seeing – all kitted out for a commando raid and then catching the number sixteen to get to the target area.'

Cámara laughed with him.

'At least no one would expect it.'

The laughter slowly died out, and they were both silent for a moment.

'All right,' Cámara said. 'No car. But what about that?'

He pointed to a motorbike leaning against the wall, partly covered in a greasy dark green tarpaulin.

'That?' Gerardo said incredulously.

'Yes.'

'It's a Montesa Impala.'

'Does it work?'

'Yes, it works, but that's not the point. It's over forty years old – it's a collector's item.'

'Are those the keys there?'

Cámara stepped across and picked up a keyring hanging from a nail above the desk.

'Yes, but . . .'

Cámara was already walking over to the motorbike, pulling off the cover to take a look.

'This'll do.'

'Lord have fucking mercy.'

Half a kilometre from Pozoblanco, he turned off the headlight and cut out the engine, coasting for as long as he could down the dark empty road until he came to the junction for the slip road down to the village. A slight slope helped him to roll down a little more until he reached the line of trees that started a hundred metres before the first houses.

He got off the motorbike and pulled it over to the verge, leaning it down on the ground on its side. No one would see it – unless they were looking for it.

He stepped to the edge of the village, remaining in the shadows beyond the footprint of the first lamp: it was just past three o'clock and the street was empty. From the map he'd worked out a way of getting around, avoiding the main square in case anyone was still about at that hour. He didn't have long, however. Within about an hour the first risers would be getting up for the dawn collection of more saffron flowers.

Colourful posters had been stuck up on the walls showing stick figures of children with smiling faces carrying balloons and riding a ferris wheel. Bold lettering at the top announced the annual end-of-harvest village fiesta for the following evening. Pozoblanco was getting ready to celebrate.

The wind was now blowing quite hard, with sudden gusts. In the end, Gerardo had lent Cámara an oil-stained padded leather jacket he used for riding the bike. They couldn't find a helmet, so he had come bareheaded, his eyes watering as the cold bit into them.

He took a side street, keeping close to the walls, walking quickly and steadily, his shoulders slightly hunched, trying, as much as he could, to reduce his presence, to make himself invisible. If someone saw him they would almost certainly see that he wasn't from the village – people in places like that always know each other by sight at least.

The warehouse was only a few streets away. Reaching into the jacket pockets he checked everything was there: a straightened paperclip and small screwdriver for picking locks, a hammer, a small wind-up torch, a folded-up paper bag, and an Albacete knife with a curved four-inch steel blade.

Past the last group of houses. A quick check to see if anyone was around, and then he stepped out across the street towards the warehouse.

Check the obvious first: the main door. You never know. But it was locked.

He looked at the padlock – not the easiest kind to pick; it would take a few minutes.

The wind almost pushed him along as he walked around to the side. The sound of the rushing air would at least help to disguise any noise he might inadvertently make, he thought, although he found it harder to concentrate, some primitive part of him keen to get out of the cold and into some kind of shelter.

He checked for other possible means of entry: side doors, windows. But they were all as securely closed as the main entrance. Coming round to the front once again he was reaching for his lock-picking tools when he caught sight of a pile of ladders left under a shelter leaning against one of the houses on the other side of the road. He jogged over to have a look: they were wooden, proper old ladders with a wide base to give more stability. He looked round at the warehouse: one window above a door had been closed, but he felt sure he could get it open. Then he might be able to reach down and unlock the door from the inside.

He lifted the top ladder up as carefully as he could, trying not to make a sound. He might not have bothered with a modern, narrow ladder in this wind, but with this one he was more confident.

In a few strides he was back at the warehouse, where he leaned the ladder against the wall. He tested the first step – it was secure. Then he lifted himself up another three steps until he was level with the small window. It opened outwards, and as he suspected, it wasn't locked. Wedging his screwdriver underneath it, he was able to loosen it enough until he could get his fingers into the gap, then he pulled it open.

It made a creaking, cracking sound. Cámara stopped. The wind, he hoped, had muffled the noise. But going unnoticed by the sleeping villagers was one thing; being undetected by the dogs many of them would keep was another. So far, he'd been lucky getting here without disturbing any. But he had to be very careful.

He listened for a moment: no barking.

Pushing himself through the window up to his waist, he leaned down and felt around in the dark for the latch. It was a slide-bolt. Grabbing it with his fingers he gave it a jerk and it slid to the side. The door almost opened on its own thanks to the wind. He pulled himself out of the window, climbed back down, laid the ladder on the ground in case anyone saw it, and then stepped inside.

His torch was little bigger than a cigarette lighter, but it cast a bright white light over what looked like a room adjacent to the main area of the warehouse. The room Faro Oscuro hadn't shown them.

He turned back to the door and closed it, trying to block out the noise of the wind outside. The bolt moved, but was now jammed for some reason and wouldn't go all the way back in. It was enough to keep the door closed, but a harsh gust might blow it open again.

In a slow, smooth motion, he shone the torch over the room to get a better look, and then stopped still. The wind was rushing outside, but set against it, punctuating the whooshing sound, was the staccato barking of a dog. It was hard to say how far away it was – perhaps two or three streets.

He cursed: he would have to be very quick. With luck the dog would be ignored, but if someone saw the light from his torch . . .

Glancing from side to side, he saw work tables set against two walls, while a third wall was covered almost to the top with hundreds of cardboard packing cases with 'La Mancha Saffron' written on them.

Opening one, Cámara saw that it was filled with fifty or sixty small plastic containers, only slightly bigger than a large coin, with no more than two, perhaps three, pinches of saffron in each one.

He took a couple and shoved them into his pockets.

Then he walked over to one of the work tables. Empty plastic containers, like the ones in the boxes, were piled up at the side. Next to them was an open box of latex gloves – a used pair, with yellow-stained fingers, had been tossed to the side, one still on the table, the other having fallen to the floor.

Three cardboard boxes were placed near the centre of the table – two much larger than the third. Next to them was a white plastic bowl. He opened each box. Inside each one was a mixture of what looked, to him, like saffron. He took a pinch from each and lifted it to smell – the first two made him curl up his nose and turn away. Only the third, of which there was a small amount, had a pleasant odour. He took a sample of each and placed them in the little bag he'd brought, wrapping each one in tissue paper first to keep it separate.

A piece of paper next to the plastic bowl caught his eye – he lifted it up to read. It was a table, showing figures and percentages. And there was writing near the top, written in a script he didn't immediately recognise. Was it Arabic? Persian? He placed it in his jacket.

Instinctively he switched the torch off. A noise had come from inside the warehouse.

He backed away, moving as silently as he could towards the door through which he'd come in. His right hand had already curled itself around the knife in his pocket and was pushing the blade out.

With his left hand he reached behind, fumbling for the bolt, but couldn't find it.

The lights had been switched on inside the warehouse – a

white-yellow glow was seeping through the gaps around the door leading into the side room where he was standing. Again he tried to feel for the metal bolt, not daring to turn his back on the intruder. He heard footsteps, a hand on the door, the clicking of a safety catch on a gun . . .

He dived forwards in the dark just as a hand reached for the light switch. Curling himself tight, he rolled on one shoulder before the momentum brought him back on to the balls of his feet and he lunged up and straight, his fist pushing hard into the man's groin. A high-pitched wail of clouded pain burst from the intruder's mouth as he doubled up, strength leaving his body, and he fell to the floor. There was a clatter; an AK-47 semi-automatic rifle hit the ground, still gripped hard in his hand.

Cámara threw himself down on the man, pinning him to the floor with his weight, trying to press his knee on the arm holding the weapon. But the man wriggled and fought back, just loosening Cámara free enough to swing the butt against his head and knock him to the side.

Dazed, Cámara swung out a kicking leg as he fell; once the rifle was trained on him the fight would be over. There was no time to pause, to gauge then strike.

His shin caught something and again there came a cry of pain. Cámara looked up and saw that he'd managed to snap the gun up into the man's face, catching his nose, which was now beginning to bleed.

The knife had been loose in his pocket; now he gripped it and lunged forwards, kicking the rifle away across the floor and pressing the blade against the man's neck.

'Hello, Reza.'

Reza's black eyes stared back at him.

'Chief Inspector,' he said.

There was a second's pause as both men understood: each one knew exactly who the other really was.

Reza's body relaxed slightly as a half-smile formed. He licked his upper lip, catching the blood and drawing it into his mouth.

'Were you looking for something?'

Before Cámara could react, Reza spat the blood up into his face. In the second Cámara's eyes closed Reza pushed him off and to the side. Cámara swiped with his knife, catching Reza's lower leg as he made to run off.

He called out in pain, but it was a superficial cut only; Reza was hurt, but not disabled. And he was making his way across the warehouse to where Cámara had kicked his gun.

Cámara looked up: Reza had come in through the main entrance, and the door had now swung open in the wind and was banging against the wall. Between Reza and the rifle there was only a large container filled with saffron stigmas, plucked and ready to be packaged.

With just a knife, though, he could do little. Once Reza picked the gun up again . . .

The wind was picking up outside, blowing stronger and stronger.

BANG, BANG, BANG went the door.

A couple of saffron strands lifted into the air from the box at his side, swirling as the currents caught them. The side room, from where he'd come, was just a few metres away on his left.

A shot rang out as he stood up and ran. The bullet ricocheted off the metal saffron container before burying itself in the wall.

Cámara was in the side room, unhurt, Reza following close behind.

The bolt came easily to his fingers this time. Easing it across, he felt the wind pushing hard against the door, trying eagerly to get in.

There was a cracking sound as the door whipped open. Reza appeared in the doorway, lifting the AK-47 to take aim.

Cámara just smiled.

The wind sailed past him, through Reza and deep into the warehouse. In less than a second it had caught up the dry, feather-light saffron and was lifting it high into the air. More air currents began to scatter it about, but the wind was travelling mainly in one direction, and now carrying its hostage away with it, it began to blow out through the main door.

The gun lowered in Reza's hand as he understood. Then with a shriek he turned and ran back into the warehouse, dropping the rifle, his hands outstretched as he tried to catch a million swarming strands of saffron disappearing into the night sky.

'No, no, no!'

Cámara put away his knife and gripped his own saffron samples in his pocket.

It was time to disappear.

TWENTY-SIX

Friday 6th November

Hilario appeared to have taken a turn for the worse, mumbling to himself over breakfast, occasionally throwing out a badly enunciated, irrelevant question and then not always waiting for the answer.

'This policeman friend of yours.'

'What about—?'

'Is he married?'

'Yes.'

'Wears a ring, does he?'

Hilario lifted up his hand and wiggled his fingers.

'Likes to wear a ring?'

Cámara had to think for a moment.

'No. I haven't seen him with—'

'But he does wear one, normally, right?'

Hilario slurped his coffee, dark brown droplets catching on his grey stubble as the cup wobbled on his lips.

'Probably,' Cámara said. 'The skin is lighter where the ring ought to be. Some policemen take it off – it's safer than—'

'Getting one yourself?'

'A wedding ring?'

'You and Alicia? Wedding bells? The Church does a nice service, I've heard.'

'Have you been on the home-grown?'

'Oh, I like that. You're the one staggering around like a blind man and I'm the one who's stoned out of his skull.'

Cámara was sitting perfectly still at the table. He looked like a model of tranquillity.

Did this happen before another attack, he wondered? Was Hilario minutes away from another blood clot lodging in his brain? What was left of it seemed to be pretty jumbled that morning.

'Are you taking your pills?' he asked.

'Don't talk to me like I was senile. Course I'm fucking taking them. It's you needs your head examining. Have you called Alicia?'

Cámara shrugged.

'You should, you know, after what you've been through together. Getting shot at.'

'How do you know that?'

'She told me. Alicia told me. She rang me up, said what a nice time she'd had. Not getting shot at, obviously. I mean coming here, meeting me.'

Cámara was silent.

'You're going to let that one slip away,' Hilario said, 'and you'll never catch another like her. Not at your age. You're turning into an old fart, you know. Bit of a gut developing down there.'

'Thanks.'

'Read your notes about the murders as well. Might use them for that novel I told you about.'

'What novel?'

There was a click down the corridor as the front door opened. Neither of them reacted, knowing full well that it would be Pilar arriving for work. Cámara glanced at the pile of dirty dishes from the night before, leaning in a tower by the sink.

'Have some guests round last night?' he asked as Pilar's footsteps grew closer.

Perhaps Hilario was merely hungover.

'Where were you? Out prowling again? And what's that motorbike doing in the front hall? That's a Montesa Impala, that is. Collector's item. What did you do? Steal it? I knew there's hope for you yet.'

'A friend lent it to me. Gerardo.'

'Oh.'

Hilario looked disappointed.

Pilar had been standing in the doorway for a few moments now, expecting them to greet her. Eventually, without turning, Cámara said hello.

'*Hola*.'

There was no reply.

'She'll have lost her voice again,' Hilario said. 'It's these strong winds.'

Then in a dramatic whisper he added, 'Her health's not what it used to be.'

'I came by,' Pilar chirped in her high voice, 'to say I won't be coming any more.'

Hilario fell silent. Cámara turned in his chair to look at her properly. And almost fell over when he caught sight of her.

Pilar had been an integral part of the life in this flat since he'd arrived as a boy. Then still a relatively young woman, she'd always appeared older than she was, not least because she'd adopted traditional mourning black for her recently deceased husband – a railway worker who'd suffered a freak heart attack in his late twenties. And so Cámara had grown up with this woman always among them, a heavy, leaden presence making their lives easier by cleaning and cooking for them, but also bringing a weight to their lives. Not that it was always unwelcome – both he and Hilario could be overly mercurial at times. But while, as a teenager, he had often wished she would disappear – or at least not burst in on him at the most inopportune moments – the truth was he couldn't envisage this world – Albacete, Hilario, his home – without her.

Yet now what struck him most – almost like a physical force – was seeing what she was wearing. For the first time in his life – and in hers, it felt like – the uniform of black had gone, and instead she was wearing a bright floral-patterned dress of thick cotton with a woollen fuchsia cardigan thrown over her shoulders. What's more, her thin, wrinkled lips had been painted scarlet, while black eyeliner framed her sunken, narrow-set eyes.

'Pilar,' Cámara said in surprise. 'You look lovely.'

'I'm going,' Pilar repeated. 'I want my wages for the month and then I'm leaving, and I'm not coming back. And if you don't like it I'll just go to the police and tell them about what you've got growing on the patio back there. Don't think I don't know. I should have gone years ago. It's a disgrace, you being a policeman.'

'Pilar, what's happened? What's the matter?'

Hilario had got up and was rinsing his hands under the tap, not looking at his house helper.

'I'm getting married,' she announced.

Cámara almost dropped his mug.

'Well, that's wonderful,' he coughed. 'Congratulations. Who's the lucky man? Do we know him?'

'No,' she said firmly. 'And I don't ever want him to meet anyone from this house of sin.'

'I see.'

Hilario moved away from the sink and made to step out of the kitchen. Pilar was barring his way.

'You'll have to let me pass if you want me to get your money,' he said.

Pilar looked shocked, as though he'd insulted her, then finally stepped to the side to let him through. She watched him as he walked down the corridor. Cámara thought he could see tears welling up in her eyes.

'Do you want to sit down?'

She appeared not to have heard.

'Pilar?'

'No, I'm all right,' she snapped, lifting a handkerchief to her face. She blew her nose like a trumpet, then sniffed.

Cámara stood up as Hilario came back into the room with an envelope, which he gave to her without a word.

She looked at him expectantly.

'Was there anything else?' Hilario asked.

She raised the handkerchief to her face again.

'Look, this is all very sudden,' Cámara said. 'Does it have to be immediate, like this? Couldn't you stay on for a few days at least? Hilario's not very well.'

'Oh, he's fine,' she said. 'Nothing wrong with him. Only in his soul. May God pity him. I gave up praying for him long ago.'

There was a pause, as though she expected one of them

to say something, but there was nothing to add.

She uttered a disgusted 'humph' as she tossed her keys on to the kitchen table and turned to go.

'¡*Adiós!*' she said sharply. And she marched down the corridor.

'Bye,' Cámara said.

The whole building shook as she slammed the front door shut behind her.

Hilario poured himself some more coffee and sat back down at the table with something approaching a grin on his face. Cámara glanced at the pile of dishes again.

'What *did* happen last night?' he said. 'You invited her to stay for dinner, didn't you?'

Hilario shrugged

'I was feeling lonely.'

'You've been smoking on your own again, you mean.'

'No, certainly not. There was plenty of food, it didn't look as though you were coming back any time soon, so I merely suggested she joined me.'

'And you had a few drinks together?'

'A few.'

'And then what?'

'What?'

'Look, the woman who's been looking after you since the beginning of time has very suddenly just stormed out on us. Something must have happened.'

Cámara stopped, a look of horror on his face.

'No,' he said. 'You didn't. I can't believe it. You didn't—'

'She only had a couple of bites.'

'You fed her marihuana cake!'

'It came out very well this time. There's some left. Do you want to try?'

Cámara sat down next to his grandfather, the strength seeming to ebb from him.

'I don't believe it.'

Hilario was chuckling.

'How did she react?'

The chuckling turned into laughter.

'You're still high, aren't you. What happened? How did she react?'

'She loved it,' Hilario managed to splutter. 'She asked for more.'

'You said she only had a couple of bites.'

'All right, a couple of slices, then.'

'Pilar ate two slices of *your* marihuana cake! I'm amazed she could even stand this morning.'

'Oh, she was full of beans last night. Really began to relax.'

Cámara gave his grandfather a look. Hilario was in his mid-eighties; Pilar was in her late fifties.

'Oh, no,' he said. 'Oh, no.'

'Oh, yes.'

'No no no no no. You're not telling me you—'

'No, of course I didn't,' Hilario said. 'I've got some scruples you know.'

'So what, then?'

'It was her. Started saying she was feeling hot, despite the window being open. And starts loosening her blouse, unbuttoning it, unfastening the belt round her skirt.'

'No no no no no.'

'And then she pounced.'

'She pounced?'

'Threw herself on me. Declared that she'd always loved and wanted me, and that it was so hard working all these years in the flat, hoping that one day I might take notice of her.'

'Was it just marihuana you put in the cake?'

'And that she never received so much as a kind word from me.'

'Well, that's true.'

'And she had to have me.'

Cámara looked at him.

'So what did you do?'

'I did what any man of honour would do.'

'Which is?'

'I called a taxi and sent her home.'

'That's not like you. Giving up a chance like that.'

'We're talking about Pilar, for God's sake.'

'Still, you are over eighty, you know. Might not get any more offers.'

'Shut up.'

Cámara paused, then sighed.

'I just can't believe she's gone.'

Yago's phone was diverting to voicemail. Cámara left a message asking him to call back.

Finding a used padded envelope, he placed the samples he'd picked up from the warehouse at Pozoblanco inside. Then he cut out a sheet of paper, stuck it over the front with sticky tape, and wrote Maragall's name and home address on it. On a second sheet he wrote where the samples had come from, and the date, and signed it. Placing the note inside the envelope as well, he stuck it closed with more tape and left it on the side. He'd go out later and get a stamp to send it.

He didn't mention Reza, or the million's worth of saffron that had blown out of the warehouse, scattering over the fields. Reza was hurt, which meant he would probably stay at Pozoblanco until the very end of his visa. And that suited Cámara well. Reza had tried to kill him twice now, and was obviously involved in the saffron scam. But there was still nothing to link him definitively to Mirella's murder. Only Estrella had talked of a Moroccan new on the drug scene. Was that Reza, posing as a Moroccan again? Had Reza fuelled Mirella's drug habit? Then raped and killed her?

After a shower, Hilario went for a lie-down on the bed.

'All this excitement.'

So Pilar was gone. It would take a while to get used to. But there was another question to think about now. Who would look after Hilario? Yes, he was an independent-minded and relatively fit eighty-four-year-old. But living on his own, with no one coming in to check up on him, help him with the housework?

Perhaps they could find someone else. But no sooner had the thought formed itself than Cámara knew it could never happen. Who else could put up with Hilario in the way Pilar had? He could see a stream of women coming into the flat, none of them staying for more than a month, then leaving in a rage, before a new one could could be found and it started again.

What could he do? Leave him on his own? Not really. Put him in a home? Forget it. Stay in Albacete himself to look after him? He'd rather die.

A solution will present itself, he thought as he picked up the envelope and walked to the door.

His phone gurgled at him as he went to open the door. It was Eduardo García, the historian.

'Can you meet? This morning? It's quite urgent.'

TWENTY-SEVEN

Cámara dropped off the samples for Maragall at the yellow postbox at the end of the road and started walking towards the city centre. The winds of the night before hadn't properly abated, and he looked up into the sky, half-expecting to see saffron stigmas floating in the air.

He thought about giving Alicia a quick call, to see how she was, to tell her about Pilar, about Hilario, about the saffron scam, the FBI investigation and Reza Amini the Iranian pretending to be a Moroccan. There was material there for an article, more than enough, and he would have called her – he really would have – if it hadn't been for the noise in the street. Just as he stepped out the city taxi drivers decided to stage a protest, driving in convoy through the streets, blaring their horns to demonstrate against a recent spate of attacks by late-night passengers. Beside him other pedestrians were walking with their hands over their ears against the noise, while police motorcycle escorts flashed blue lights in front and behind the taxi cavalcade, herding them along.

'No more violence against taxi drivers!'

'We have a right to make a living too!'

If this were taking place in Valencia, Cámara thought, someone would be setting off some firecrackers about now as well, adding a few extra decibels to help get the point across.

He smiled to himself. Valencia. He almost missed the place.

And the phone stayed in his pocket, unused.

Besides, the saffron thing had been a sideline, a diversion. What he was really interested in, what made him stay, apart from Hilario's health, was the Mirella Faro case. And on that he'd made little progress. Should he try and talk to Inspector Jiménez? He wouldn't react too well to another homicide policeman trying to barge in on his murder.

Too many questions unanswered, too many unknowns. Tying things up, making the world neat again – he knew it was one of the urges that drove him, that made him a policeman. And it was a never-ending task: messiness, chaos, came at you again and again, like a barking dog in the night. And he'd pushed against that for as long as he could remember – tidying up, trying to clean and reorder, force things into place, unravel the knots, bring a semblance of meaning to a universe that forced the questions on you: Why her? Why him? Why us? Why me?

But to ask 'why' implied a belief that some kind of 'because' existed in the first place. And he'd always needed that – he'd needed to believe in a reason, a cause, something he could point to, something he could blame, and hopefully fix.

Yet was it any more than that? A need, an emotional need?

It made so many things easier to cope with to believe in 'something' – even if it was just a target for his anger and frustration. From the first moment that he'd woken to the world, from the moment he'd discovered his sister's rotting body on the rubbish tip, he'd needed to believe that something was responsible. First it was the murderer himself – but no one had ever been found guilty. Then it was his parents in some way, and their own rapid exit from life following Concha's murder. Later it became a collection of people and ill-focused concepts: Hilario, Albacete, Destiny, the world itself. All of them potentially guilty and responsible for his mess, his fucked-up life.

And so he'd gone about fixing it, mending what was broken: joining the police and working his way as quickly as possible to *Homicidios*. It was what he'd always wanted to do – where he was 'destined' to be.

Then the murder cases came, and he started having some success – big investigations, his name even in the newspapers – although not always for the right reasons. But he was becoming a name at the Valencia Jefatura – he could tell by the number of enemies he seemed to develop of a sudden.

It felt good for a while – he was fulfilling an ambition, he was doing what he'd dreamt of, what he was meant to be doing. And he thought of himself as a policeman – that that was his true identity, that he was realising himself in some profound way, although he wasn't entirely sure what the phrase exactly meant. He brought healing to a torn, bleeding world. He couldn't stop a murder taking place, but he could help clean up afterwards and perhaps – yes, definitely – in some cases prevent more killings taking place by arresting a murderer before he could reach his next victim.

And he was kicking against whatever it was that brought pain and fear. The chaos. It was as if he believed in it like a force of nature – it was there, a kind of evil. It had touched his own life and it circled through the world, its fingers reaching out to cast blackened spells. It was his job to slow it down, to restrict and restrain it, to slap it round the face, to chain it down, to curtail it. Wasn't that what he was doing every time he apprehended someone, every time he brought them in for questioning, interrogated them, brought charges, sent them to jail?

They were individuals, yet somewhere in his mind they were merely actors, puppets of the destructive force he struggled against every day – the cause, the void.

Now, though, there was a change in him. He couldn't see it clearly yet – it was more a sense, a feeling – but it was there. For the first time he was becoming aware of this belief in himself. Before, it had simply been how he thought, how he saw things, and so it had been all but invisible.

So what had happened? Did he not need that belief any more?

La pera dura con el tiempo madura. A hard pear ripens with time.

For the first time in his life he could almost grasp the concept – emotionally, not just intellectually – of a world where cause and meaning did not exist, or if they did were beyond ordinary understanding: a world that did not provide reasons for his or anyone else's suffering.

The truth is only ever what you perceive it to be.

For some reason he could hear Hilario's voice inside his head, as though he'd been listening in on his thoughts.

Yes, that was probably what he would say. He wondered how much longer he'd have his grandfather around to talk to. Perhaps he'd never really listened to him. Not properly.

Eduardo García had a pile of papers next to him on the table at the bar where they'd arranged to meet. Cámara sat down next to him, ordering a *café solo* from the waiter. García had already started on a *café con leche*.

'Bring me another one as well,' he called out to the disappearing waiter.

'Caffeine hit?' asked Cámara.

'We've got a lot on – lots of things to sort out and finalise.'

Cámara shuffled in his chair, making himself more comfortable.

'So what's up? What's so urgent?'

García patted the papers on the table.

'We've got the green light at last. The regional administration has agreed and we can go ahead with the dig at the cemetery. We're starting tomorrow morning.'

'Yes, I saw the tents up.'

'We've been set up for a few days now, waiting for the final word.'

'What's the rush?'

'The opposition right-wing party are against it – say we shouldn't be digging up the past, that the Civil War is over, we need to move on, that kind of thing. And that we shouldn't be spending our money on things like this.'

'So?'

'They're planning on taking this to the regional supreme court, trying to get it stopped. So we have to move fast before we get some kind of injunction on us.'

'I see.'

The waiter brought their coffees. Cámara took a sip.

'And you needed to see me because of this?'

'We have to get the families' permission to dig up their relatives. It's a formality. I know you said you were happy for this to go ahead, but we really need someone – either you or your grandfather – to actually sign the paperwork. I tried calling your home number a couple of times, but there was no reply.'

'It doesn't matter,' Cámara said. 'Here, just tell me where.'

García gave him a pen and passed over the papers one by one, signalling where the signatures were required on each one.

'What will happen to the body?' Cámara asked. 'Assuming you find it.'

'There has to be an identification first. That's where a DNA sample would be useful. And there will be a forensic examination to formalise cause of death.'

'And then you hand the body over to us?'

'These aren't normal cases. We understand that. If you want to be given the remains and hold a private burial service – that's what some people opt for. Others – most people, in fact – are happy for a collective ceremony to be held for all the individuals found in the mass grave. The decomposition has reached such an advanced stage, you see, and it's not always possible to separate one body from another. We were thinking of some kind of memorial, perhaps a plaque in the park.'

'I see.'

'I'm sorry to be so frank like this.'

'It's all right. I mean, Maximiliano was – is – a relative of mine. But I never met him – he died a couple of decades before I was even born.'

'It might be harder for your grandfather.'

Cámara shrugged.

'Perhaps.'

'You don't have to decide now. With these papers – and the others I've got from the other families – we can get started on the dig. In the meantime you can be thinking about how you might want to proceed afterwards. There's a plan to create a special park commemorating everyone who was a victim of the reprisals.'

'There was something I wanted to ask you,' Cámara said. García leaned an elbow on the table, anxious to get away with his signed papers.

'Of course.'

'How much do you know about Maximiliano? About how he was discovered and imprisoned? My grandfather said he was a *topo* for a few years, living in secret inside their home.'

'Many papers have been destroyed,' García said. 'But for some of the victims we can piece together an idea of what happened. Thankfully, Maximiliano is one of those cases.'

'My grandfather said something about him being betrayed.'

'Maximiliano went into hiding right at the end of the war,' García said.

'That's right.'

'I assume he had nowhere else to go. The city was surrounded.'

'But someone else must have known he was at home? From what Hilario said, the soldiers simply walked in and took him away, as though they'd known all along.'

'From what we've learned, it seems they were tipped off,' García said.

'Who by?'

'Another *topo* in the city was discovered just a couple of days before Maximiliano. He was tortured and from what we can gather he began to talk. The authorities suspected other Republican supporters were hidden away in the city, and they wanted to find them all. It was all part of Franco's plan to eradicate the "other" Spain, the one he'd beaten in the battlefield. Now he wanted to make sure he'd rooted them all out from their hiding places.'

García picked up the papers and tucked them under his arm.

'So yes, we think Maximiliano was given away by this other *topo*. He must have known that Maximiliano was hiding at home as well. Perhaps they told each other before going into hiding, at the end of the war, before Franco's troops marched in. I'm not sure.'

'But who was it? Who told them where to find my great-grandfather?'

'A communist called Francisco Faro Cordero. He was an administrator in the Republican government here in Albacete – just a young man at the time. But for giving names his death sentence was commuted to life. Then in the fifties he was released under one of the amnesty plans.'

'What happened to him?'

'He moved to a village not far from here. Pozoblanco. Just a small place. Started growing saffron. Became mayor. His son's mayor there now. Paco Faro Oscuro. Odd fellow – runs the place like a collective, they say. Funny – your grandfather asked me about this when I first spoke to him.'

But Cámara wasn't listening. He was already out the door and running down the street.

TWENTY-EIGHT

The flat was ten minutes away; he couldn't lose any time. Yet already, the moment he opened the front door and ran up the staircase, he could sense that Hilario had gone.

He checked every room – the kitchen, the bathroom, the living room – but Hilario was nowhere to be seen. Perhaps he'd popped out for a stroll. Yes. Or perhaps instead he was out seeking revenge for his father's murder years before – a murder he had tried and failed to stop.

He started pulling open the drawers, two at a time. Where had Alicia found the Luger? The gun had been here all those years and yet he'd never discovered it himself. Had Hilario hidden it better when Cámara was a young boy living here with him? Perhaps he'd taken it out of its hiding place and put it somewhere more immediately accessible. Did he have it on him now? Was he about to use it again?

Cámara pulled out every drawer he could see, frantically searching through the papers and random household goods for any sight of the old pistol. A dusty pack of cards, Hilario's birth certificate, old telephone bills, letters from Eduardo García about the excavation work planned at the cemetery . . . but no gun. It had gone.

If Pilar were here he could ask her. Wasn't it strange that she should have left them only the day before? She had been with them for years. Why did Hilario do that? Had he really got her stoned? Had she then made a pass at him? Why now?

Hilario had made the story up, he thought. He'd wanted her gone, out of the way. He'd been planning this for some time. Remove Pilar, and then he could go ahead with whatever it was he had in mind.

Which was what, exactly? Cámara couldn't say. All he knew was that his grandfather was somewhere in Albacete with a loaded gun on him, bearing a grudge that had dogged him for decades.

Paco Faro Oscuro's father had betrayed Hilario's; it was Francisco Faro Cordero who had told the Francoist authorities about Maximiliano's hideaway in his flat. And while Maximiliano had ended up getting shot, Francisco Faro Cordero had escaped death and had gone on to become a saffron farmer in Pozoblanco. And now his son, Paco, was running the village like a cult leader, heading an international saffron mafia from this unprepossessing village in La Mancha.

Hilario hadn't known any of this. He could only have guessed that someone had betrayed his father. Then Eduardo García had shown up, talking of digging up Maximiliano's remains, and telling the story of how he had been arrested.

Only then, over sixty years after the event, did Hilario find out the truth about what had happened. Had he been hiding that Luger all those years for this? Had he been secretly waiting for a chance to avenge his father's death?

Was that what Mirella's murder had been about? The thought remained in the back of Cámara's mind, only partially formed. He couldn't bring himself to think of his grandfather as a raper and killer of a fifteen-year-old girl.

Yet he had to find him, urgently. First Pilar's dismissal, now his disappearance, almost certainly with the Luger. Something was afoot and Cámara had to reach him as quickly as possible. Otherwise he feared the worst.

A settling of scores. The phrase passed insistently through his mind as he dashed down the stairs again and out into the street. Juan Manuel Heredia had used the phrase when he'd gone to see him in jail. And someone else recently, although he couldn't remember who. That's what this was about, though, surely. Years later, there was a settling of scores from way back in the Civil War period. Perhaps the people who criticised the opening up of these old mass graves were right – the country wasn't ready for it; the wounds hadn't healed; all they were doing was stirring up bad blood. Hilario had a right to know how and why his father had died. But was it really such a good idea if it led to this?

Cámara tapped out a number on his phone and a police operator answered.

Put out an alert – an armed man is out somewhere on the streets of Albacete, current location unknown. He may be heading to the village of Pozoblanco. Inform all units. He's dangerous. Yes, dangerous, even though he's over eighty years old.

The weight in his voice overrode the doubts in the operator's mind. You didn't come across that many armed and dangerous OAPs. But the caller on the other end of the phone appeared to have some experience and seemed to know what he was talking about. He might even be a policeman himself, from the way he talked.

As soon as he was confident that the message had been received, Cámara ended the call and dialled another number.

'Jiménez speaking,' came a leaden voice.

'It's Cámara. I've got something for you.'

Jiménez listened as Cámara explained about his grandfather, the Luger, and the Civil War connection with Faro Oscuro. Something appeared to click inside the inspector as Cámara spoke. Yes, this was something he could understand, and there was an urgency to it. The adrenalin was starting to move, the rush, the moment all desk-bound policemen are always hoping will arrive.

'Tell Yago,' Cámara said before Jiménez could put down the phone.

'He left,' Jiménez said. 'Twenty minutes ago.'

'Where's he gone?'

'Dunno. He was in a hurry. Got a call when we were in a meeting and just left.'

'Did he say anything?'

'Something about his wedding ring. Not sure. He was mumbling. Said someone had found his wedding ring, I think.'

The line went dead.

Cámara stood still on the pavement. Cars cruised by, elderly women brushed past, dragging their shopping trolleys behind them, a man walking his dog smiled as he stopped and then crossed the road.

An ordinary street scene, a city going about its business. Yet Cámara's world had just stopped, as though some beating pulse that pushed it along had seized up and frozen.

Who else had recently talked to him of a settling of scores?

It was an easy way to explain away a murder, as Heredia had said.

Was that why Hilario had asked about the wedding ring?

And those pills, the ones that made you lose weight rapidly . . .

Slowly he lifted his hands to his face, covered his eyes, and then dragged his fingers down over his cheeks, smoothing out the skin and drawing it tight.

He had been stupid and blind. Blinded by his own grief, his own beliefs.

But now he knew. And more importantly, he had a very good idea of where he would find Hilario.

He had to run, though, as quickly as he could. He'd already lost a lot of time.

The narrow pavements were too busy with other people, so he hopped out on to the street and began skipping in and out of the cars. There was a furious honk as he narrowly missed the wheels of a bus, but he was quickly round a corner and almost out of earshot before the driver could start shouting abuse.

Down side streets where there were fewer cars, the doorways and shop windows flashing past in a blur.

A dead end: the road had been cut off for re-tarmacking. Only a tiny pathway had been left for pedestrians and it was now packed with a group of small schoolchildren holding hands as they walked and giggled their way on an outing with their teachers.

Cámara vaulted the barricade and leapt over the patch of hot fresh asphalt.

'Hey!'

'You can't do that!'

The roadworkers were excited out of their normal lethargy by the sight of him sailing through the air in front of them.

'What the hell's going on?'

Out and away from the tight, crowded streets and on to

a wider avenue leading away from the city centre and towards the industrial quarter. Already he could see the warehouses in the distance, and next to them, on the left, a patch of ground, still empty of buildings after all these years.

He had to cross a busy thoroughfare to get to it. The traffic was heavy at that time of day but he couldn't wait for the lights to change in his favour. Holding out his hands he waved for the cars and lorries to stop as he stepped out. There was a screeching of tyres and a bump as one car crunched into the back of another, not reacting in time to the sudden halting of the flow. Another car almost caught his hand with the wing mirror as it swept past him, but Cámara just managed to pull his arm away in time.

No insult was too good for the idiot who had leapt in front of them and almost caused a serious accident. But Cámara's mind was elsewhere – on the wasteland a few more yards ahead. The weeds and crumbling wall meant he still couldn't see inside, but with one more leap he could make it.

If he was right Hilario would be there, Luger in hand. Cámara just hoped he could get there before Hilario's target showed up as well, and stop another murder from taking place.

A settling of scores. He should have seen it himself before.

TWENTY-NINE

Yago was standing by the rubbish container, his arms hanging by his sides, his head lowered, but his eyes fixed ahead, flashing with an animal keenness at the threat now facing him. Five yards in front, with his back to Cámara, stood Hilario, his right arm outstretched with the Luger clutched in his hand.

Cámara moved as quickly and as silently as he could. If he surprised his grandfather he might cause him to pull the trigger. He had to get to him before it was too late.

He dropped down and started scampering through the tall weeds. Hilario was talking, saying something to Yago, but Cámara couldn't hear. As he drew closer, though, he could see that Hilario's arm was beginning to shake – he was incapable of holding the gun still in his condition. Any shot would almost certainly miss its target.

Which Yago would notice and be aware of.

Perhaps distracting Hilario might be the best thing to do.

In that gap he might just be able to get to him before Yago did.

There was a crackle as his foot pressed down on a tin can half-buried in the dirt. He looked up, silently cursing. Yago had heard it too. Cámara dropped down further. Had he been spotted? Spying through the weeds he could see Yago's eyes were darting between the elderly man with the gun in front of him and the stretches of wasteland surrounding them, checking to see if anyone else were there.

Hilario twigged that something was up as well. For a moment his head turned to the side, as though wondering what Yago was looking at.

Yago didn't waste his chance. Seeing that the old man's attention had been distracted, he broke into a sprint and charged headlong at Hilario. At that same moment, from down in the weeds, Cámara too leapt up and ran towards the two men.

CRACK!

Over half a century since it had last fired, the Luger went off. Cámara was still a few paces away, but he saw Yago and Hilario fall to the floor as they grappled with one another, disappearing into the dead grass and broken debris.

In a heartbeat Cámara was there as well, reaching down Yago's face and thrusting his fingers into the man's eye sockets to pull him away. There was a scream as Yago's vision left him and he felt a kick in the side as Cámara pushed him away from Hilario. His grandfather.

Hilario looked pale and dazed, but there was a smile in his eyes as he saw his grandson leaning over him.

'Oh, it's you,' he panted. 'What a pleasant surprise.'

Cámara quickly checked for bleeding.

'I'm fine, a bit winded, that's all.'

'Where's the gun? Where's the Luger?'

'I found a wedding ring down here, after Concha was killed. Those policemen are useless.'

Cámara looked at him.

'Mirella. You mean Mirella? Faro Oscuro's granddaughter?'

'Yes. He said it was his. Said he lost it.'

'The gun!'

Hilario looked him hard in the eye.

'That's how I knew it was him. Who else would it have been?'

'Where is it?'

But the smile had turned to fear.

'It's too late.'

Cámara swivelled on his heel. Yago had managed to pick himself up and, staggering, was pointing the Luger in his direction. Blood was pouring from his left eye, but his right eye, the one he needed to shoot with, could see clearly.

Cámara looked at him squarely. For an instant they were two young boys again, cutting their way through the weeds and waste with sticks, chatting, singing, playing and hoping . . . until they had reached this spot, and childhood had been brought to a grubby, naked end. They had become almost like brothers in that instant, joined by an experience so dark and intense that it welded their emotions together.

'I never liked you.'

But Cámara wasn't listening. Without thinking he dived to the side to draw Yago's fire away from Hilario.

CRACK!

Yago fired, the gun recoiling in his hand.

And in the split second before he could pull the trigger again, Cámara was on him, tackling him at waist height and pulling him to the ground. Yago smashed the butt of the gun down on to the side of Cámara's head, but a bull-like force had entered him and he barely felt the metal pushing down and tearing into his scalp. Reaching up he ripped at Yago's ear, catching the side of his face with his forehead as Yago lifted his hands up in pain.

Cámara stood up, blood beginning to dribble through his hair and down his face. Hilario was still on the ground behind him. He held up a hand and signalled with his thumb that he was all right.

Yago was curled up in a ball by Cámara's feet. Cámara thought about landing a last kick in the man's side, but held back. His breathing was getting heavier and heavier as his chest began to tighten.

From the ground, Yago glanced up. The Luger was still in his hand. Shaking, he lifted it as high as he could for a final shot. Cámara watched as his finger pressed against the trigger, the barrel pointing directly at his chest.

There was a click, but nothing happened. Yago tried again, but the gun refused to go off. It had jammed.

Weakness from the head wound was overcoming Cámara. He was incapable of fighting any more.

Taking a step, he staggered closer towards Yago, looked down into his good eye and then slumped down, crushing the thinner man with the weight of his body.

It was finished.

THIRTY

A Couple of Days Later

He'd seen dead bodies before – plenty of them. But never like this.

Slowly, for fear of breaking them, the bones were uncovered, exposed and finally liberated from the earth.

'You think it's him?'

'A DNA test will tell us for sure. We'll take a sample from you then do the procedure, just to be a hundred per cent.'

Eduardo García put his hands on his hips and looked over at the body.

'But for my money, that's Maximiliano.'

Cámara stepped down into the pit, dirt pushing into the creases of his shoes, blood pulsing underneath the scabs on his scalp. The doctors had had to shave off some of his hair to apply a couple of stitches, but apart from the oddness of his appearance, and a few bruises, he'd come out of the fight better than he'd expected. Or at least he'd suffered nothing that half a bottle of brandy couldn't sort out.

He was sober now, however, very much so, skidding down the side of the hole and pacing towards the dead man. The technicians moved slowly out of the way to let him past. It went against protocol to let family members in while they were in the middle of a dig. But they knew he was a policeman, a murder investigator; they could trust him.

The bones were practically clean by now, the soil brushed away. And while the browning bones were partially rotten and crushed from having spent so much time in the earth, the form and shape of his great-grandfather was visible. Round glasses, their frames almost rusted away, lay broken over the lower section of what had been his face. The jawbone lay open and had fallen to one side, giving him a wild, almost hysterical laugh. He tried to imagine the eyes that had once rolled and shone from the empty sockets. Small clods of chocolate-brown mud, still waiting to be cleaned away, had taken their place.

And he wished he could reach out and let him know in some way. We've found you – you'll be all right now. We'll do this properly, at last.

Just a collection of broken bones. Maximiliano had gone years before. Neither a photo nor his mortal remains could bring him closer to him.

For that, he had to look inside himself. If Maximiliano was to be found anywhere, it was there.

THIRTY-ONE

Jiménez was waiting for him outside the cemetery with a dark-haired woman.

'This is Inspector Silvestre,' he said sternly. 'From Madrid.'

The woman held out her arm and shook Cámara's hand.

'Internal Affairs.'

Cámara smiled; he could have guessed.

They crossed the street and headed towards a café on the corner. It was cold, the first taste of winter in the air, and so they ignored the tables on the pavement and dived into the relative shelter inside. Cámara ordered three *cafés con leche* and a shot of Torres 10 brandy for himself on the side.

'Faro Oscuro's handed himself in,' Jiménez said. Still head of the local murder squad, he had temporarily been asked to cover Yago's old job in charge of the whole of the investigative police force until they could find a permanent replacement. There was something beaten, if not quite broken, about him: every policeman in the city – as in the rest of the country – was in a state of shock over what had happened.

'Is he talking?'

'Oh, yes,' Jiménez said. 'He may have tried avoiding capture at first, but there was nowhere he could go. Drove himself to the Jefatura last night. I've just come from seeing him now.'

He rubbed his eyes and took a slurp of coffee as though to emphasise his lack of sleep.

'And the link with . . . with Yago?'

'As you said, it's there. Faro Oscuro says he was paying Yago off – probably to keep quiet about the saffron scam. We're waiting for the bank to send in details of his accounts so we can confirm, but there may be other accounts with different banks, so it will take some time.'

Methodical and slow, even now when it came to investigating his own superior.

'What about the shooting?' Cámara asked. 'Has he mentioned that?'

Jiménez scrunched up his nose, wringing his paw-like hands together. It pained him to say this.

'Yago . . .' He cleared his throat. 'Yago asked Faro Oscuro to get rid of you. As a favour. Said you were dangerous and could blow the whole thing.'

The phrase Yago had used at their meeting at the cemetery trickled back into his mind: 'You should be dead.' He had really meant it.

'Which is why he sent me to Pozoblanco,' Cámara said. 'Not to see what I could find out – he knew it all already. He wanted to have me disappeared. So what happened? Why did they botch it up?'

'You showed up with someone else – a woman,' Jiménez

248

said. 'They weren't expecting that. Some journalist from a national newspaper. They checked her out while you were still in the village. She was a real journalist, not a fake one like you. So they couldn't just kill you. That's what Faro Oscuro said. Said it was too dangerous. They'd create more danger for themselves.'

'But they still tried to kill us.'

Jiménez shuffled in his seat. Beside him, Inspector Silvestre listened intently.

'Faro Oscuro told us he called Yago as you were leaving. He was angry you were still alive, so he ordered – that was the word Faro Oscuro used – ordered to have you killed.'

'So that's when they tried to shoot us in the car.'

'That's right.'

'Which Reza the Iranian did.'

'Reza, Ahmed. Whatever his real name is.'

'Any sign of him?'

Jiménez shook his head.

'None. Vanished. Probably out of the country by now. We've issued an international warrant. People in the village want to find him as well – they're really pissed off. Say masses of saffron has gone missing. That's their livelihood. They reckon Ahmed ran off with it.'

Cámara kept a straight face. There was no point mentioning his encounter with Reza now. It would come out eventually. Or not.

He knocked back his brandy and took a sip of the coffee. It was cooling now, but it seemed to burn his mouth as it mixed with the alcohol lingering on his tongue. Lifting out his packet of Ducados, he offered them cigarettes: Jiménez took one; Silvestre declined with a smile.

'We're looking at the others,' Jiménez said, blowing out

smoke. 'That list you gave us of the killings with a similar MO.'

Cámara nodded.

'They fit. And Yago could have done them. He was either in the city at the time or near enough to get there and back without anyone missing him. Guadalajara is a short drive from Madrid.'

'And all of them either unsolved or attributed to men who could quite easily be set up,' Silvestre said.

'Drug dealers, a homeless guy, Gypsies.'

'A settling of scores,' Cámara mumbled.

'What's that?'

'Nothing.'

'It's going to take time,' Jiménez said. Cámara smiled: it was the inspector's favourite phrase. 'We'll have to go through the records pertaining to those cases, bring in other units. It's a wide net.'

'But it will be done,' Silvestre butted in. 'And done thoroughly. This is the most serious case we've had for decades. The Ministry has given it top priority. The *Policía Nacional* is one of the most respected institutions in this country. We can't have that image spoiled by one rotten egg.'

'And I think it is just one egg in this case,' Cámara said. 'It was just Yago. No one else. At least as far as these cases are concerned.'

Silvestre leaned back in her chair.

'I'm glad you think so. I'm of the same opinion. You knew him, though. From back when you were children. Your comments will count for a lot in this.'

'We hadn't seen each other for years. Not since academy.'

'Nonetheless, you shared a harrowing experience when you were boys together.'

'How is he?' Cámara asked suddenly. Anything to avoid the inevitable questions about why, about the past, about the 'psychological scars', or whatever the lingo was at the moment.

'You mean Yago?' Silvestre asked, surprised.

Cámara nodded.

'He might not get full sight in his left eye again, but we're expecting the all-clear from the doctors later today,' Jiménez said. 'We'll start the interrogation straight away.'

'You doing that?'

'I'll be there,' Jiménez said. 'It's a murder inquiry, plain and simple.'

The butt of his cigarette burnt brightly as he sucked hard and then blew smoke out through his nostrils.

'This is a complex case,' Silvestre said, correcting Jiménez gently. 'There's the murder to investigate. Thanks to what you've given us I think there's a substantial advance on the Mirella Faro case. There's no doubt in anyone's mind about Yago's guilt on that score. The wedding ring places him at the scene of the crime.'

'The pills,' Cámara said. 'Said he was losing weight very quickly.'

'It was clever of you to find that. Can't think how it got missed.'

She threw a glance at Jiménez, who ignored her. The *Policía Científica* was another department. He might be temporarily in charge of the investigative police, but he wasn't taking the fall for cock-ups by the crime scene lot.

'Years of experience,' Cámara said. And he thought he might get away with it. Just. OK, so it was Hilario's experience he was really thinking about, but they didn't need to know that. *En boca cerrada no entran moscas*. Flies can't enter a closed mouth.

Silvestre threw him a quizzical glance, as though he might be making fun of her, then continued.

'DNA testing can confirm the rest. We're scouring Yago's home, office, car. Then there's the semen traces found on Mirella's body. If it matches . . .'

'All we need is a hair or something from Mirella and we've got him,' Jiménez said, almost spitting out the words.

'His wife?'

Silvestre looked at Jiménez, as though expecting him to answer.

'With relatives,' she said when Jiménez refused to speak.

'I've spoken to her once,' Jiménez burst out. 'We'll be getting her down to the Jefatura again in the next few days, mark my words.'

'I don't think there's any—'

'No. But there'll be something. Some detail that will help bring that cunt down. A dinner date he was late for, a late call-out he then couldn't explain properly. I don't fucking know. But there'll be something.'

They sat in awkward silence for a moment. Jiménez was right to be angry, but for some reason Cámara couldn't share his feelings. It was too close to him. Mirella – Concha – Maximiliano. There was a chain of death in his life, one that seemed to wrap itself around him and weigh him down, like a heavy, wet, rotting blanket. And yet now, for the first time in his life, he felt capable of casting it off, discarding it and leaving it here in Albacete for good.

It was a time for cleaning, patching up the rips and tears as he always tried to do. But not for rage. Not any more. That had passed.

Concha. He could barely remember her any more. Except, perhaps, for a smell he associated with her – something woody, like pine, and a sweet waxy scent that perhaps came from some perfume or a candle. He wasn't sure. It was the smell of her room. He always caught it when he walked past, in the weeks and months after her disappearance. Someone had spoken of clearing her things out. But no one had ever got round to it. And then other things had started to happen – his mother's breakdown, the pills, the drink, the loneliness. And Hilario, picking him up and taking him with him. At that moment he'd hated him, of course. But then he was the only one it made sense to hate – back then, at least.

Hate. It felt like such a distant emotion now, as though he were seeing it through an inverted telescope – reduced in size and importance.

He wondered about ordering another brandy, but the barman was looking in the opposite direction, catching the highlights from a recent football match on the TV news.

'They'll be dragging the psychologists into it,' Jiménez said, flicking his head in Silvestre's direction.

'It's inevitable,' she said. 'Jiménez has already made his feelings clear on this—'

'Waste of fucking time,' Jiménez mumbled.

'—but there's no loose ends with this case. We've got to tick all the boxes.'

Cámara breathed deeply, stifling the groan that jargon like this always provoked in him.

'A team will be coming down from Madrid later this afternoon,' Silvestre said. 'They will be wanting to talk to you.'

Cámara shrugged. Did he have a choice?

'Your . . . your shared history. It will be vital for providing a complete profile.'

'I'm not the one being investigated, right?'

Silvestre looked shocked.

'N-no. Of course not.'

Jiménez grinned cheekily.

'It's all right,' Cámara said, smiling. 'Sure, whatever they need.'

'There may be a link.'

'Course there's a fucking link,' Jiménez said.

'Mirella's murder – and perhaps the others, if they can be proved – stem from some trauma Yago suffered as a boy. I understand he was with you when you found the body of Concha? Your sister?'

'That's right.'

'She was found on the same patch of ground.'

'Thirty-two years ago,' Cámara said. 'They haven't built on it.'

'Yes, well, that will all be covered in your interviews with the psychologists, no doubt.'

'What they need to work out is how a fucking psycho like him got into the police force in the first place,' Jiménez said. 'It's all very well doing the profiling now, coming up with a "narrative" after he's been on his killing spree. What about before? I ask you.'

He threw his hands up.

'We're all upset,' Silvestre said. 'I know that. And if you want some time off—'

'No fucking chance. Time off now? When I've got the biggest case of my career on my hands? No way. I'm seeing this all the way through. And I'll be there when they fucking throw away the key as well.'

But I won't, Cámara thought to himself.

THIRTY-TWO

He'd call Alicia. Soon. They still hadn't spoken. Was he avoiding her? Perhaps. Avoiding her, the situation, everything. It was what he tended to do. But no more. Things had changed. Something in him . . .

It would be good to hear her voice again.

Besides, there was something he had to tell her.

'Is there anything else I need to know about you?'

Hilario's face was grey, his lips thin and dry. A drip dangled from his arm, which looked thinner and weaker than Cámara remembered.

'There's always something else to know about people.'

Of course, Cámara thought with a smile. He could have answered the question for himself.

He pulled up a chair and sat down at his grandfather's side, holding his hand. A nurse came in and checked the amount of fluid left in the drip bag.

'Come and get me when it drops below this line,' he said to Cámara. 'Then we'll change it.'

He left the door open behind him, and the sounds of a hospital ward filtered through. A bunch of flowers had been left on the floor, a gaudy collection of yellows, oranges and pinks.

'Got an admirer?'

'They're from Pilar,' Hilario said.

'I don't believe it.'

'It's true. Check the card if you like.'

'Did she—?'

'No, they were sent. She wasn't going to show her face round here after what happened. No, the beautiful Pilar has left our lives for good, I fear. I asked around – the story about her getting married is true.'

Pilar had been such an integral part of life at the flat that Cámara wondered what things would be like without her, whether he would actually miss her, in fact.

Hilario, he felt certain, hadn't even gone so far as that. Once Pilar had walked out the door life had instantly moved on. It always did for him. No looking back, no wondering what if. Pilar leaving barely registered as a hiccough.

Although there was the question of how he would look after himself. Would he be all right on his own? Some solution had to be found.

'Gerardo was here,' Hilario said.

'My mechanic friend?'

'His dad's a mate of mine. Taught him a few things years back. They've always been a generous lot.'

'Yeah . . .'

'Well, until you filled his prize BMW with bullet holes, that is.'

'He told you that, did he? Couldn't be helped.'

'He's all right. Got over it. Must have, or else why would he have come round?'

'What did he say?'

'If I needed a helping hand, that kind of thing. Everyone seems to have heard about Pilar leaving.'

'We could always find someone to replace her.'

Hilario shrugged.

'Something will come up.'

He grinned.

'You'll be pleased to know,' Cámara said, changing the subject, 'that your name will not be appearing in any police reports.'

'Thank Christ for that.'

Cámara laughed.

'You're the anarchist detective,' he said. 'Invisible to the authorities, silently solving the crimes that have them tied up in knots.'

'It's got a ring to it.'

'So I was the one who found the wedding band, not you.'

'Right. So why didn't you hand it in as evidence?'

'Because of the doubts Yago sowed in my mind about the corruption in the Jefatura. I didn't know who I could trust.'

'OK. But why didn't you realise earlier that it was his wedding ring?'

'Because my attention was being distracted by this saffron scam thing.'

Hilario pursed his lips.

'Maybe. Or you're just fucking stupid.'

'Well, there's that as well.'

'You know your problem?'

'Here we go.'

'You never suspected Yago because he's a policeman. But that's precisely why I had my doubts about him from the start.'

He tapped his finger on his temple.

'You've got to be smart, see? Got to see the prejudices and assumptions that stand in the way of you seeing what's really going on.'

'Hang on, you're just as prejudiced as I am. You're prejudiced against the police.'

'And I was right.'

Cámara groaned.

'You going to start giving me lessons on how to be a detective now?'

'This is just the beginning.'

Hilario grinned, then coughed. There were droplets of blood on the palm of his hand where he covered his mouth.

'We still don't know who killed Concha.'

Hilario looked him in the eye.

'You've come a long way,' he said. 'You're slow, but you've made some progress these last days. I've seen it.'

'What are you talking about?'

'It's loosening its grip on you, bit by bit.'

'What is?'

'The fear, the anger. All this rushing about, wanting and wanting.'

'It's all very well saying, don't be angry. But you never told me how.'

'I've never shown you anything but.'

Hilario turned away.

'Many years ago I made a deliberate decision about how I was going to live my life. When they shot Maximiliano I told myself that nothing was going to crush me or push me off the course that I decided to be on. And I've stayed there. And you know the shit there's been. But you keep on, you just keep on. God knows I've been trying to tell you this for years. And there are times when you've almost got it, but you slipped back, got caught up in your own self-pity.'

He sat up in bed, leaning in towards Cámara and squeezing his hand.

'That's what's changing in you. It's there, in your eyes. They're quicker these days. Perhaps it's Alicia, or maybe it's been coming back here, this case. I don't know. It's probably not important. The point is, you're close to becoming who you really are.'

Cámara smiled.

'Another anarchist, like you?'

'Call it what you like. There are a thousand tyrannies, and the majority of them exist inside ourselves. Free yourself of them and you can call yourself any name you want.'

'Even a detective.'

'Even a detective. But one who solves crimes not for the State, but for a greater good. One who isn't afraid to break the law, even, if it helps him get where he needs to go.'

'Oh, I don't think I have much of a problem with that.'

'See? Some things have managed to rub off, then.'

He closed his eyes and lay back on the bed.

'You should read Ernst Jünger and his ideas about the anarch, a sovereign individual.'

His grip around Cámara's hand relaxed.

'Why did you confront Yago like that? Why didn't you—?

'Get you to do it?'

Hilario's eyes were still closed.

'For example.'

Hilario shrugged.

'Seemed like a good idea at the time.'

'That Luger is ancient. You didn't even know if it would fire.'

'I took my chances. German engineering – the best in the world, they say.'

'You could have been killed.'

'Life, death. What's the difference?'

'I think I know.'

'What? The difference between life and death? Dead people don't move very much, it must be said. And they smell pretty bad.'

'No. I mean why you went off to meet Yago like that.'

'Go on.'

'He tried to have me killed.'

'So?'

'So you were taking revenge, or trying to protect me, or something like that.'

'Is that the best you can do?'

'What I'm trying to say is that for all your talk you really are a sentimental old man who wants to take care of his own.'

His eyes still closed, Hilario took a deep breath, and sighed.

'Might be,' he said at last.

'Thanks.'

'Bugger off.'

The drip bag was almost empty, so Cámara got up to call for the nurse. After a few minutes he appeared with a fresh supply and attached it to Hilario's arm.

'Has he fallen asleep?' he asked Cámara.

'Just dozing, I think.'

'He looks paler. Has he said anything?'

'Said anything?'

'Complained about pains or anything?'

'No. Not to me.'

'I'm going to call the doctor.'

And he rushed out.

Cámara sat down again in the chair, reaching out for Hilario's hand.

'Are you awake?'

He shook his hand slightly.

'Grandpa?'

There was no response. Cámara squeezed harder, standing up to look Hilario in the face.

'Hey!' he called.

Hilario's eyes flickered. After a pause, he opened them; they looked bloodshot, with a creamy film covering them.

'Are you all right? The doctor's coming.'

'I was having a vision,' Hilario said quietly. Cámara raised an eyebrow.

'It's time to leave Albacete. I've been here far too long.'

Cámara tightened his grip around his grandfather's hand, looking pleadingly into his eyes.

'Somewhere new, a different place. I can see water.'

'Water?'

'The sea.'

From the corridor Cámara could hear hurried footsteps; the doctor was on his way.

'Time for new horizons.'

He closed his eyes again.

'Yes.'

ACKNOWLEDGEMENTS

The initial idea for this book came from my friend Toby Follett, who told me about the very real saffron scams that are taking place around the world. I have him to thank for that tip-off, and for setting things in motion.

My contacts in the Valencia *Policía Nacional* were as helpful as always, passing on details about police work – Rafa Campo, Sebastián Roa and Esther Maldonado.

Once again, everyone at Random House has been very supportive. My thanks to Becky Hardie, Clara Farmer, Parisa Ebrahimi, Alison Hennessey, Bethan Jones, Vicki Watson, Roger Bratchell, Jane Kirby and Monique Corless for all their hard work on the Max Cámara series.

Thanks also to my agent, Peter Robinson, for his kindness and support.

Mary Chamberlain performed copy-editing magic, as ever, while Jenny Uglow remains the rock on which these books are built. I can't thank her enough.

Now read the first chapter of the next
Max Cámara book, *Blood Med*.

Out now in hardback and ebook

ONE

The story was moving so slowly it made him want to reach for the remote and hit the fast-forward button. But the more trivial details the correspondents gave, the more general anxiety was produced and the more important the man lying in the hospital at the back of the shot was seen to be. This could go on for hours or even days. He should nip out and have a decent lunch; there would still be no developments by the time he got back.

Nonetheless, there was a curious fascination about it – a moment in history. They would all remember this, years later. He could imagine the future conversations now: Do you remember where you were when you heard?

The King was not dead yet – not quite. But the message had been repeated endlessly by the media: he had had a massive heart attack and was undergoing emergency surgery. And while no one was saying it openly, few expected him to be leaving the hospital anything but 'feet first'.

Cámara had been on the beach with Alicia when the news reached him, enjoying one of the premature summer days that early May sometimes brought, seducing people to expose their winter-white skin for a few hours before a cool wind scattered them home in search of warmer clothes.

No te quites el sayo hasta el cuarenta de mayo, Hilario, his grandfather, had reminded him, trotting out the traditional proverb. Don't cast a clout 'til 40 May. But that was before they heard.

Now the temperature outside barely registered. The King's sudden and life-threatening condition had cast a chill – and semi-paralysis – over the whole country.

Everyone in *Homicidios* was watching the television in the corner of the office as, in faraway Madrid, the authorities struggled with questions of what happened next. The Constitution was clear when it came to a simple death of the monarch. But what did they do if he was left lucid but incapacitated? The doctors might be able to keep him alive, but would he be able to function as head of state? Could the Crown Prince step in? The word 'abdication' had been often repeated in recent years as the King visibly aged, but the idea was viewed as a taboo subject for many: the Spanish monarchy was too fragile an institution to even contemplate such a thing.

Outside, the streets of Valencia were virtually silent, as they were throughout the country. The man who had overseen the building of their nation, who had guided them from dictatorship to democracy, hovered on the edge. And it could not have happened at a worse time. For how much longer could things hold together?

Standing near the back of the office, peering over his colleagues' heads, Cámara watched the pack of journalists gathered at the expensive private clinic in the capital. Occasionally members of the Royal Family – at least those who hadn't been tainted by scandal over the previous years – passed in and out, refusing to comment on developments inside. Through the window of an official car the Queen had been witnessed raising a lace handkerchief to her eye. Was she genuinely upset? No one could say.

The anxious tears among the thousands of Spaniards gathered nearby were more clearly heartfelt. The camera alternated between shots of dignitaries arriving at the hospital, and the worried faces of ordinary people in the street. He was a father figure for them, a central icon around which the country could – albeit tentatively and not without some stress – come together. But Catalonia was already edging towards independence; if the King died it would inevitably fuel the separatist movement there and in other parts of the country – as well as the determination of those bent on keeping Spain united.

Minds were already turning to plans for the funeral. It would be a big and complicated security operation. Police from Valencia and other parts of the country would almost certainly be bussed in to help make up the numbers. Foreign kings, queens, presidents and prime ministers would all attend. The King was a friendly and popular man – the best asset that 'the Spain brand' had, as one television commentator kept repeating. What the State-run media did not mention, however, was the Republican demonstration being held on the other side of Madrid. Cámara had seen references to it on the police intranet. Similar demonstrations were planned for Barcelona and parts of the Basque Country. No one had a clue how many might be showing up. There was talk of tens of thousands.

The door behind them clicked open and someone walked in. Cámara did not need to turn around. Chief Inspector Maldonado, head of the Valencia murder squad, had an unmistakable way of moving that announced his presence, strutting where others walked and pulling on doors as though they were obstacles to his relentless climb where others merely opened and closed them.

'Morning,' he called out, a little too loudly. No one answered, their eyes fixed on the screen.

Cámara could sense it in his blood before he even heard the words.

'Torres and Cámara – I need you in my office now.'

They were back in the old police headquarters – the Jefatura building on Gran Vía de Fernando el Católico; everyone had seen it coming. The sci-fi fantasy building that had been their home for the past few years was impractical and too expensive to maintain. Valencian architect Jaume Montesa might have won international awards for his spectacular white-concrete designs, but the place had not even survived a decade before serious-looking cracks started appearing up the walls. And every time it rained for more than five minutes the cellars got flooded. Torrential downpours were a common problem in the area, but local-boy appeared to have forgotten that when drawing up his plans. Now, if anyone could find any money, they were going to turn it into an art museum, which was what it had been intended for in the first place – never a police station. No one missed it.

But being back at Fernando el Católico meant they were stuck in their cramped office again: two small adjoining rooms on the ground floor for the entire murder squad.

Maldonado had decided it was not enough and had requisitioned another office on the floor above – which he kept for himself.

The three men exchanged no words as they took the lift up. Cámara glanced at their hazy reflection on the scratched steel surface of the doors. Maldonado's jutting jaw and Torres's thick black beard and rounded shoulders were just visible. And himself? He was taller than the other two and looked . . . well, he looked pretty good, he had to say. He was taking care of himself better than he could remember – living with Alicia made certain of that – and it showed.

Along the corridor, Torres edged past and walked into the office directly behind Maldonado. Someone else was there waiting for them.

Maldonado walked to his desk and began shuffling papers with his fingertips, as though moving pawns on a chessboard.

Cámara looked across to the fourth person in the room.

'Oh yes,' Maldonado said as nonchalantly as he could. 'You know Chief Inspector Martín, don't you?'

Torres grunted an acknowledgement. Cámara walked over and shook hands.

'I think I've seen you around.'

'I was on leave for a while,' Cámara said. 'Only been back a few weeks.'

'Interesting time to return.'

'Right, we need to get on,' Maldonado interrupted them. 'Cámara, in case you didn't know, Laura Martín is head of the *unidad de violencia de género*.'

'I *am* the sexual violence squad,' she said. 'It's just me.'

She wore a grey skirt and beige blouse – almost a regulation uniform for a senior female officer – but he noticed multicoloured bracelets hanging loosely on her wrists and a couple of studs in one of her ears. She was two or three years younger than him, he thought, still in her early forties, with hazel green eyes that simultaneously smiled and held back, as though hiding and yet still reflecting some recent horror she had seen. If she had made head of the sexual violence squad – albeit with a team of one – she was ambitious if not necessarily capable; that would become clear later. Her clothes were conventional, but the cut of her red-brown hair and an ironic tone in her voice suggested something more complex.

'OK, listen,' said Maldonado. 'I know it's a difficult day for everyone, but as luck would have it our quiet run has come to an end. Right now. Four months without a murder in a city this big just isn't natural. Anyway, I didn't want to bother the others. Both cases look straightforward . . .'

'We've got two?' Torres said. 'Four months and then two come in at once?'

'One's a clear murder case. The other's a suicide attempt, but we need to check it out. And as you've so gallantly volunteered it's yours.'

Torres rolled his eyes. No one liked a suicide: they left a nasty taste in the mouth. Especially the jumpers. All those mangled body parts. It never got easier, no matter how many you saw. And besides, there was nothing really to investigate. It was all clearing up.

Maldonado passed him the file from his desk.

'Hang on,' Torres said. 'Suicide attempt? What do you mean?'

'Well, he's not dead yet. Not quite.'

'So why am I looking at it?'

'Look, he's in intensive care, in a coma. But by the time

you get your arse in gear he'll probably be dead anyway, right? So we're getting ahead of the game. Just go and check it out. God knows all hell might be breaking loose soon what with the King and everything. Get going now before questions of national security start interfering with ordinary police work.'

Torres shuffled on the spot.

'Why are we involved, then?' he said.

'What?'

'I'm a murder detective. Isn't it clear if it's a suicide attempt?'

'It's in the file. The man's called Diego Oliva. He was broke, about to have his flat repossessed. The usual story. I'm telling you, it's almost certainly suicide . . .'

'An attempt.'

'Whatever. He jumped from a second-storey window – his own. You know what I'm saying. Just go and check it out.'

Torres slipped the file under his arm.

'Well, go on then!' Maldonado barked.

Torres and Cámara exchanged a conspiratorial glance and Torres left the room.

'Right, next case,' Maldonado said as the door closed.

'Cámara, Chief Inspector Martín will be joining you on this.'

Maldonado thrust the file in his direction. Cámara nodded to Laura – they were roughly equals in the police hierarchy, and he was already thinking of her by her first name.

'There's a sexual element to it, then.'

'Looks pretty simple, on the face of things,' Maldonado said. 'Young woman in her home in the Cánovas area. The husband called it in. He's still there.'

He did not need to spell it out; the implication was understood.

'The *científicos* from the forensic medicine department are already there. Go over, get a confession, whatever you have to do, and let's see if we can wrap it up by the end of the day. With a bit of luck you might just do it.'

Laura made to leave.

'One other thing –' Maldonado sat down in his chair and looked over the papers on his desk. 'The woman's American. Young – only in her twenties. The husband's a local. Probably won't complicate things too much, but it's not normal, obviously. At least not for us. More likely to have been shot had she stayed at home, what with all the guns in America. But there you have it.'

He shrugged. Laura walked to the door; Cámara did not move.

'The chief inspector will be along with you in a moment, Martín,' Maldonado said. 'He and I have something to talk about first.'

JASON WEBSTER

A Death In Valencia

MAX CÁMARA BOOK TWO

Detective Max Cámara is under pressure.

A renowned paella chef has been found dead; the town hall is set on demolishing El Cabanyal, the colourful fisherman's quarter on Valencia's seafront; an abortionist has been kidnapped and with the Pope due to visit the city, the police are summoned to offer protection from crowds of the faithful and the danger of anti-religionists alike.

When one of Cámara's long-term adversaries is put in charge of the missing abortionist case, tensions quickly run high, and with ominous cracks spreading across the walls of his flat, Cámara soon has nowhere to turn.

'Jason Webster has made Valencia his own . . . This is Max Cámara's second outing, and his colourful personality is every bit a match for the vibrant but often troubled home of paella he has to keep safe'
Henry Sutton, *Daily Mirror*

'It brings to life Valencian living, evoking the people, the food, the drink and most of all the atmosphere . . . Highly recommended'
Eurocrime